ALSO BY MICHAEL VENTURA

Night Time Losing Time

Shadow Dancing in the USA

*We've Had a Hundred Years of
Psychotherapy and the World's
Getting Worse*
(with James Hillman)

Sitting on Moving Steel

Letters at 3 A.M.

THE ZOO WHERE YOU'RE FED TO GOD

A Novel

MICHAEL VENTURA

Simon & Schuster
New York London Toronto Sydney Tokyo Singapore

SIMON & SCHUSTER
Rockefeller Center
1230 Avenue of the Americas
New York, New York 10020

This book is a work of fiction. Names, characters, places and incidents are either products of the author's imagination or are used fictitiously. Any resemblance to actual events or locales or persons, living or dead, is entirely coincidental.

Designed by Paulette Orlando

Manufactured in the United States of America

1   3   5   7   9   10   8   6   4   2

Library of Congress Cataloguing in Publication Data
Ventura, Michael
The Zoo where you're fed to God: a novel/ Michael Ventura
p.   cm.
PS3572.E5Z43   1994
813'.54—dc20   94-7997
CIP
ISBN 978-1-5011-1143-3

Acknowledgments:
Chris Crosby led me to many places, many animals, and many books about them. Some of these books deserve particular mention: *Tigers—The Secret Life*, by Valmik Thapar and Fateh Singh Rathore; *Tigers—How They Live*, by Rupert Matthews; and the tiger book in the Jane Goodall's Animal World series, by Ruth Ashby and Jane Goodall. I must also thank Steve Erickson, Jodie Evans, George and Dixie Howard, Cathy Marable, Jana Johnson, Naunie Batchelder, Zanne Devine, James "Big Boy" Medlin, Bridget Adams, Paulette Taix, Kit Rachlis, Dawn Rae Davis, John Powers, Deborah Milosevich, Diane Wolkstein, Ron Stringer, Dave Johnson, Melanie Jackson, and especially Bob Asahina of Simon & Schuster, a faithful editor who showed me where my story needed me.

For Christine Ellis Crosby

PART ONE

THE SECOND TIGER

Hunters cannot have their own way, they must fall in with the wind, and the colours and smells of the landscape, and they must make the tempo of the ensemble their own. Sometimes it repeats a movement over and over again, and they must follow up with it.

Isak Dinesen

A
VISITATION

He became a surgeon because he was afraid of knives. He got married because he was afraid of women. He had a child because he was afraid of responsibility. Now, his marriage over and his child no longer speaking to him, he turned off all the lights in the house because he was afraid of the dark.

In the dark he sat at the kitchen table, naked but for a towel on his lap. (He was shy that way, even when alone.) The desert wind had blown over Los Angeles all day, all night, for three days and nights, hot, incredibly clear, charged with static—a dry steady rush of air with only the slightest of gusts. There was no need to daub himself after his shower; the Mojave wind lapped all moisture into nothing in minutes. He sat before it near an open window, and it was like being licked by a cat's tongue.

The refrigerator kicked in, startled him. The house was so quiet, now that he didn't have to run the air conditioner for the wife, for the boy. He suspected that conditioned air weakened the immune system, and in any case he worked in it all day and it was dehydrating. "Drink lots of water," he used to tell his wife and son so often it had become a family joke. Not that he was obsessed with health, but it was his profession and he was a thorough man.

The wind was almost soundless, rustling the trees and bushes only slightly, steadily, a distinct and pretty whisper amidst engines revving on nearby streets and the incessant hum of the Golden State Freeway a mile or so off. But sitting still like this in the kitchen, and the refrigerator starting and stopping suddenly as it did—when on, its motor seemed unusually loud, probably needed repair, and it shut the city out; then when it turned itself off each small sound felt separate and near, within reach. The man enjoyed that moment.

He found himself waiting for it. And when it came to him, as he sat in the dark, naked, with a towel on his lap, alone, he felt suddenly, unaccountably, *happy*. This startled him. Then the feeling passed as soon as he realized he was having it, as though the realization had driven it away. And his happiness, gone, left a new hole, a new space, for his fear; and he felt his fear rush in and fill where the happiness had been. It was terrible to feel its swift movement.

He must have been sitting there longer than he realized, because the refrigerator kicked in again, startling him again. He longed to get up and do something recognizable and simple, like turning on a light and having a glass of water. But then he'd have to turn the light off again, which would be worse; or leave it on all night, which would be much worse.

He could hear what Elizabeth, his wife, his *ex*-wife, would say: "If you feel better with a light on, *keep a light on.*" And she'd think it was "macho," or something, his not being able to do that, and they'd get into one of *those* discussions, arguments she would inevitably win because she believed in her words while he didn't believe in his own, in hers, in any. Somewhere behind all the words was something words could not bear. And it wasn't far behind, it was right behind, eating at the backs of the words as they came toward you.

In any case, he knew (though he could not explain) that how he felt about the dark, and about whether turning lights on or off would make it better or worse, had nothing to do with "macho."

"Look at you," he said aloud, "arguing with her—and she isn't even here. You can't say Beth started *this* round."

If Elizabeth had come into the kitchen right then, in a loose housedress, her body still so good at age forty, and her mood in his presence poised precariously between bitterness and tenderness, she would have asked what she so often asked: "What are you thinking?"

And he would say the noncommittal kind of thing he usually said, something like, "Just kind of letting my mind breathe, I suppose."

Then she might tease him, say, "You mean you're meditating?"

She knew the word embarrassed him, and when she caught him, as she would put it, "in this space," she'd insist playfully that he was meditating but that he didn't know it. Not that he disapproved of meditating, or of any of his wife's, his *ex*-wife's, interests in that vein. As a surgeon he earned his living ministering to a procession of sufferers; he was all too knowledgeable about the diabolical variety and absolute certainty of suffering. He couldn't disapprove of anything that relieved anybody's. Meditate, if it helped. Legalize heroin, why not? Pray. Drink. Still, the word "meditation" embarrassed him. It was part of a whole area of topics his wife talked about with her friends—lovely people to whom he could never find anything to say.

Did he miss Elizabeth? No, his scalpel-like honesty cut through that. He didn't want to mistake a dependence on old habits for "missing." He'd discovered that at the age of fifty this is the sort of mistake you cannot afford. No, he had conjured her into their old kitchen, had made up a typical argument ("discussion," she would have called it) not because he missed Elizabeth, whoever *she* was—for they'd been strangers, he knew now, for the longest time; he had conjured her there because it frightened him to be alone in the house in the dark.

As for missing—he didn't even miss his son, though he loved his son. He trusted his love for his son, whether or not anybody else did. But you could love someone and not miss them, the way you could miss them but not love them. Life was easily complex enough for that.

As for the fear—it would have been understandable, even in some way acceptable, if he were afraid of intruders. He knew, of course, that there *were* intruders, and that they did intrude, and that, if you believed the papers, they were more dangerous and intrusive every day. But he had never been afraid of people in that way.

He told himself that he was afraid of the dark, but that's not quite what he meant. It was more as though his fear awoke in the dark. Yes, he understood that much. It was as though he'd been afraid all day but light kept his fear, not down, but preoccupied, distracted. Later, in the dark, alone, the fear in him could notice itself, notice other things, move within him, and move *him*, move him around the house, from the living room to the den to the shower to the kitchen chair in front of the open window where he had not moved a muscle in a while.

This had to do with why a man, though afraid of the dark, felt compelled to turn off the lights (and it was also why he was relieved that his marriage was over, though it hadn't been his idea to end it): because darkness let his fear move from the terrible place where it had been locked inside him, and its movement was less awful than the hidden leaden weight of its stillness. Now that there was no longer any need to hide it, no one to hide it from, it was a great relief simply to feel it, finally; not suppress or attack or test it as he always had. There was nothing to prove anymore, there was nothing to do but get through the rest of his life. A certain number of surgical procedures, a certain number of meals, a certain allowance of small pleasures. A useful and self-sufficient and bearable way to be.

But fear is fear. Fear *is* fear. Nobody likes it. He didn't like it. He wished he enjoyed drinking more than he did, to dim the fear, but he had never been a drinker. His profession required a delicacy that drinking blunted. He wished he liked sitcoms and talk shows, but he was actually offended (prim as it sounds) at the pointlessness and quantity of their words. Television didn't make him sleepy, it made him angry. Movies rarely held him. So he usually ran out of things to do before he ran out of energy, and then his fear would arise, as though it lived where his energy could not satisfy and had never satisfied itself. His fear would arise, and he'd let it arise, making the firm distinction that this was fear, not panic, and that as long as he gave it a little room, a little quiet room, it wouldn't be panic, and as long as it wasn't panic it was fine and could be lived.

What he didn't know, and didn't want to know, was that he was waiting for his fear to move him further, further than from room to room in a house of painful but uninteresting memories; waiting for his fear to move him toward or away from a *something*, a something that attracted and repelled him at once. Perhaps it was the something that was behind words—the thing that words couldn't bear. He was waiting for his fear to move him further toward, or away, from that.

This made him, in a way, a dangerous man—which is something else he did not suspect about himself.

And just a few minutes ago—or a half hour, or an hour, whatever it had been, he'd lost track—there'd been that truly disturbing moment, because it was so strange, when he'd felt a flush of happiness, happiness with the sounds, with the wind and its electric feel on his skin and its faint smell of the desert. Happiness being what it is, he couldn't help but want that feeling back, so he tried to sit very still to let it come again, and sitting very still like that he fell asleep in the kitchen chair with a towel on his lap, in the dark.

It was a lively dark. More so than he'd ever noticed. He was not aware of the family of possums who scouted his yard almost every night, looking for tidbits and to see if the Outside Cat (he had no other name) had left anything in his dishes. Nor was the man aware of how that cat would sit where the cellar window had broken during the last earthquake and watch the possums carefully, but never go near them. Nor of the huge raccoon, for whom the tall tree in the yard was a regular stop. The man would hear dogs sometimes, when the garbage cans were out, but never the coyotes (because you don't hear coyotes unless they want to be heard). But coyotes rarely came down this far anymore; they tended to stay in the Hollywood Hills, like the deer, or in the mountains around Glendale and Pasadena. As for deer, no one had seen a deer in Echo Park in many years, even where his house was, on the steep hills of the affluent area to the west.

He had smelled skunk but had never seen one, though he might have if he'd sat quietly in his deck chair late into the night—a skunk came through there now and again. The skunk tended to arrive later than the possums, and alone; the possums usually came as a family. This night, while he was still sitting at the window, and still awake, he didn't see that the mama possum had come with four little ones hanging from her, two on her back, one clutching her side, and an albino at her neck. The babies had their eyes tight shut; they seemed born scared. The albino surely would not live long, and though all possums see poorly the albino was probably blind. (Many animals are born blind. Tigers, for instance.)

The Outside Cat watched the baby possums with special interest, especially the albino. But cats like easy kills, and no mama animal is an easy kill, even a possum.

The possum finished the leftovers in the cat's dish, then went away. The Outside Cat sniffed their trail, but did not follow. He was a somber, dirty-gray creature who had shown up one day in the yard, very skinny, not quite fully grown, very frightened. The man had noticed him, put food out for him, but the cat wouldn't touch it until long after the man had gone back inside. The man watched the cat feed. The woman hadn't left yet, the day the Outside Cat had come, and she noticed the man looking out the window and came to see what he was looking at. "That one has a history," she'd said of the cat. "It seems to," the man had said.

This night the cat was also being watched, and may well have known it. High in the tree an owl, unusually large for Southern California, was looking down—but grown cats are too big for owls. Lower in the tree, the raccoon was watching too. A cat is no match for a raccoon, but it's much faster; this raccoon had no particular interest, except the interest of all animals in anything occurring in their area. The owl and raccoon both happened to be watching the cat from their perches when they saw it freeze, suddenly, then run so quickly for the cellar window that it was a blur even to them. Animals protect each other by spreading the fear of a predator from one to the other; the fear of the most alert is a signal for the rest. The owl and raccoon took the signal and watched.

The coyote seemed simply to appear in the yard, as coyotes will. Two nights of desert wind had excited it, perhaps, to go beyond its usual range. But you couldn't tell about coyotes. They'd sometimes appear on golf courses at night in the middle of the city, and no one knew for certain how they got there—except that they, too, traveled the freeways, running in the grassy, bushy slopes on either side of the Hollywood, the Santa Monica, the Pasadena, the Ventura, in the wee hours, rare to see even if you knew how and where to look. Occasionally you'd pass one dead in the morning, struck by a car.

This coyote was big for a coyote, larger than most dogs, though it had entered the yard as easy as you please through the same fence that kept dogs out. It inspected the premises carefully, casually, with no fear. It knew everything it wanted to know, could smell the procession of the possum, the ways of the cat, the raccoon in the tree, the man.

Who awoke, as they say, "with a start," as you do when you've fallen asleep sitting up and you begin to slump over. His startled jump at waking made the towel slip from his lap, which he reflexively grabbed for as he opened his eyes into the eyes of the coyote, not four feet from him, in the yard.

His heart beat madly a moment.

The pain that shot through him was too strange—even with all his experience and training he didn't know if it was physical or not. He snapped his eyes shut against it, and when he opened them, only an instant later, both the pain and the coyote were gone.

He took his pulse. Fast but steady. The coyote could easily have been a dream, but then he said aloud: "It can't have been a dream, you don't have a hard-on." Males always have erections when they dream, whether or not the dream is sexual—among all the scientific facts he knew, this was one of his favorites. He scanned the yard for a trace of the coyote, but the beast had gone.

He stooped, picked up the towel, which was white, wrapped it around his waist, then realized he had broken out in sweat, all over, when his heart had beat so hard. The sweat of fear, the sweat of effort, the sweat of sex, and the sweat of heat, all have distinct smells if you pay attention, and this was a man who paid attention—he considered it necessary to his profession. The scent on him now was fear, with a whiff of sex. If the coyote was anywhere nearby, and the wind in the right direction, it would smell his fear. (The other animals smelled it, too, but he didn't think of this.)

And suddenly he was aware of the crickets. He'd taken them for granted all night, everybody in Los Angeles does, but they seemed, just then, louder. That was probably an illusion; it was just that the coyote made him notice. When he'd first moved from New York to Los Angeles the crickets kept him awake. It had seemed so strange, a din of crickets wherever you went in the most modern city in the world. You didn't see the crickets, you couldn't imagine where most of them were, but you heard them all night in season. The way, in the morning and all through the day, no matter where you were, you heard birdsong. But he had never spoken of these things, and had never heard anyone else speak of them.

Something *was* wrong with the refrigerator, its motor was too loud, he'd have to get it fixed. He thought this when it shut itself off again, and the cricket racket, by virtue of his awareness of it, became almost unbearable. It sounded just like panic. For a moment. Then it was only crickets again.

He would have to take another shower. He couldn't go to bed with the stickiness of dried fear on him. The digital on the microwave read 3:49:43. Its precision irked him. He watched the seconds pass in the moment he was irked, and *that* irked him.

In the shower, under its cool spray, he knew that everything beyond words had somehow taken a step toward him.

A VISIT

The difficulty wasn't at night, it was in the morning. No matter how late he fell asleep, he woke just before first light. An owl woke him. (Not the owl of last night, which he had never seen, but another nearby which he had also never seen.) It gave two low throaty hoots, over and over, with insistent and unchanging emphasis. Just as the owl would finish, a mourning dove would begin its round-toned, three-note call, just as emphatic, just as unchanging. One mourning dove or another kept it up almost all day, almost anywhere you went in the city, and if you were conscious of it, if for some reason your ear fixed on it, it could get on your nerves badly by nightfall. There were always mourning doves calling in the hills of Echo Park, where the foliage made thick cover for birds.

He lived on steep Cerro Gordo Street, at the crest of the hill. Not a neighborhood where you'd expect a surgeon to live. Movie stars lived here once, but that was seventy years ago and more; now even the affluent hilltops were worn—"the genteel side of shabby," Elizabeth used to say. Toward the end she'd hated it. Surrounded by streets where immigrants legal and illegal lived five and ten to a room, and with gang graffiti everywhere, the steep hills of another era were like islands in a swamp of poverty and confusion. Elizabeth was afraid for their son. But the man was reluctant to live

where he could easily afford—Santa Monica, Brentwood.
He had grown up on the streets of Brooklyn among a rough
people ("shanty Irish," they were called) who gave no quarter and expected none, but did both with a natural humor
and ferocity that he respected more than anything else and
had found nowhere else. He had been an anomaly on his
own streets, a quiet, brilliant boy who held his own when
threatened but for the most part just looked on. Still, as he
had said to Elizabeth so often, "This is as high as I want to
rise." It was incomprehensible to her, and those fights were
probably the beginning of the end of their marriage. How
could he explain that to distance himself too far from the
realm that she called "shabby" was to leave forever the only
people he had ever trusted: people who insisted on survival
for its own sake, without hope of betterment or comfort or
any victory at all—nothing but the defiant fact of their survival. To rise higher would be to remove himself from the
last feelings that had even the slightest claim on his alle-
giance. And far from protecting his son by moving to, say,
Brentwood, he felt it would be a betrayal of him—not for
any fuzzy liberal reason, not for any reason he could name.
He didn't trust reasons much anyway.

One mourning dove called alone for a while, then others
joined in, and then the sparrows with their piercing cheeps,
and then other cries of birds he could not name, and then
the ravens in that big tree down the hill with their incredi-
ble racket of caws. The man would lie awake, or half awake,
listening to the same progression of birdsong every morning, cut through by the first sirens of daylight, and the first
police helicopter. Once he had been able to sleep through
it all till the alarm.

It wasn't the divorce. This "sensitivity," as he had named
it, began well before. The difference was that when he was
married he got to sleep earlier. During that pathetic exer-
cise called "marriage counseling," which he'd endured under protest, it "came out," as they say, that he had often gone
to bed early in order to be alone. Had often been in bed by
nine-thirty, while she preferred eleven-thirty or even later.
Getting into bed then was truly delicious. It was the one

time of the day that he didn't have to deal in any way with other people. He felt as content, then, as children are supposed to feel when they're tucked in. And sleep would come swiftly.

In counseling he had admitted, when pressed, that these early bedtimes constituted an escape, and that it was the *escape* that was so restful and welcome—escape from the woman, escape from the boy, escape from what the counselor called "the real world." They were convinced, the counselor and his wife, and he agreed with them because it was the easiest way to shut them up. Otherwise he would have called it "the insistent" rather than "the real" world: "insistent" at least had a meaning, while he'd been involved in science all his life without understanding the word "real." And he would have preferred "exit" to "escape," because while he admitted his early bedtimes constituted a leaving, there was nothing fugitive in his feeling. Didn't "escape" assume something fugitive, something wrong? To agree with that word, he soon found, was to agree to being wrong. But who were these invisible beings standing behind the counselor and his wife, standing in their very language, who set up this criterion that judged him so?

Exit from what, into what?—wife and counselor might have asked that. I don't know, he would have said. The counselor would have concluded that his very way of thinking was an escape, while his wife, who prided herself on being fair, would have given him the benefit of the doubt, which is the benefit of respect. And so she had, always. But finally she'd decided he was lost. Perhaps he was. Yes.

And then she admitted to having a lover. And that was painful, but not as painful as he himself thought it should have been. (Again, he wondered, who sets the criterion?)

In any case his sensitivity to the dawn had begun well before the marriage counseling. Months before. At first it had been pleasant. Waking with the birds. The delicate early light. The woman asleep beside him, a woman he had once loved (even the resignation of *that* took on a not unpleasant tinge at dawn). But gradually dawn became like a barrier he could no longer cross when asleep. Light would come and he would wake, and there would be nothing he could do with that waking. Nothing but stare. And if he closed his eyes, awake, it was still a kind of staring. And so his difficulty with dawn would become—he wouldn't use the word "torture" because he knew something about torture, had been on a commission to Latin America to examine victims of torture; but it was torturous enough so that the word would come to him before he rejected it. What did the dawn want of him? He found himself asking this now and again, almost petulantly, then retreating from his question.

Now that he was alone, now that he usually couldn't sleep till the wee hours, waking near dawn was hurting him. Threatening his work. It made for a fatigue that came and went in waves, so that suddenly, while seeing a patient on his rounds or in the middle of a surgical procedure, all energy would drain from his limbs, the least gesture would require an act of will, and he would feel again as he'd felt as a young man in the hospital at Cam Ranh Bay in Vietnam, as though all of life were one great mangled body which he must operate on endlessly, endlessly cutting and suturing and sewing, and it did no good.

He recognized that to protect his work he might soon have to resort to sleeping pills. He hated that. It was the very last thing he wanted, yet he couldn't have said quite why. He had no objections to the pills; he hadn't his wife's suspicion of all chemicals. He was a pragmatist: prescribe anything that gave relief, and be alert for side effects. It was his experience that serious side effects were rare. No, it wasn't any philosophical or medical objection to the pills, it was— he stopped the thought, let it fade, couldn't say it to himself. It made no sense. It made no sense to *want* this restlessness in the evening.

In any case, surely all he needed was a rest. He hadn't taken a vacation in a long, long time. A month without work was unthinkable, but a week. Two. Then see. Wednesday was his last scheduled procedure. And today he didn't have to work, unless the beeper sounded, today was Sunday. It was his day to visit his son.

He ate lightly, shaved closely, dressed carefully. Dark shoes, tan slacks, a well-pressed light-brown shirt. He pressed it himself. He enjoyed ironing his own things. His father had taught him when he was a boy. His father had been a laborer who prided himself on looking spiffy. "Spiffy" was his father's word. His father was a drinker and a worker, bitter and raucous by turns, who agreed with his mother on one, and only one, issue: that their only child, "Jimmy," as they called him (and as he hated to be called since), should and would become a priest. "You'll have to do this for yourself even when you become a bishop," the father told the seven-year-old when he taught him to iron. (Where his father got such notions of the Church, he never knew.) But his father's zest was catchy, and the precision of his ironing skill was impressive, so what became their weekend ritual of ironing the clothes was the best memory he had of the old man. The other memories were of a preening self-confidence that fell apart before every challenge except an argument or a fistfight. But even now he himself found few things more gently pleasurable than the smell of a steam iron on good cloth. He had tried to do this with his own son, but the boy resisted it, resented being taken away from Sunday morning cartoons; it had become a battle, useless, stupid. Yet he remembered when the battle was over, when he'd given up trying to pry his son from cartoons, and on Sunday as usual he was ironing his things for the week, enjoying the detail work around cuffs and collars and creases, claiming again for himself the chore he found so oddly satisfying—"The motions are a *little* like surgery, but without the blood," Elizabeth had laughed, "that's why you like it. Or that's why you like surgery, one. Do you know how strange Rosalita thinks it is, that she's not allowed to iron *your* things? 'Por *qué*, señora?' 'Mi esposo es loco en cabeza, Rosalita' "—but he remembered the first Sunday the battle was over, and his son walked through the laundry room, to or from his cartoons, and the odd lilt of loss when the boy said, "Hi, Dad." Strange, what you remember. The moment had evaporated at the time, but months later it came back to him and stayed with him—had become, in fact, one of his most vivid memories of his son. No matter how old either of them became, somewhere in his heart that boy would always be walking through that laundry room saying, with an odd inflection, "Hi, Dad."

So that now when he ironed, his father and his son joined him, each very differently, but very much there.

And so this Sunday he did his ironing. Then chose a white Panama hat, to shade him at the zoo; he'd buy the boy a baseball cap on the way there, the kid would like that. Eleven, or was he twelve? That didn't seem too old to go to the zoo. And they hadn't been to a zoo in a long time, years, not since the three of them had stopped in San Diego on their way to or from Mexico. That was his last vacation, in fact. He wondered if zoos were more a mother thing than a father thing. It was with his mother that he'd gone to zoos as a boy, in Central Park and the Bronx. She was quiet and little, very dignified, very tough. "Nuns shouldn't get married, my dear, or weren't you informed?" his father would say on a tear, and he probably had a point. His mother rarely smiled in their tenement flat. She pretended to be proud. It wasn't pride, actually, it was anger; she was always angry. Expecting no more than she had, she nevertheless hated what she had: the little, stuffy rooms, too cold in winter, too hot in summer, with their cracked linoleum, and water beading on the wallpaper, and always more work to do, and never any money, and her steely silence meeting her husband's taunts as they remained locked in mutual loneliness— she hated everything except her only child. He never saw her relax except when they were alone. For memories of his mother smiling he had to think of places like the zoo, where her reserve (which he'd inherited) would soften, where she'd make up stories about apes and tigers, and beam with an almost unsettling pleasure when he rode the camel and the elephant on their bulky saddles. He would feel the lurch of the beast beneath him, as he clutched the saddle desperately, always afraid, always trying not to show it, trying to be worthy of his mother's rare happiness, the joy she showed as she watched him.

"Ah, Jimmy, *ah*, Jimmy!" she'd say as the attendant helped him down and she'd clutch him to her and rock him back and forth and kiss the top of his head.

The animal stories she told were Bible stories. This was easy when speaking of camels and lions, or lambs and the donkey in the children's zoo, where you could touch them. It was easy when speaking of the horses that the zoo police rode: all those chariots in the Bible were pulled by horses. And the reptile building had plenty of serpents, that was easy. For the rest—the only animals that God seemed to have created *specifically*, besides man, were whales and cattle. They're the only ones named in Genesis, the rest are "beasts of the field" and such; but there were no whales and cattle at the zoo. In fact for most beasts she had to depend on Noah's ark, and when she read him that story it confused him, because children tend to be literal and the only beasts actually mentioned in the Noah story are cattle and doves. His mother had an illustration of giraffes and elephants and others in a long line, two by two, going into the ark, but that illustration also left many out. There were no apes, for instance. There were rhinos but no hippos, leopards but no tigers. "Every creeping thing," it said in the Bible, as his mother would read it to him, but there were no creeping things in the illustration. All the animals walked. They didn't creep. Then she found another illustration which left out some of the animals in the first and put in others. He wanted to know which was right. He remembered this as his first serious discussion, remembered the depth of his puzzlement and the pain of her consternation, a pain she'd tried to conceal. It may have been the first question for which she'd failed to provide her son a satisfying answer.

The man whom "Jimmy" had become thought of these as happy though "serious" memories, when he thought of them at all. He and Mother at the zoo, of *course* it was happy. Actually, it was perplexing, and he would, the rare times the memory came to him, be perplexed without letting himself realize it.

All parents are terrifying to their children. This was something the man assumed. He didn't think it unusual, so he doubted it was unnatural. He had seen so many average, middle-aged adults at the bedside of a terribly frail, dying parent—seen the grown children only barely able to contain their terror, but clearly more afraid of the parent than of the coming death.

To be lost is to be *lost*. The man didn't even know he was thinking these things; or rather, they had no emotional weight or content, the memories were simply pictures to him, the thoughts simply words, an activity he took as no more specific or portentous than sweating in heat or growing hair, processes that happened inexorably no matter what was going on, no matter if you went into the garage, got in the car, checked that you had your beeper, put the Panama hat on the back seat, and backed the new maroon four-door Buick down the street. He put the car in forward gear, then hit the brake almost at the same time. The Outside Cat was in front of him in the street.

He felt a surge of rage.

And was surprised. He wasn't a man who felt surges of rage. The cat darted off.

And now he just felt numb. No. Stupid. No. Frustrated very nearly to the point of tears. No. Frightened. From the moment of waking to the moment of hitting the brake, he had somehow managed to forget that for three weeks now his son had refused to speak to him, refused even to acknowledge he was there.

For the first time in many years he wanted a cigarette. Just to sit in the car and smoke a cigarette, before driving off to what would probably be a futile and humiliating scene. He thought of calling first, to ask if the boy would see him. Why make the trip to Pasadena otherwise? But it didn't seem right to call. It seemed, somehow, cowardly. He was a father and he should show up at the appointed time. Even a degrading ritual was a ritual—*some* sort of connection. Was a connection of any sort better than no connection?

"I have no fucking idea," he said aloud.

He looked at his hands before him on the steering wheel

of the large car. "The hands of a priest," his mother used to say, holding them in hers. His fingers were long, well formed, aristocratic, strong. The palms were muscular. The veins stood out on the backs. "I'm a laborer like my father, I work with my hands," was a saying of his, and people would think he was joking, but he wasn't. A fine surgeon had to have a touch, like a fine pianist. He could be very good at cutting his son open, in a difficult procedure, feeling through his fingers, through the gloves, through the steel, the tiniest layers of his son's skin parting, it would be a local anesthesia, his son would be awake, aware of his great skill. Perhaps the boy would have an accident between now and when he arrived in Pasadena, and he would have to operate right there. Far from the old saw that a doctor shouldn't operate on his own family, he couldn't imagine letting anyone else do it. Perhaps—

The backs of his hands broke out in a light sweat. His son on an operating table, that was alright, he, the man, would be there, in control; but his son in an accident—that was a sickening picture, and the little he'd eaten for breakfast balked in his stomach, he could taste it in his throat. None of this was making sense. Like putting the car in gear, as he was doing, and going forward to an encounter nobody wanted.

He wondered was she watching him. It was a strange enough thing to wonder, since both were convinced that they no longer loved each other. He seemed to be walking toward the house in slow motion; it seemed as though she had all the time in the world to study his every feature, though after fifteen years of marriage why would she be interested? But perhaps, now, he seemed as foreign to her as she did to him—a disconcerting clash of the alien and the familiar disturbed him whenever he saw her. So perhaps, concealed at some window, she had been watching for his approach (he was always punctual), and perhaps now she watched how he carefully locked the car, how, near the "Armed Response" sign, he almost stepped on the grass, then chose not to, walked instead the few steps up the side-walk to the cobble pathway that went in a slow curve across the lawn, then paused to look at the flower garden that high-lighted the porch. Even in what had become his accustomed state of uninterrupted distraction, the brilliance of her gar-den penetrated him—especially those flowers with petals so black he thought they glowed. He could not name them, nor the yellows near them, blazing in contrast, nor the del-icate blues beside the yellows . . . and he looked at each flower, not knowing really what he was doing, nor that a half-smile played on his face. His only conscious thought was to wonder if she watched, if she noticed his walk, if she judged its slowness or its step. If she was judging. Was she noticing whether there was more gray in his thick hair that had once been black, and wondering whether that might make the gray of his eyes more or less intense? Did she look at him, in other words, the way he could not help but look at her, for some sort of clue?

To what? To every last thing.

The flowers seemed impossibly bright—or what seemed impossible? *Something* was impossible. The notion of mo-tion, no more than that, of taking a single step. The black petals glowed, he stared into them, he felt a vertigo, while without words the part of his mind that had catalogued thou-sands of symptoms examined himself (lack of food, lack of sleep, stress)—and did not understand. The only familiar feeling, among all he was feeling, was embarrassment. Had it come to this, his fifty years, had it come to this teenage sense of awful expectancy, was she or was she not *watch-ing* him? And if she was not? And what was his name?

"James? Are you alright?"

There is one's name, and there is where one's name takes place in another's voice. His was at the very edge of her voice, as though she didn't really want it in her mouth.

"I'm admiring your garden."

"For ten minutes?"

"Am I on time?"

"You know you're on time, you're always on time. Are you going to look at me?"

There were colors all over her. Paint stains on her hands, and on her bare feet—spots and splotches of all the colors. And a smudge of green on her left cheek. She wore an old white shirt of his, rolled up neatly to the elbows, very big on her like a smock. She had on tight blue jeans that fit her well still, very frayed, with holes at the knees and tears at the thighs (not for fashion, though torn jeans were the fashion that year, but because she hated to throw away any clothing she worked in). Her black hair was pulled back in a ponytail, while her one silver streak shined in the sun with a glare. Her eyes were gray like his, but her skin was a Welsh creamy white, while his was an Irish tawn. She was slight without being little; her features, like his, were strong and finely shaped; and in her arms she held the enormous Inside Cat, the cat that hardly ever moved, orange-red, with its eyes closed as usual.

They examined each other frankly up and down, each with a slight smile—almost the same smile. His look paused at her lovely feet, which he still found entrancing somehow, and always had.

"You're looking at my feet again."

"I'm looking at your feet again."

It was a couplet they'd said often.

"You look . . ."

" . . . spiffy?" he said.

"Only short men can look spiffy. Actually, you look tired." He shrugged.

"And I look?" she said. Her head came up to his shoulder. She stood with her feet apart, a firm, alert stance.

"You know how you look," he said.

She gave a kind of snort—a little like a laugh and a little like a curse.

"What do you think of that?" she said to the Inside Cat, so huge it seemed nothing but featureless reddish fur as she held it in both arms. "I really can't stand you, James."

"I know."

"But when I see you, the first moments, I'm really pleased to see you."

"Me too. The pleased part, not the can't-stand part."

"Oh? Come on."

"Only sometimes. I'm not as consistent as you are."

"You're a thousand times more consistent than anybody. Sort of."

"I'm not, actually. So. Is Eddie ready?"

"Ready Eddie. No, he's not."

"That's OK, I've got all day."

"Eddie doesn't want to see you, James. He asked me to tell you."

"Eddie's going to have to tell me himself."

"Why make it more difficult?"

"Why make it less?"

They held each other's eyes a moment, then each looked down, he at the flowers, she at the cat in her arms. Without looking up she said, "Who are you punishing?"

Without looking up he said, "I'm not punishing anybody."

"Why are you forcing yourself on him?"

"I'm not forcing myself on anybody. I just want to say, 'Let's go to the zoo—' "

"The zoo?!"

"—and hear whatever he has to say, and if he doesn't want to go I'll leave. That's not forcing."

"The zoo?"

"Look, I'm not going to barge into your house if you don't want me to come in. But—it's not about the legalities, it's—I think I have a right—to see him, to hear it from him. It's—I know you dislike me now, or whatever, I—I'm not a bad person, Beth."

"I know. I do know. It's just I see you, and I keep wanting to—chip away at you. If I was doing that, I'm sorry."

"You don't have to be sorry about anything."

"About fucking somebody else?"

"I don't really care about that."

"I *know.*"

"I don't mean I don't 'care' care, I mean—you don't have to be sorry. It's all just a bunch of words anyway, it's—"

"*No.*" Her eyes were bright. "We're not going to talk about *that* again, not going to talk like *that.*"

They looked each other in the eyes, and in their looks

pleaded with one another and with themselves not to be speaking as they were speaking. He closed his eyes a moment, opened them, looked into hers again. Closed them. The outline of her head floated in his vision, with the splotchy glares of the bright sun, under his closed lids. He opened his eyes again.

"Are you alright?" the woman said.

The man nodded, reached out, stroked the utterly unperturbed cat in the woman's arms. Its fluffy soft fur felt very good. Then with the tips of his fingers he gently touched her arm. He could easily feel, with his great sensitivity to flesh, the differences between skin that was open to a touch and skin that resisted. Long ago, when lovemaking had mattered or had even occurred to him, this had made him a wonderful lover for her. Now his fingers were surprised at her skin's sympathy toward his touch. He traced an arc on her forearm, around the rough patches of green and blue paints. The cat had purred when he touched it, and it continued to purr loudly.

The man said, "Hello, Elizabeth."

"Hello, James."

"Same old Inside Cat."

"Cats don't change."

Cats don't change? he cried in his mind. And felt again a kind of vertigo, an utter disorientation. Who was this woman? Where was this garden? She'd said it so casually, almost brutally, as though it didn't mean anything: Cats don't change.

Cruel to go around making absolute pronouncements as though they don't mean anything. While you're holding a cat in your arms. In the bright sun. And— And—

The woman, for her part, was startled by the sudden blankness in his eyes. She had spent so many years trying to bring him "back," as she put it, from disconnections much smaller; she didn't know what to make of anything this drastic, she could only say his name:

"James."

"*Eddie*, Elizabeth. Can I speak to Eddie?"

"Come in and sit down. I'll tell him you want to talk to him."

"Thank you."

"OK."

She turned and was up the porch stairs before he took a step—a step that made him feel how stiffly he'd been standing, and how the sun had heated his shirt and pants, which still felt freshly ironed.

He sat in a living room hung with her new paintings. In the world where things like paintings mattered, Elizabeth Cairn-Abbey was well thought of. Her paintings hung in good galleries, got decent write-ups, and sold, when they sold, for decent money. She had always been involved in art, both during and after her education, but had never been attracted to the so-called artist's life, the bohemian life—had said in an interview, "They [the bohemians] make art too special, too removed from the way everyone lives—a painting is a part of everything, a Monet or a Pollock is so strong that it takes its place with *everything* in life. That's what's so wonderful about good painting: it joins the world. It's thrilling to try to make something that does that." The man admired this quality in the woman more than he could say—and, in fact, more than he did say. He had watched this part of her life intensely, but from a distance. He thought of her paintings the way he thought of his operations: as procedures, each requiring its own dexterity, its own knowledge, its own audacity, and each leaving a scar.

These new canvases were large, aburst with colors, colors conveyed on jagged rhythmic lines. Yet for all their movement and energy they were intellectual. Willed. It was almost as though that was their point and their strength, a quality of will which, more than the colors, made them attractive. "Very Elizabeth," he said softly.

The huge Inside Cat lumbered its orange-red bulk slowly across the room, another bright thing in the bright room under the bright canvases.

"There are no cats in the Bible," he said softly to the animal. "I'll bet you didn't know that."

The man James Abbey knew it because his mother had

forbidden him cats based on their absence from the Bible.

The cat ignored him, as it always had, and sat on his foot, as it often had.

There is something about an eleven-year-old boy saying the word "fucking," when you hear only the voice, the high round sweet voice, strained in anger, in fury even, but still with that boy-sweetness which cannot carry fully the weight of any curse, especially the curse "fucking," which, the man knew, was derived from a word his ancestors had spoken, a word that had nothing to do with sexuality, a word that meant: "May you die before you make your peace with God."

"The fucking ZOO? THE FUCKING ZOO?"

"Eddie, please, damnit."

The voices came from upstairs.

Downstairs, on the couch, they made the man feel boyish, small.

"I'll talk to him, I'll talk to him, I wanna hear it from him about the fucking ZOO!"

They were the words of a grown man. But he knew how lovely the boy's face was, the astonishing swift beauty of the boy's smile. But the boy wasn't imitating a grown man's sentence, he was saying it.

The clumping downstairs was heavy too. And he saw why. The boy had on thick round-toed black boots—they made his feet seem enormous. And he'd shaved the sides of his head. And his black hair stuck up in little spikes. And even this was comical and sort of lovely. But not the expression on the boy's face, contorted consciously, it seemed, to broadcast his rage.

The boy stood planted before him, able to look down at the seated man. The woman, breathless, followed him, and looked frightened.

"You wanted to see me—OK, you see me."

"Hello, son. I guess you don't want to go to the zoo."

He was clearly a boy who was past being taken to zoos. If the boy had permitted the man to see him the last couple of visits, the man would have known. Yet only several weeks ago the boy had looked utterly different and had still been a boy one could take to a zoo.

"How could you think it? How could you think?"

No answer would satisfy the boy, that was obvious.

The man was glad in his heart to see his son. But he was also frightened of his son, and he felt ashamed of that. And the boy, for his part, felt the fear in his father's body, without knowing what he felt, but it made him all the more enraged.

"I don't know, I—there was a coyote in the yard last night, for a second we looked straight at each other, I guess it made me think of zoos."

"It's insulting."

"What?"

It made him so disoriented to hear the boy speak like this.

"You're insulting me," the boy said.

"I don't get it."

"You'd never go to the zoo by yourself, you never would. But you'd go to the fucking zoo—"

"Eddie, please," his mother said.

"—with me, I'm dumb enough to take to a zoo, you'd *never* go by yourself, you're not *interested*, it's phony."

The boy had always been articulate, from when he was quite small. The man had always delighted in it. Some part of him wanted to smile even now. There *was* something comical in this, the man felt it, and perhaps that was why he said something he had no intention of saying:

"That's not true, I *would* go to the zoo by myself."

It was a lie, and all three knew it, and all three were shocked that he'd said it—he most of all.

The boy did not react with rage, as the man for a moment feared; no, the boy became completely crestfallen, suddenly all his bright energy left him, and, full of hurt, he said softly, "That's not true."

The boy's gray eyes, the woman's gray eyes, the man's gray eyes, each softened, as though together, full of pleading.

"It is," the man said. "I would."

The boy burst into tears and ran from the room.

"This didn't have to happen," the woman said. "You could have taken my word for it, James. You—"

"It did. It had to happen. You are wrong."

"What?"

He dislodged his left foot from underneath the hot weight of the Inside Cat, and stood up.

"When's my next visiting?"

"A week, you know that. Don't think you're going to repeat this."

"I am unless you want to go to court to stop me."

"You're crazy."

It was the first time the possibility had occurred to him. He rejected it.

"Take care of yourself, Elizabeth. I like the paintings."

And he walked out of the house. She sat down on the floor next to the cat and looked at her paintings and sobbed. The boy lay upstairs on his bed on his stomach with his face to the wall. The man didn't notice the garden this time as he passed it. He had an odd sense of purpose, very strong, very urgent—something he hadn't felt in the longest time.

The car felt good. The wheel in his hands. The easy gliding power of it, down the shaded street past houses like hers, old wood houses from early in the century, solidly built, with wide windows, built by people who expected a very different century from the one that came to pass— there was a generosity to the porches and large windows, an expansiveness to the way a breakfast nook would jut out the side of a house, or a corner room on the second floor would be turretlike, three windows at an angle, just because somebody felt like it, somebody who expected to live there till death, and their kin to live there after. People had expected such things once, not long ago, though it seemed terribly long ago. Elizabeth's "new" house, new for her, had been built around 1910. The house they'd shared, the house he still lived in, up the steep hill on Cerro Gordo, dated from not twenty years later, and already things had changed, there was no expansiveness, it had been built for privacy, built to avoid, to shut itself off from its neighbors, from its street; the large fence around the house was part of its design, windows situated to look no further than the yard—a house at the top of the hill that didn't even face the street, but out over the steep drop so that from the front windows you could see into the distance, see the hills of Glendale and Pasadena, but you couldn't see a neighbor. And all the houses now, on whatever block, his or hers or anyone's—each sported a little sign about "Armed Response," or whatever system people were using to convince themselves of the possibility of safety. James Abbey could not be convinced. And, when there was no longer a child who deserved at least an illusion of protection, he'd canceled the service. "You can't protect anyone from anything," he used to say, until an explosive argument when Elizabeth, with the authority of pure fury, forbade him to say it "ever again." She said such things were "an excuse." She was wrong, and she was right, and perhaps she was more right than wrong, but he hadn't tried to sort that out; her fury won, he'd agreed. He couldn't remember if he'd ever told her *why* "you can't protect anyone from anything." It was just that one day even the most protected would come under his knife, or someone's knife—and those were the lucky ones, the ones who could afford a skilled and helpful knife to gain a few more months or years to do whatever it was that made life so worth holding on to. "I see everything through the knife now," he said aloud, surprising himself, as he drove slowly in the shade of the great trees that had been planted early in the century, and then turned left into the bright, bright sun and up the west ramp of the 210, the Foothill Freeway, when without realizing he speeded to seventy miles an hour, his hands tighter on the wheel, changing lanes sharply, passing cars, passing trucks, full of a purpose he did not question, from the Foothill to the Ventura west, down from the Pasadena hills, the skyscrapers of downtown L.A. in the distance behind another row of hills to the south, the hills where he lived—and everything so pinpoint clear after two days of Santa Ana wind, the air full of static, sparks had ignited when he touched the car door, if it had been dark he could have seen them, they would have been blue.

As he drove and looked across the hills he could see several miles and how many people? A quarter of a million? More? He had no idea he was doing seventy-five in the big maroon Buick. Where the freeway cut through the colorless clutter of Eagle Rock the siren startled him. He hadn't looked in the rearview at all. Now he saw the flashing lights as he heard the officer, angry through the loudspeaker: "Pull over *immediately*." How long had the cop been after him? He pulled over, stopped, turned off the ignition, not worried. Police are usually polite to doctors. Nevertheless he sat with his hands on the wheel, as one does in Los Angeles, where police tend to be excitable. A male and a female. The female, who'd been driving, stood behind his car, her hand on her revolver. The male approached on the passenger side, and asked him to get out on that side because of the freeway traffic. Shocks of wind as cars and trucks went by. He slid across the seat and got out. Showed his license, registration, proof of insurance, as asked. They were in their mid-twenties, the officers. Young enough to be his children. They had decent faces, not intelligent by his standards but not unintelligent either. They were marked people, marked by their profession, marked by their time; they tried to look earnest but they were merely anxious. Those were the lines in their young faces. They were on their way to the knife, and they knew it. He liked faces that knew it better than faces that didn't.

"Take your hands out of your pockets, please."

It was the female, from over his right shoulder, standing at the trunk of his car. He hadn't realized his hands were in his pockets. He took them out. The male was checking his papers.

"Hands *out* of the pockets, sir."

"I'm sorry." How had they gotten back in? He just didn't know what to do with them. He folded his hands in front, at his belt buckle. If he'd bowed his head, it would seem an attitude of prayer.

"We're citing you for speeding, Dr. Abbey, and for failure to wear a seat belt," the male said.

Failure to wear—the phrase struck him oddly, made him want to smile, his first smile of the day, was it? But Dr. Abbey had grown up in Brooklyn, where one does not smile at the police.

"If you don't mind my saying so," the female said, "a doctor should know better."

"I don't mind your saying so."

"Doctor," the male said, "when was the last time you had an alcoholic beverage?"

"Weeks ago. I don't remember."

"Are you on any kind of medication or drugs?"

"I didn't do those kinds of drugs even when I was your age." This time he did smile. These were children. He felt, beside them, a hundred years old. "I'll take any test you like. You're free to look in the car."

"We're already free to do that, sir. You were driving erratically. Were you upset, sir?"

He wanted to say: What a good question, yes, I was upset, but I would never think of it that way, I'd never use that word.

"Sir?" the male prodded.

"I—suppose I was."

"And what was the nature of your upsetness?"

Abbey wanted to laugh. He wondered vaguely if the question was constitutional, and knew certainly that this boy's nervous invention of the word "upsetness" couldn't be grammatical, but in an odd way he found himself having a good time. So he answered: "I just visited my ex-wife."

He had known how the line would play. It was like something on a talk show. He had finally said something they could recognize, which in turn would compel these two kids, armed and anxious, to enact a completely predictable reaction. Abbey saw it as though in slow motion, the slight smirk of the male, his quick glance at the female, her ever-so-slight grimace back, reactions they had no control over. It seemed horrible to him that they *had* to have this reaction, there was nothing they could do about it. He was scared for them. Poor babies.

"Well, two citations are enough for one day, I suppose," the male said. "Do you feel able to drive safely now, Doctor?"

"Yes. Thank you."

As he pulled back onto the freeway he glanced in his

rearview and saw them laughing in the front seat of their patrol car, the second stage of their reaction. Insane, the predictability of it. Insane, wasn't it? As he drove, carefully, consciously, at the speed limit, he thought of those two kids going through their days responding, responding, one predictable response after another, even their emergencies were predictable, and their shop talk, and their home talk; and all the while they believed they were having a life, even a life of high drama—while to him they spent their days *doing* nothing, *truly* nothing, the operative definition of nothing: they were puppets pulled this way and that by thousands of strings they couldn't see.

His heart broke for them. He was close to tears for them. And beneath that, something inchoate, not grief or fear or rage, but an animal sense that he was moving in the center of a million, of tens of millions, of responses, of lives that were only responses, automatic, puppetry, a living that was dead. It was one thing to think this as a thought, but it was fearsome to feel it in his body, to feel on his skin a near-unbearable physical unease at being in the midst of such beings. It was as though there was no mercy. How could such a city be capable of mercy?

The man James Abbey drove on, still with his sense of purpose, and when he saw the sign that he was looking for he wondered what the police would have thought if he'd told them he was going to the zoo.

AN
OUTING

He had never seen creatures of such delicacy. They were some kind of antelope. They had the name "gerenuk"; it seemed not to fit them at all, Americans would pronounce it as he was tempted to, some sort of Germanic "jer-rer-nuke" or "ger-rer-nuck." What was the language of the namers? He'd never seen nor heard of the beasts. He stood transfixed by their delicacy.

There were nine. Such long legs, so thin it seemed you might snap them with no more than a hard grip. Compact torsos, sweetly rounded. Sleek fine fur. Long-necked, necks fully as long as their legs. And a tiny, fawnlike face. With long, long ears, pointy-tipped, turning precisely toward each new sound. Small curved horns on one. The lightest shade of brown on their legs, flanks, and necks—brown just before it is white; their backs a little darker, and mottled; white bellies. And every step taken, and each turn of the head, was dancelike, as though they moved to a light, airy music of clear small notes and sudden, very still silences in which they stood with nothing moving but their modest tails, dark-tasseled, flicked with quick snaps to keep flies off the anus.

They stood at their enclosure—hard ground, sun-dried grass, some rocks, surrounded by a high wall, with trees and vines overgrowing the wall from the other side. They stood straight and almost unbearably alert in a group, each facing a slightly different way, such that the field of vision of the little herd covered all possible threat from any side. They were beings who could not feel safe, never felt safe, even here, where if you coughed their flanks would twitch, if a motor revved far off they'd register it, so with all the children's cries at this busy day at the zoo—the gerenuk constantly blinked, flicked their ears, twitched their flanks, and gave little sharp kicks with their impossibly thin legs, tiny hooves stamping the ground as though about to flee. Clearly in the wild anything could hurt them. They lived by virtue of their alertness—an alertness, a sensitivity, excruciating to watch. How could they bear it? And here, in this enclosure, they were denied the only act that could satisfy their fear, the all-out running for which they were made, for which they longed. He didn't understand how such creatures could be. They shocked him. That was it. Their delicacy was shocking. So he stood there for the longest time.

Most people, mostly children, looked at the gerenuk quickly and went on. In the raucous atmosphere of the crowded zoo, the air shrill with children calling to parents, parents calling to children, children calling to each other, it would take a special child to gaze long at the gerenuk. The man James Abbey felt like that child. Surely they couldn't be this way *all* the time, surely no creature could bear to be *that* frightened? He took his eyes away long enough to read the sign again. They were from Kenya and Somalia. There was famine in Somalia now, drought and civil war. Thousands of human beings dying every day, millions expected to die, the images on the news so terrible even he would turn away. Little children with their mouths hanging open because their jaws were too weak to hold them closed, eyes abuzz with flies—their tiny arms, thinner than the legs of the gerenuk, could not brush the flies away. Before his eyes, if he did not turn his head, each child would become his son. In the footage there were no animals at all. The cats and dogs had no doubt been eaten by now. With all this, and the drought, the fantastic delicate gerenuk must be gone from there.

That was merely tragedy. Tragedy moved him, but it did not impress him. Tragedy was business as usual. But this

creature, this gerenuk, truly impressed him. Even after, finally, he tore himself away. And wondered if, in his well-
made, well-pressed clothes, with his new Panama hat at a
slight tilt, and the healthy tinge of his skin, wondered if he
could possibly look the way he felt, haunted by the delicacy, the delicacy, of the gerenuk.

Lion food, that was the gerenuk. Cheetah food. Leopard
and hyena food, food of wild dogs. The man James Abbey
sought out the lions.

It had been reported in the *Los Angeles Times* not long
ago that a man had committed suicide by jumping into the
lion enclosure. It must have delighted the lions, the moments following quickly one after the other: threat, attack,
victory—the devouring, before anyone could interfere. What
interested Abbey were the fantasies the suicide must have
nursed, perhaps for weeks, who knows, even years: of the
moment of leaping, of being overpowered by the beasts, of
being torn. Of people watching. Children watching. That
must have been important to the suicide, the watching, for
he'd chosen a crowded day.

Abbey approved of it as a way of death—all except the
watching. He couldn't like or admire anyone who needed
that much watching.

Abbey wondered if the suicide had read up on such
things, had read, as Abbey had when a boy, Dr. Livingstone's
journals of Africa: "Starting and looking half round, I saw
the lion just in the act of springing upon me. I was upon a
little height; he caught my shoulder as he sprang and we
both came to the ground below together. Growling horribly close to my ear, he shook me as a terrier dog does a rat.
The shock caused a kind of dreaminess, in which there was
no sense of pain nor feeling of terror, though quite conscious of all that was happening. This singular condition
was not the result of any mental process. The shake anni-
hilated the fear, and allowed no sense of horror in looking
round at the beast." That was the dazed look one saw on
antelope or water buffalo being eaten alive by lions and hye-
nas in the National Geographic films. Clearly once the feeding started they were in another state, no longer afraid. Was
this the state the suicide was seeking, moments of pure con-

sciousness, painless, unafraid, wonderful clarity as he experienced and even watched the creature ravage his body? Or was he ignorant, did he *expect* pain, but find instead a terrible purity of seeing that he had not sought? And did he know things in those moments that were revelation, and worth it all; or was there something in that dreamlike clarity that told him, as he died, he was a fool?

James Abbey reflected that few gerenuk had the luxury of achieving that gifted state of dying. They were too delicate, their slender necks could be broken too easily; simply the impact of the pounce of the cheetah or lion would probably, to his surgeon's eye, either kill them outright or knock them unconscious. What, then, could be the joys of the gerenuk? Their coupling? The company of one another? To nibble sweet fruit, perfectly ripe, during a pause between threats? And is this what made them our brothers and sisters?

"Is she right? Am I going mad?"

He said it almost aloud. His lips moved. He remembered the sudden shock and concern in Elizabeth's eyes.

He had arrived at the place of the lions.

It was not much of a place. A moat of still, scummy water between the barrier wall and a flat half-circle of hard ground, a few rocks, a little shade—more comfortable than a cage, perhaps, but surely, for the likes of a lion, no less boring. And possibly more confusing. When Abbey was a boy, zoos had cages, not enclosures or "habitats." He remembered a huge tiger who paced the cage incessantly, rubbing his nose against the bar as he paced. The skin of the nose had been rubbed away, it had to be a painful wound, yet the tiger never let it heal, rubbing the open wound against the bars every day. That tiger knew where it was, knew it was in a cage, knew it wanted to get out, and it was doing something you wouldn't expect an animal to do: keeping its fierceness alive by intentionally causing itself pain.

Nothing like these two, these lionesses, sitting listless in the sun, beset by flies. The man knew that predators in the wild spend most of their time resting—it wasn't that the beasts were still, it was the helplessness of the lioness before the flies. They were being tormented, flies on their faces, at the eyes, at the tails—yet aside from some twitches and blinks (or simply closing their eyes for a time, though one kept her head erect with closed eyes) these lions did little. Huge beasts, but ragged looking; they had a hopeless air. You can *see* when energy comes off a being—the gerenuks were so very alive—and this is true of people as well (all doctors know this); but no life energy came from these lions. Or had they been drugged because of the suicide? It hadn't been more than a few months. You'd think the zookeepers could have done something about the flies; Abbey couldn't imagine why there were so many flies here, and far fewer at other enclosures (no more than seemed normal at the gerenuks). What was it about flies? They bothered the people too, people carrying soft drinks, people eating cotton candy. And there were yellow jackets, not pestering the lions, but hovering about people with sweets, especially children with sodas, who would panic, swat wildly, scream and run, and their parents or grandparents would yell and run, and everybody would be upset, though neither lioness registered any of this commotion—children boosting themselves on the barricade, yelling, "Lion! Lion!" "Here, kitty, kitty, kitty!" Clicks of cameras. Daddies with minicams. (He saw no mommies carrying minicams.) Would Daddy go home and watch on his television, and show to his children, and show to his neighbors, and show to his relatives, the flies abuzz about the head of the lioness? That man is a Daddy and I am a Daddy and my father was a Daddy, James Abbey said to himself; and in Somalia, as at this place, flies are the only privileged; and I cannot fit these pieces together. He was glad Eddie had not seen these lions.

As he walked away from the lions, past the stench of the camels, who were, if anything, even more beset with flies, he noticed, for the first time in detail, the people he was in midst of. And the peacocks.

The peacocks were everywhere—not obtrusively (though it is difficult for a peacock not to be obtrusive), yet everywhere. They were not obtrusive because of the thickly growing trees and brush, but if you happened to raise your head and look at the roof of a snack stand, there'd likely be a peacock on the roof; or in the branches of the larger trees, or on one of the work buildings, or down a path past a sign that read "Closed to the Public," there was a peacock, this one was a male, with its outlandish plumage, those long feathers with circular tips like eyes and then feathery protrusions from the eyes, in the brightest purples and greens. And another on the roof of the toolshed.

"Oh, my god! Look at that cockadoodle on the roof!" This from a white boy of about twelve.

"*Cockadoodle?*" This from his father, in his mid-thirties, twisting the word so derisively, his voice full of contempt.

"Uh—uh—*peacock*," the boy said.

"*Cock*adoodle?!" The father laughed harshly. And the two walked on.

I am going mad, perhaps, it is mad, perhaps, to want to stop that man and shake him by the shoulders and beg him for mercy—not mercy for myself, I don't especially need mercy, but just: *mercy*. Let the children play in the shade of mercy.

And as though that had torn a veil, suddenly the voices of the children were deafening. There were, everywhere, children, and it seemed none of them were silent, all were calling, calling, *Mommy, Daddy*, each other's names, the names of the animals, words in many languages for candies, for bathrooms, for wee-wee, for who did what to whom, for Mommy, for Daddy, it seemed more piercing now than at the lions, and all you heard as English were the white-toned voices and the black-toned voices standing out (because he could understand them) in a sea of Spanish, or rather Spanish-Indian, and Portugese-Indian, from all over the Americas—they were most of the crowd, two-thirds at least, possibly more, and for every adult there must have been three to five children, sometimes more, and every voice . . . if you stood still, and listened, as James Abbey was now doing, every voice was a different timbre, you could stand and close your eyes, as he was doing, and keep track of every one at once, so many children, by the difference of the timbres, then open your eyes and see them, so many with bags under their eyes, dark circles, circles he knew the meaning of, not enough sleep, not enough good food, too much tension, but eyes so bright, such a terrible amount of laughter, of yelling.

Abbey was dizzy. He sat down on a bench. This meeting place of children and animals, this place where the children are brought to see the animals, this place that is the last refuge of so many of the animals, this place which exists, is supported, by the fact that people bring their children to see the last of the wild animals . . . even sitting down he was dizzy. The world was ending here. Right here. Where the children are brought to the animals. This place could exist only by virtue of the fact that the last twenty thousand years of history—perhaps more, perhaps the last twenty *million* years of history—were ending. And the children called to their mommies and daddies, and were happy one moment, and inconsolable the next, as children are, and had no idea; and the mommies and daddies directed and coddled and scolded the children, and were hassled and delighted by turns, as parents on outings are, and had little idea; but every one of the animals knew. Every one. Absolutely. The man James Abbey understood this with every nerve. I thank You for the privilege of this knowledge, he said sarcastically, silently, to something unseen.

Sitting on this bench I cross a certain line. It is as though this bench were a raft, and it has gone a certain distance, crossing a boundary unmarked on the water. This is the line I cross: I do not care any longer whether or not I am mad. I cared when I stood at the gerenuks. I cared when I stood at the lions. I cared when I heard, truly and finally *heard*, the cries of the unknowing children. But I do not care any longer about being mad.

And, thinking this, he was no longer dizzy. He felt his strength return, he stood up with an odd new vigor. And realized: I am the only person here, as far as I have seen, who is not accompanied by other people.

It was true. As he walked, just looking at the people, ignoring the animals (unable in these moments to face *their* knowledge), he realized that almost nobody came to this zoo alone. Today, as far as he could see, he was the only one. Adults bring children; or teens come together—mostly junior-high age, the gaggles of teens here and there; or lovers come. Some old people. A few old people come together. But now he saw there were many couples. Of varying ages. Some in their teens. Some middle-aged. Some holding hands. Most, in fact, hand in hand, strolling, stopping a little at one exhibit, a little at another, the way people pause at paintings in a museum, long enough to register them, not long enough really to look—but they go, as it were, to be *among* the paintings, the animals, to walk in the atmosphere of "we are at the museum," "we are having a day at the zoo," holding hands, holding hands. "What did you do this weekend?" "We had a nice day at the zoo." Where the world is ending. A world. And some of the couples look "in love," as they say, consuming each other, consumed by each other, loving it, each feeding in their soul upon the other's properties, needing it—such an active, nourishing, exhausting form of delight. The animals understand this. And when each, or one, has had his, or her, fill? Elizabeth? Did we once look at each other that way, yes, we did, just that way, like those two there, standing by the giraffes but looking at each other with looks of such overwhelming generosity. Ah, Elizabeth, generosity is not mercy. One learns this. Or fails to learn it. Isn't that so? Let the lovers learn in the shade of mercy.

I don't want to talk to you anymore, Elizabeth. Nothing personal. It's only that we've reached that place where neither is capable of understanding what the other says— though we'd understand the same things readily from someone else. Elizabeth, Elizabeth—I fear this has nothing to do with psychology. I fear it may even be more basic than that. But don't worry, I may be wrong, since there appears to be a possibility I've gone mad. "Crazy," was your rather panicky word. And you would say it has something to do with the look in my mother's eyes when I rode the camel when I was small in the Bronx Zoo, where my mother was as she was nowhere else, where her fierceness took on a strange brightness. But look at all these mothers, Elizabeth, all these children. Your mother took you to the zoo, too, I imagine, of course she did, you spoke of it—and your mother had eyes too, all these mothers appear to have eyes, bright eyes. Let us posit that "because" is a silly word, "because" is a word not worthy of me, not worthy of you, but if we're going to use such a silly word, even, as it were, for argument's sake (all our arguments, Elizabeth!): then it (I mean: my condition) is *because* my mother took me to the zoo, *because* it's *because* ALL do, and we were part of the ALL, of this noisome crowd, *I was that boy right there*, I wanted Eddie to be that boy too, in this raucous procession that would not exist but for the end of the world. A world. It is not simply who touched who, do you see, not simply that Mama took me to the ladies' room to pee, and we in the stall together, doing wee-wee, she holding my tee-tee so tenderly, and then sitting down herself, and I had to stay so I wouldn't get lost, but I got lost looking at the blood swirl down the bowl, and she got so angry that I saw, so up-set—to use that young policeman's word—so upset with me, not angry, the policeman is correct, *upset*, and I had just ridden the camel, and she had watched so proudly, and I have seen so much blood since, Mama, and Elizabeth, so much blood, you can't imagine, enough to know beyond any possible words how every *because* is washed away sooner or later in the unending unstoppable rivers of every person's and every creature's blood. How many reasons have to combine into any single reason to make it *the* reason or even *a* reason? And how arbitrary are those combinations? How silly any reason seems, when, if you follow it up the river of all blood, it leads to nowhere but another reason, which, if you follow it up the river of all blood, leads to nowhere but another reason, which leads to nowhere. Let the reasons rest in the shade of mercy.

Giraffes are better than reasons. Once he had seen a black giraffe. "Melanic" is the word zoologists use: a melanic giraffe. At the Wild Animal Park in San Diego. From the tram that circles that park. And he'd held Eddie up, compact five-year-old Eddie, held him in his strong surgeon's hands. "Eddie, look! Look at it run!" The black shine of it in the sun, the grace of its stride, and little Eddie caught his excitement, said, "Mommy, it's running!", and Mommy had said, "I didn't know there were black giraffes," and Daddy had said, "Neither did I." They went again a year later, it turned out to be their last visit, and the black giraffe was gone. He'd even dreamt of it a time or two. You cannot forget a black giraffe.

Somewhere giraffes are running now; the sign here says they are not "endangered," merely "rare." They'll run a little while yet.

The sign here says that the first zoo ever was the idea of a queen of Egypt, Queen Hatshepsut, worshipper of Isis, three thousand five hundred years ago; and that, by order of Queen Hatshepsut, a giraffe was brought one thousand five hundred miles down the Nile for her zoo. Not on the sign, but from his voracious reading and in his infernal memory, was that Hatshepsut was the daughter of Thutmose I, and she married her brother Thutmose III, who seized the throne from their father, but it was Hatshepsut who really ruled, and she ruled for decades—and created the idea: *zoo*. "Incestuous patricide," he said aloud, enjoying the taste of the syllables. Nobody noticed he'd said it, halfway through the fourth millennium of the modest invention of a place that would become the crossroads where creatures would meet us at the end of the world. Their world.

Nobody noticed as he said the slippery syllables again, "incestuous patricide," after which Queen Hatshepsut left his mind, and he gave himself up to the charm of the giraffes. His mind could not stop chattering roots and reasons to him, but there was a part of himself it chattered to that did not chatter back, the part that had no need of roots and reasons, indeed no belief in them, knowing giraffes are better than reasons.

There were four. An enormous male—the sign said 18 feet high! "One of the strongest creatures in the world." It is a tribute to that strength, the man James Abbey thought, that we don't think of them as strong. "They have been known to kick the heads off lions," the sign went on. The female was perhaps two feet shorter than the male, and there was a young one, and a child. A family. ("Look, Eddie, a family," he said to the five-year-old Eddie of the past.) The giraffes stood at the far wall of the enclosure, where trees and thick bushes hung over, the adults and the young one close together nibbling leaves, the child a little ways down the wall, also nibbling, and each seemed oblivious to the large numbers of people who stopped and stared (or, like the lovers, didn't stare) and oohed and aahed. Something about giraffes

gentled the crowd—they were charmed. And then the female made her feces. A series of neat tidy pellets, surprisingly small, almost dainty, they spurted like little blackish
eggs from her anus—an anus (if one were standing near it)
at least a foot or two higher than the tallest people in the
crowd. And there were titters, and there was laughter—but
not derisive; pleasant, really. Surprise and enjoyment. It was
even charming to watch giraffes shit.

People started saying his name. They were nearby.

"*James!*" a strong voice called out. A female voice, very
sure of itself, casting forth the name with the force of a spear
thrust. "James," a male voice added, not as sure. "*James!*"
the female called again. A mature voice, yet young, perhaps
not thirty, "*James!*" He couldn't make them out, couldn't
even determine the direction—four walkways met at the giraffe's enclosure, one coming down from an elevation, another rising up, two more from twisty lanes, there was a
snack bar and rest rooms, many many people in motion,
every sort of person, five races, fat skinny short tall, all in
little groups, trying to keep track of each other, many grown-
ups pushing strollers, and in the midst of it, somewhere,
"*James,*" one name of many names, now that he was listening for names. Extraordinary how many names people were
calling, or simply saying, if you tuned yourself to that, in
many languages, mostly Latin, but *English* English as well
as American English, and several accents of American English, and Japanese, German, Arabic, Hindi, Hebrew, even
American Indian, it was actually sort of fun, a kind of game,
to listen for one's name in all that, the word one answered
to, "*James!*" But now by the sound he knew the caller was
no longer coming toward him, had turned, would not come
in sight. And he found himself going in the direction he
thought or hoped the caller had gone. How long had it been
since he'd given himself up to such whims? So he followed
his name.

And in response he heard "*Come on, James, come on!*"
from the weaker voice, the male, turned toward him again;
but not by the end of the phrase, by the end of the phrase
the caller was already looking forward. He tried but could
not pick them out from all the heads of hair, most shorter

than he, most Latin American dark-hairs—the stronger caller might have been that yellow-haired lady down the way, he couldn't say, passing the elephants, and the elephants looked so sad; no, desolate. Truly they looked desolate, in their great concrete pen, smelly, no foliage, a ball and chain—huge ball, thick chain!—around a foreleg of each. And a heavy steel fence between the male and the female. They swayed from side to side. All they could do. Spirits meant to travel in great herds, unchallenged, many miles a day, whose brains were said to be larger than ours, they swayed from side to side at the end of their million years, the very last moments of their million years. He looked about. No one enjoyed watching these creatures. Was he imagining, in the crowd, a sense of respect for the elephants' immense air of desolation? A parent tried to work up enthusiasm for her child: "See the elephant?!" But the child *did*, that was the trouble—a puzzled little girl who wanted to go on.

But where was his name? He'd lost it. He hurried on.

There were many other names. Nadine, Danny, Jesus, Juan, Maria, Brendan, Esperanza, Rachel, and Asian names he didn't recognize as names except by the way they were called, and in all that, occasionally, the *James*, and it was as though he were being led by the hand, in a game of names, to teach him *where* his name might be among all the names—a knowledge he had lost so long ago he no longer knew when, no longer even knew if he'd ever had such a knowledge. He felt ever so much younger, listening for his name, hearing it, moving on. And while with one part of himself he understood very well that this was not normal behavior, he was so glad, so relieved really, to be beyond the grip of that very understanding that he had a bright sort of flush that one could only call happiness. There it was again! The sound of his name delighted him. He did not know that he was smiling.

Past the lone Sumatran rhino, collapsed in sleep; past the hippopotami, standing in water—and one hippo, a whitish goo oozed from its eye, collecting at the edge of the socket, and the man wanted somehow to comfort it, but there was no comfort, at least none that was in his power. "No comfort in my power but the knife." And he went on toward his name.

There was a stupendous cacophony at the chimpanzees! They were screaming and careening, running this way and that over their great rock with its caves and crannies, bumping into each other, yowling in each other's faces, hopping up and down in little circles as they cackled, it was a disconcerting din—*almost* scary, just this side of scary, the cries of the chimpanzees seemed to endow them with power beyond their size. And it went on and on, their excitement. The crowd caught it. The children got giddy and made like the chimps, screeching at them, hopping up and down like them doing sudden spastic little runs, and the parents couldn't get control because they couldn't be heard above the animals and the children, except for the tiny shrill voice of one little girl pointing at one chimp on a high perch, "He's looking straight at us! He's looking straight at us!" While the man James Abbey, the sound of his name lost to him in this great racket, remembered that human beings and chimpanzees share ninety-nine percent of their genes. *Ninety-nine percent of our genes are the same as theirs.* In a normal speaking voice, which could not possibly be heard in that commotion, he said, "The difference between their fate and ours is one percent. One percent of something makes *that much difference.*"

And he pushed his way through the crowd to see if that information was on the sign, and he was offended that it was not. And a keeper came, standing above the enclosure, and she began throwing bananas at the chimps, and you wouldn't think their din could get louder but it did. One percent.

The man walked away in fear. One percent of something? The meaning of this was clear. The meaning of this was:

Anything.

One percent of any being, any situation, could change. That seems well within the bounds of statistical probability. And if one percent of change could make as much difference as the difference between a human being and a chimpanzee, between the *fate* of human beings and the *fate* of chimpanzees—this means that anything can happen. Anything *at all*. He remembered the words of Kierkegaard: "With God, All things are possible. God *is* All things are possible. All things are possible *is* God." And it took just one percent. In any given situation, being, world.

He wished he could hear the woman call his name.

Ninety-nine percent of the genes of humans and chimps are the same. God needs only one percent to make *All Things Are Possible*.

Why didn't the woman call his name, now that he was nauseous with Anything? But now he could hear nothing, not the chimps, not the people. It was all going on in front of him, calming down actually, but he didn't hear it, hardly noticed it. No wonder Kierkegaard died at age forty-one. How long can you bear the thought that all things are possible?

For if all things are possible, then the world man has made, the possibilities we have chosen . . . are an abomination.

"The life I have made, the possibilities I have chosen . . . are an abomination. A travesty." James Abbey stood in the midst of the crowd with his eyes open but seeing nothing, speaking out loud. Some people noticed him and edged away; most did not. "I knew this fact, I've known it for years, about the genes of chimps and men. Why did I wait so long to *know* it?" He didn't notice those who noticed him. He just walked off in the direction he happened to be pointed in, wishing the caller would call his name.

He did not walk, he stepped. One foot placed after the other, puppetlike, as though a string lifted the leg at the knee. The gliding street kid's stride that was still his walk (all that was left him of his beginnings) was, for the moment, no longer his. He walked as he would walk as an old man. Stepped so slowly the peacock almost didn't get out of his way, and its long tail brushed his trousers when it did.

That touch startled the man. The feathers felt stiff and hard through his pants along his right calf. He saw where he was, that he had wandered onto one of the service paths, past a sign that said he shouldn't be there. It was an odd sensation, to remember seeing the sign, walking past it, and

yet not really to have noticed; it didn't register, he didn't
care. He had even stepped over a low chain, without being
aware.

The path curved behind a high hedge. The din of the
crowd was muffled through it. You couldn't really see them
through the leaves, just a mottled moving rhythm, like sunlight reflecting off a fast stream. He was alone.

He took a deep breath. Musty smells of foliage, of animals nearby.

What had he been thinking?

Oh.

He remembered what it was but he couldn't think it here.
There was a resistance to such thought in this leafy solitude.
Insects buzzed about. In order to keep thinking, and he felt
he must keep thinking, he would have to go back upon the
walkway, among the many creatures. By "creatures" he
meant people, too. He meant himself, as well. So he turned,
and realized how oddly, stiffly, his legs were working. He
shook one, then the other. He took another breath. Then
walked slowly, but with his own walk again, out from behind the hedges.

Back among the people, the children and the adults, the
colors and the calls, he felt easier. What had closed briefly,
on that path, opened again—by which movement he realized, with a small rise of nausea, how closed he had been
for so long. Closed was: his life. Open was: this walk in the
zoo. There seemed no way the two could be brought together. He must take this walk, then, while it was his to take.

Eddie? Son? Who is holding who by the hand? You
brought me here, in a way I could not possibly explain to
you. Eddie: All things are possible.

He noticed there were fewer people. He had no explanation. It was just as hot. Perhaps more time had gone by
than he'd thought. Time was a viscous thing today, as likely
to ooze one way as another, at one speed or another. He
wore a watch, of course, and a beeper too, as men of his
profession were expected to, but he didn't raise his arm to

look at the watch—that was a gesture that didn't seem, what was the phrase? Relevant to the proceedings. It didn't seem relevant to the proceedings.

I know quite clearly that I am in a state of what would be called, and perhaps should be called, a nervous breakdown. I have heard of such clarity in others and now I am experiencing it. I feel perfectly fine about it. I am certain that its effects are confined to the zoo. It is something between me and the zoo. When I leave the zoo, I can leave this state. If I wish to return to it, I have only to return to the zoo. I was called by an elaborate series of events—elaborate is perhaps not the right word. Elegant. An elegant conjunction of events. Coincidence or not is beside the point, isn't it? I find myself falling, but certainly not from grace, yet I am falling, but not like just anybody, I am falling like an acrobat, like a stuntman, it's a controlled fall. (I wonder if they all say that.) I will land safely. (I wonder if they all say that.) I will pick myself up and go on about my life. (I wonder if *we* all say that.) I will pick up the knife and go about my life, my travesty, my abomination. I wonder.

There is something called Anything. All things are possible. And the corollary to All Things Are Possible is: Everything Is Inexorable.

All Things Are Possible. Everything Is Inexorable.

Why were, are, there no people watching the polar bear swim? And the Barbados sheep, atop its machine-tooled mountain, the kind of factory-trademark "nature" you see at Disneyland, don't children want to see Barbados sheep? The male with its great horns? And the peacock some feet away from it, visiting the enclosure? Have we become accustomed to peacocks, then, so soon?

He had never seen creatures of such authority. Or rather, seeing them, he had never been open to their nature. The word they are called suits them beautifully, though he had no idea where it came from, who named them, unless it was Adam: "tiger." He had heard of these beasts all his life, pictures of them could be seen everywhere, anywhere, he had seen the pictures, seen the beasts before, in other zoos, but he stood now as though he had never seen, stood as stunned before the tiger as he'd stood before the gerenuk—held in thrall between them, the tiger and the gerenuk, as though between them lay the spectrum of all beauty.

"*James.*"

He was glad to hear the caller again, and the voice seemed quite near, but he did not turn around. He was watching the tiger in the shade of its enclosure. A Bengal. Magnificent. It was too bad the gerenuk was at the other end of the zoo; it would have been a kind of rapture to look from one to the other. "*James?*" For this the tiger had in common with those fragile, gentle antelope: their essence was not changed by their surroundings. You did not get the sense that they were "in captivity"; they were simply tigers, they were simply gerenuk, in this place. Undiminished. Where the lions and elephants were ragged and defeated; where the chimpanzees were frenzied; where the giraffes, like most of the other creatures, seemed in a sort of gentle daze, as though they still couldn't believe, and would never quite believe, they were here—the exquisite gerenuk were absolutely here, taking nothing for granted, you saw that in their bodies. "*James.*" And the tiger, its fur shining, its immense strength radiating, its certainty of its powers evident in each step, evident now in its languor as it lay down and rolled slightly and took in everything with a sweep of its great head, then set its head down on the grass and closed its eyes—the tiger was present. As though waiting. Waiting with the same certainty with which it walked.

"*James? James!*"

He had been looking at the far end of the tiger's enclosure, where the beast had lain down in the shade. He had not noticed other people, and there hadn't been many others in any case. A few children with their "Mommy! Mommy! A tiger!," but the blend of languages and footsteps and cries was not a cacophony anymore, now that the crowds had dwindled—it almost seemed hushed compared to before. So the caller's voice stood out—strong, not far off, and hard to tell now if it was male or female. The man James Abbey looked around, looked for that yellow-haired woman he thought it might have been, whom he'd seen from a distance and behind, but there was no yellow-haired woman.

He turned back to the sleeping, or napping, tiger. The enclosure was sunk deep beneath the level of the walkway. One looked down over a wire-mesh fence—a rather high fence, taller than many children, which seemed odd; the fence ran in a long curve, and your view of the enclosure changed subtly but significantly depending on where you stood. Beneath the fence there was a wide moat of green, scummy water on which floated many fallen leaves. Past the moat the enclosure was comparatively wide and deep for this zoo, the best enclosure he had seen yet. It had leafy bushes and thick green grass, and two large palm trees for good shade. Further back there were gray boulders, and lots of leafy branches hung far out from the walls for more shade. From its perspective the tiger could see only heads peering over a fence high above it and yards away, and birds flying over. It was not exposed to the full hustle and bustle of the place like the chimps, the elephants, the giraffe, the gerenuk. The man wondered what the tiger could hear down there. The depth of the enclosure, and all the foliage, must protect it some from the cacophony. "*James.*"

He almost jumped. It was as though his name had been spoken softly but sharply not far from his ear. He looked around quickly. There was no one who could possibly have said it. The two families at the fence near him spoke a Latin American language. Somewhere far within him a quiet "no" turned back on itself before it reached his consciousness.

"*James.*"

Yes, that was quite clear, his name spoken plainly. In a soft firm voice. Hard to determine the gender from a single word. It could have been a gentle male voice, but he knew women with deep strong voices, it was hard to tell. Female, he'd guess. There was no possibility it was coming from anyone he could see, no. He stood then with his back against the fence, facing now away from the enclosure, suddenly as tired as he had ever been, with not a word in him, not even the "no" deep down, with nothing but a fear so fundamental he couldn't even tremble. There came the thought that he would not leave the zoo under his own power. That the time would come and people would take him away. And he thought of Elizabeth getting the call, and Elizabeth having to tell Eddie, and Elizabeth or the police or someone calling his office, and the receptionist having to call his patients, his colleagues, whomever. He turned slowly back to face the enclosure, and his strong hands gripped the fence so that his knuckles were white. He looked at the tiger resting in the shade of mercy.

The man James Abbey did not expect, could not expect, any mercy for himself.

"*James?*"

In the moments before sleep, when he was a boy, he would hear his name called—in various tones, seemingly from various distances, and with all sorts of inflections. The name stated simply: "James." Or called: "JAMES!" Or questioned: "James?" Or the way kids will call it: "Jaaaaaaayyyyyyy—aaayyyymmmmes." Or very very soft: "James." And not once, each night, but often and in many ways: "James? James. JAMES! Jaaaayyyyy—aayyyymmmes." In the moments before sleep. He had never, as a boy, thought it unusual—it had been merely what happened as one fell asleep. He'd assumed the same calling-of-names happened to everyone falling asleep. He'd also heard, in those moments, scraps of conversation, fragments of sentences, as when it's a child's bedtime during a party, and the child is put to bed and can't sleep, and hears from the other room bits and pieces of the grown-ups' talk that the child cannot fit together, and this continuous patter of fragmentary sentences soothes the child in an odd way, and puts the child to sleep. Never had he been frightened or disturbed by any of this.

The man didn't remember when the voices had stopped. Around the age of ten? Thirteen? He hadn't noticed; the stopping of the voices hadn't been an event. Occasionally, now and again, he heard them still, but this was very rare and didn't seem important. Certainly not disturbing. On the contrary, it had a soothing familiarity, and brought with it a feeling of sweetness. In those rare evenings when the voices came again as an adult—and sometimes years went by when he didn't hear them—he'd slept wonderfully.

But now, toward the end of a bright afternoon, gripping a fence, staring down at a tiger, and hearing his name again, softly and simply, "*James*"—he felt, though there was no threat in the voice, as though all of existence had threatened him.

But in this moment he surprised himself. He would later think of it as the defining moment of his life, the moment when something in him answered:

"What?"

Just that. An answer commonly given to a question not understood:

"What?"

"*Remain.*"

His surprise was total. He had asked and been answered. Ask and it shall be—given, yes, but *what* shall be given?

"Here? Remain here?"

"*Here.*"

"At the zoo, or—right here?"

"*Here. For a time.*"

He looked about and saw, with an almost overwhelming gratitude, that nobody cared that he'd said a few words. A few soft words. To his right and left were Central American families, then further to his right an Anglo family, and nobody cared, even if they'd heard. He suddenly liked these people very much. And the world felt surprisingly safe, in a small sort of way.

He was to remain here. For a time.

It was then that he noticed the second tiger.

He was sure it hadn't been there, hadn't been visible, before. It was at the back of the enclosure, behind a large boulder, and shaded by much long overhanging foliage—there was a square opening into a dark space, a kind of man-made cave, where the tigers could rest and be cool. He suspected that behind the enclosure the zookeepers had access, and that's how the creatures were fed and tended. And now, lying in that space, was the second tiger, its great head raised, and looking straight at him.

It could have been there all the while, but lying back a bit from the opening, in the dark, and then he wouldn't have seen it; still, it could have seen him. Could have been watching him this whole time—though why would it? There was nothing extraordinary about him, except that he was here alone, and was taller than the Central Americans, and was wearing a hat. Could the sunlight on the hat have attracted the attention of the tiger? He didn't see why it might. Yet he had the strongest impression that the tiger was looking at him.

Tigers hunt by sight, not smell or sound. How long ago had he read that? When he was a boy, no doubt, and his mother had subscribed to all those animal books, which they couldn't afford—so he'd read them, he had to. Read them aloud to her. Tigers hunt by sight.

Well, he was remaining. It was the oddest sensation. It made him *very* much want to leave, but he couldn't. He had, he felt, somehow agreed to remain, though he'd uttered no word and had had no thought of agreement.

Agreed with whom? With what?

With the second tiger. That much was clear.

With one part of himself he knew that this could not and should not be happening. He knew it meant he was mad. ("Are you alright?" Elizabeth had said. "You're crazy," Elizabeth had said.) But with another part of himself he had a certainty that he'd heard the voice of the second tiger, was obeying the will of the second tiger—nothing had ever felt more *so*. And with still another part of himself he observed these parts, the part that resisted and the part that surrendered, and wondered that they could exist side by side, both of them whole, both of them him.

And now he felt under the protection of the second tiger. No one would take him away. He would sleep in his own bed.

He watched the beast. The enclosure went so deep that the zoo had installed one of those coin-operated binocular stands, where you put two quarters in the slot and got three

minutes' seeing time. One parent after another had lifted a
child up to the viewer (it was adult size), and they chattered
on about the tigers, the one resting in the shade, the other
watching from the dark opening in the wall. It was all very
pleasant, all inane, in accents of English and Spanish that
now seemed soft to him, and distant, and soothing. But he
had no inclination to look through the viewer.

Rather he wanted to see the beast as the beast was seeing him. And he folded his arms on the fence, rested his
head on his folded arms, and, with no thought crossing his
mind, stared at the second tiger. Sometimes he would shift
his gaze and look at the first tiger. Then again at the second.
With no thoughts whatever, neither waiting for instructions,
nor wondering if the tiger would speak to him again, nor
worrying that he was mad, nor thinking what he might do
next. It was a carefree state of mind. There was a wild happiness at the heart of it. He just looked from tiger to tiger,
and the world as he had known it became less and less significant. And it was through this strangely happy feeling that
he knew the beast had his best interests at heart, for it had
given him good counsel by telling him to remain.

The tiger said one more thing to him when closing time
came and they began to shoo the visitors away:

"*Return.*"

Of course. Of course he would return.

All the world seemed to be exiting the zoo as he was, and
every accent from every corner of the world, in a scene that
made him think of a reversal of the ark: everyone leaving
instead of everyone boarding. While still in the zoo he
stopped at a public phone.

Elizabeth's hello was distant, efficient.

"It's me, Elizabeth."

"Well?"

"I want to talk to Eddie."

"I don't know if he'll come to the phone. I don't know if I want you to talk to him."

"But you'll *let* me talk to him, won't you?"

"I will now. But something's got to change here. Fair warning."

Something *is* changing, he said to himself as she went to fetch Eddie. The boy picked up the phone without saying anything. The man heard the rustle of it.

"Eddie?"

"Yeah."

"I'm at the zoo, Eddie."

"What?"

"I just wanted to call you and tell you I've spent the day at the zoo. It's closing time now and I'm about to leave. I wanted to call you from the zoo."

The boy gave out a kind of bark or grunt—hard to tell if it was a clipped laugh or another sort of involuntary kind of shock.

"What are you trying to prove, Dad?"

"I just wanted to tell you. OK?"

"Yeah, *OK*, what am *I* supposed to say?"

"Goodbye, son."

" 'Bye."

But even that didn't shake the state of mind the man had entered during his time of watching the tigers. As he walked out of the zoo and through the parking lot he thought again of Dr. Livingstone's words: "The shock caused a kind of dreaminess, in which there was no sense of pain nor feeling of terror, though quite conscious of all that was happening." He knew he would sleep well tonight, deeper than he'd slept in many weeks. Wake rested, relaxed, and spend his next two days cutting human flesh.

AN
ECHO

Human flesh is many-layered. These layers are named, for the benefit of science, with long words, each composed of a harsh combination of syllables. "Epidermis," "subcutaneous"—that kind of thing. When you get to the organs, the heart, the liver, the stomach, and such, the layers get ever more delicate—outer walls and inner walls, and walls between the walls, membranes named by the contorted consonants of scientific designation. These words serve their purpose. The work gets done in a brightly lit, cerebral atmosphere, bounded by its own strict protocols and even more so by the language composed for the work and its tools. Beneath the glaring light and the professional propriety, and by means of the language and the tools, flesh is cut, stripped away, fastened back; blood is drained, sopped, and pumped; and organs are taken, manipulated, repaired, replaced—while the body, usually drugged asleep, pulsates, circulates its juices, tries to comprehend, many steps below words, the drastic changes it is being subjected to. Many heal. Some die. Some live on in a half-life that is neither healing nor dying; for some, this grasp of a few more moments or years matters; for others it is terrible, a gift they are in no position to use. Civilization in general takes all this activity to be one of its greatest achievements. The man James Abbey sometimes tried to remember when he had stopped taking civilization's word for that.

A great surgeon (and this James Abbey knew himself to be, though after Vietnam he no longer cared whether anyone else knew it) can feel the parting of each tiniest layer of tissue under his instrument. In the war they would run out of surgical gloves often enough to give him what he called the "classical" feel of surgery, holding the instruments in your bare fingers, feeling the patient's blood spurt on your skin and the organs slick against the sides of your hands as you went in. These sensations made him feel thousands of years old—that is how long people had been trying to do this, and in the last hundred years, the last sixty really, people had learned how at last, and he was the dispenser of all that effort across all that time, and the patient was the inheritor. But he loved, too, the ghostly feeling of the gloves. It was a different class of sensation, hot blood on the plastic, the smoothness of mucus-slick membrane against the thin glove, like making love with a condom.

When James Abbey performed surgery in his dreams, which he did regularly, he usually wore no gloves. It was his bare fingers touching steel, massaging organs, slimy with body juice, slimy but not sloppy. Sometimes, dreaming, he would invent fantastic procedures which he could never completely remember in the morning. Sometimes he would be in full surgical dress, sometimes in work clothes, sometimes he would discover that he was operating with no clothes on—he would suddenly notice this because his feet were icy cold on the tile, or the patient's blood would splatter onto his belly and feel so warm as it trickled into his pubic hair. The shock of his nakedness might wake him. Sometimes, with his hands deep in another's body, he would see that they were caked with dirt. He would be horrified, he would want to jerk his hands out of the body and go wash, but he would be in the midst of a procedure where suddenly letting go would be fatal, and he would be all alone, no staff to help. The last time that had happened he'd had his hands in a woman's breast, he was taking something out, an object he couldn't identify, a little square box about an inch long and wide, black, how could it be opened? What could it contain? A key? A ring? A stone for a ring?

Sometimes the bodies of patients in dreams would change under his hands. From this he would wake in terror. To be operating on a woman and to see suddenly that she'd become a small boy or an old man, or that an old man had grown a young girl's breasts, or that a woman was growing breasts all over her body or a man growing cocks and he had to cut each off one by one. Waking, Abbey would clench his fists to resist touching his own body, his genitals, his body hair, his nose, to be certain he too had not become a changeling.

Not that he dreamed this way every night, or even every month. The surgical dreams tended to come in clusters, and a long time would go by, even a year or more, without one. Then in a matter of days he might dream several a night. The most shocking dreams (yet they were dreams that in a way he looked forward to, or rather: anticipated) were those in which he operated on himself. Sometimes he, as patient, would be asleep, sometimes awake—sometimes awake with a local anesthesia, sometimes without. He experienced every permutation of this scenario, Abbey as patient, Abbey as surgeon, his awareness leaping from one to the other. From this he'd wake with a brutal headache.

Long after he had the dream of the little square box in the woman's breast, he had another where he searched his own body for the box. It was like performing an autopsy. He went into every nook and cranny and couldn't find it. He'd sewn himself up well, Abbey the patient had lived, but that dream left him in a strange, even humorous place: in his actual waking operations thereafter he would sometimes fantasize, Ah, perhaps here, in this intestine, or this spleen, or this breast, or between the folds of these muscles, will be that little black box! I know this is a stomach operation, but I wonder if they'd mind very much if I looked in the lung as well. Then he would smile to himself as he cut and probed, glad that in his profession one wears a mask.

On the night of his excursion to the zoo he had a new dream. He was dressed in the dream as he'd been dressed at the zoo—even wore the hat. He went into a small room, very old, with polished wood floors, and wood walls, and windows on the east and west walls—he knew they faced

east and west, even though for some reason he couldn't see
through the windows, though the glass looked clear enough.
In the room the light was bright but gentle and it had no
source. His surgical instruments sparkled on the tray. And
on a huge stone block, rather than an operating table, he
himself also lay, in the same clothing—except for his other
self's hat, which he noticed had been hung on a peg on the
wall. The patient James Abbey seemed to be asleep, breathing evenly. The surgeon James Abbey took the patient's
pulse. It was strong. He began his procedure. He cut through
the clothing as though it were a part of the body, feeling, in
the cutting, how coarse was cloth compared to the fineness
of skin. Then the delicate layers of flesh parted under his
blade. There was a little blood, not much. He opened the
heart. In it, very small, slept the head and much of the neck
of a gerenuk—but not as though the animal had been de-
capitated, not as though the organs were dead. The size of
a figure on a charm bracelet, the head, with its eyes closed,
breathed sweetly, the slick fur of the neck shined with life.
Abbey closed the heart again. He opened the lungs, and
found there: the full-sized paw of a tiger—he gasped to see
it. He opened the stomach and found: the feet of a chimpanzee. Like the tiger's paw and the gerenuk's head, it was
not as though it had been amputated—they had the calm
presence, with motion so slight as not to be perceptible (unless it is absent), of living things. How thick were the nails
on the chimp's feet—as though of a being immeasurably old.
Abbey knew now that any organ he opened would reveal
some sleeping part of a creature. How strange that his body
had become an Ark! And such an Ark. A vessel of the incomplete. And now he was supposed to open his skull. But
he could not. What if *there* a completeness lurked, what if
the skull were full of flies? Or one great shiny fly? Or, if it
too must be incomplete, then only that fly's many-lensed
eye?

   And with that thought he woke.

   It occurred to him to pray. He couldn't, of course. He remembered the last conversation with his father and mother,
the last time they sat all together at the small round formica-
topped table in the kitchen of their tenement in Brooklyn—

it wasn't their last conversation ever, but it was their last on that street, and their last about the priesthood: when he told them with a finality that they could neither dispute nor avoid that he would under no circumstances become a priest. He was seventeen. His father had said, "What are you then, Jimmy, too proud to pray?" They all knew that in his heart the answer was, at least in part: yes. And his mother had said: "Remember this, then. A man who cannot pray when he is happy should not pray when he's afraid."

He believed then and he believed now that she was right.

The day after the zoo was a day of easy cutting. Now he sat in his kitchen over an evening cup of tea.

It was his habit to have his tea at the kitchen table (strong Irish tea, no lemon, no sugar, no milk), then shower, then sit with a book, or with the paper, or simply sit, letting the house darken. Then would come his fear in the dark, of the dark, which he would set himself to withstand.

Shock is a strange thing. Yesterday he had heard voices, had believed absolutely that a tiger summoned him, a tiger spoke to him. Last night he had dreamed what he had dreamed. You'd think today he would have been upset, registering some kind of shock. Instead he had gone along calmly, competently, quite himself, saying the proper things in the proper tone of voice as he performed the proper acts at the proper time. The events of yesterday would occur to him, but as though he'd seen them in a film—until he stood in the steam of the shower, and its enveloping sound of water, and the almost-too-hot spray pouring over his long body. And it was as though he'd stepped out of the zoo and into the shower, with nothing in between but the dream.

"I know," he said aloud, his voice lost in the water sound, "that a tiger did not communicate with me yesterday. The only trouble is, I believe, absolutely, that it did."

In the steam and the roar of the shower stall he stood and for the first time breathed in, with the hot vapor, what had happened.

The compulsion rose in him to return to the zoo, and as

it did he heard familiar bells—the ringing of the door chimes. Elizabeth had chosen them, wanting chimes loud and penetrating enough so that even when she was gardening in the back or painting in her little studio near the garden she could hear them. They were deep yet tinny, an irritating sound. They rang again.

He stepped out of the shower dripping, puzzled—wondering, too, if he *really* heard the chimes. Anxious to answer the door now, to see if someone was actually there, he wrapped a white towel around himself and made his way through the dark house.

"Beth!" He was so surprised, he said the name he'd called her when they were younger and in love.

"Jim," she said back, but tightly, as though he had volleyed with her old name and she had swatted back the serve with his.

"I'm sorry to bother you," she said. "Why are all the lights out?"

"Turn one on, if you like. Turn as many on *as* you like. What's going on?"

As she went to the lamp by the sofa and switched it on a wave of nausea unsteadied him as he said, "Is Eddie alright?"

"Yes and no."

"Elizabeth, I'm a little—shaky, as you made a point of noticing yesterday. I need straight answers. Is Eddie alright?"

"It's not so bad that I don't have the time to enjoy *you* needing a straight answer for a change." She savored that. "There hasn't been any sort of accident or trouble yet, I didn't mean to frighten you. Didn't think you *could* be frightened. If I'd thought that . . ." Her voice trailed off. "Frightened of anything but being a human being, at any rate. I . . ." Her voice trailed off again.

"It seems my turn to ask: are *you* alright?"

"Would I be knocking on your door like this if I was alright? *Jim?* I'm scared stiff. So scared I haven't been able to *say* . . . It's not an *emergency* emergency, if you know what I mean."

"I haven't got any idea what you mean, as a matter of fact."

They stood a moment looking at each other.

"You're dripping wet, James."

He'd wrapped the towel around his waist. His skin was pale under dark but graying body hair. No flab on him yet, though his chest had sunk a little and his belly hung slightly. She wore a dark green skirt and a shiny long-sleeved gray blouse that set off the gray of her eyes and the lovely gray-white swatch through her black hair. She wore sandals, and the nails of her feet and hands were painted bright red.

She said, "I can make tea while you put something on."

"I'm fine, but make tea if you like," he said, sitting on the sofa.

"I'd really rather—I feel so stupid saying this. Put some clothes on, alright, James?"

"Elizabeth . . . what . . . Fine."

And he went into the bedroom, daubed himself dry, put on a pair of blue jeans and the white shirt he'd worn all day. The shirt smelled stale on his fresh skin. He didn't bother to button it. He heard the water pot whistle, a shrill and annoying sound—and there they were again, the two of them, as though nothing had changed after all, she with that odd habit of letting the pot shriek louder and louder as she calmly arranged the cups and the teabags and creamer, getting everything on the tray just so, until it seemed the only sound in the world was that infernal whistle. It was always such a relief when she lifted the pot from the flame and the whistle died.

In the yard the Outside Cat, the owl, and the birds (who had been sleeping)—and also the rodents living mostly in the basement and the walls, and the dog in the next yard—reacted to the whistle each after their fashion.

He was remembering what she'd said, that cats don't change. But the lioness yesterday, buzzing with flies, was a broken being. No lioness is born broken. Something had changed. And the tiger was undiminished—and must not something have changed for the tiger to be as undiminished in captivity as in the wild? *Cats change, Elizabeth*, he said to her without words, as she brought the tea tray into the living room.

"Eddie said you called him from the zoo yesterday," she said as she prepared the tea—lemon for her, milk for him, as he used to drink it. She'd forgotten that he'd been drinking it black for some time now; since before they split. He noted that little change of habit as a marker for the time when she must have stopped really looking at him, seeing him.

"Yes," he said, "I called him from the zoo. I'm glad he thought the information important enough to pass on. You never know whether he's taking something in or not."

"But that was hours after you left. You were at the *zoo* that whole time?"

"I was at the zoo—a long time."

"I'm sorry. I don't mean to be drawing this out, but—nobody's very good when they're afraid."

"True."

"You know you say all the right things, James, but you don't *show* anything anymore. Do you know that?"

"I sort of do know it, actually." Then: "I wish you'd tell me what you came for." And suddenly: "You know, Elizabeth, I never say things like that to you. Those cutting, authoritative observations—I never do."

"Lack of interest?"

"No. It's not a lack of interest. No. I think—I guess I think it's rude."

"Rude!"

"A strange word to use during the last decade of the twentieth century, I know, but, yes: rude."

"Eddie is hearing voices."

"He . . . " Abbey couldn't finish the sentence.

"Is hearing voices."

There didn't seem, at the moment, to be a sound in the world. The father and mother of Eddie, creators of that silence, shared it.

She said after a while: "Do you realize that you're smiling? Because you look like you *don't* realize it."

"It happens. I smile."

"This is something to smile about?"

"Smiles come from many lands."

"I don't like you, James, I don't, I don't."

"I know, I know."

"It's so *fucking* frustrating that I'm the artist and I'm the practical person, and you're the surgeon and you're the dreamer."

"It frustrates me, too. Eddie is hearing voices?"

"You were shaky when I came in and you're not at all now."

"It's interesting, isn't it?"

"Was that 'rude' to point that out? Do I care?"

"What sort of voices is Eddie hearing?"

"What *sort?*"

"And I'm at least as scared as you are, Elizabeth. Yes, what sort? There are voices and there are voices—aren't there?" He flushed with the fear that he'd let on too much.

"People are saying his name."

"People?"

"Voices."

"Oh."

James Abbey's eyes filled slowly with tears. Elizabeth Cairn-Abbey watched this quietly.

"James?"

"I'm alright."

"Sure. We all are. The whole family."

She understood, below the reach of the words which she depended upon so fiercely, that he was feeling the same terrible apprehension she felt: what have I cursed my son with? What awful thing have I passed on?

But there was something Elizabeth could not have said, for to say it or even admit it to herself would have violated her strict sense of fairness—and yet it was there, buried beneath what she would have called her thoughts, buried even beneath what she would have recognized as her feelings, and it was this: she didn't think Eddie's voices came from her, not really, she thought they came from James somehow.

In the same way, with the sense of fairness that was a large part of what held Elizabeth together, she would not admit that she had longed for Eddie to be a girl, and had kept on longing even after he was born, for she'd felt

squeezed between two such strong and willful male pres-
ences—Eddie had had an extraordinary willfulness even in
the cradle. She'd felt every day since his birth that she was
in a quiet and unrelenting struggle for her very soul against
one or the other or both. Not that they wanted to harm her,
but that either one held the emotional center of a room so
much more firmly than she, and she was always pushing
against that, and this constant effort threatened to exhaust
her capacities for empathy. It had been such a relief to have
one of these males, James, out of her daily life.

For his part, James too had wished for a girl child. He had
no confidence in his ability, much less Elizabeth's, to teach
a boy to be a man. On the operating tables of the war he
had seen, beyond any rhetoric or belief system, exactly what
was expected of boys and men, and how little value civilization finally placed upon the meeting of its expectations.
So James Abbey felt almost guilty for offering a son to his
civilization. Especially since he could not, in conscience,
want his son to grow up to be like him. So he, too, had se-
cretly wished for a daughter.

And now they sat in a dimly lit living room, mother and
father, unable to admit many things, to each other or to
themselves; unable to say almost anything; with someone
they loved but had not really wanted, in their mutual charge;
and with so many strands of love, and of what had been
love, and what was no longer love, woven between them in
that room that it was an effort to move even slightly, an effort to breathe.

In slow motion, then, simply to move, Elizabeth slipped
the sandals off her pretty feet. Odd, to notice that, even now,
James thought. Odd, still to be moved, as though her feet
were not a part of all that had happened and all that had
failed to happen. She saw him noticing. She knew, vaguely,
that it was a suggestive gesture between them. They both
still wanted so much from each other, and knew how to take
so little.

Two people sitting in a room.

"Where's Eddie now?" he finally asked.

"At a friend's. They're doing a science project. He's sleeping over. I brought him there, gave them some help with the

project awhile, building it. Then I came here."

"What's it about—the project?"

"Gravity. What will we do, James?"

"You already have a plan or you wouldn't be here. You came to recruit me for something, Elizabeth, not to ask for my help. You don't trust me enough to ask for my help."

"I don't have to speak to that."

"Right."

"Do you want to hear this or not?"

"I don't want to, no; I must."

"Yes."

"So?"

"He tells me that in the moments before sleep—"

And she went on to say what he knew she'd say. The same voices Abbey had heard so often.

"How long has this been going on?" he asked.

"Not long. Weeks, he says."

That's why he's frightened, Abbey thought. Mine began when I was so little I thought it was normal, they never frightened me. On the contrary, realizing they'd gone disturbed me a little. Gone till yesterday.

"Did he tell you anything else about the voices—the way they said his name, was it hostile, threatening?"

"He said they were soft—even said some were 'lovely,' which is not an Eddie word—and some were frightening. I mean, it even upsets me that he used the word 'lovely.' It's *really* not an Eddie word."

"And you want what of me, Elizabeth?"

"Family therapy, the three of us. I don't mean *technically* 'family therapy,' I mean the three of us in session with someone my friend Karen—"

"I'm sorry, but your friends all kind of blur together for me. Which one is she?"

"You don't care anyway, why ask?"

"True. So she said what?"

And Elizabeth went on to describe what Karen said about a particular sect of psychotherapy while James made a show of listening, though he barely heard a word. For silently, intently, he was saying to her: I am betraying you, Elizabeth. And I may be betraying our son. My son. I cannot tell you about my voices. All these years we've known each other. Loved each other once. Had, have, a son together. And I've never told you, and cannot tell you. And I don't know if I am being, as you would say, "fair," or not. Probably not. Must I tell my son? I do not think I can.

"Well?" she finally said after her description was done.

"Well what?"

An exasperated silence was like static between them.

In the silence, Elizabeth, I love you. When we speak I don't. Back and forth. So strange.

Elizabeth, for her part, did not permit herself the words that would have expressed her frustration and her fear, words that would have said: I have tried to protect my son from your strangeness and now it seems I've failed and I don't know where to turn.

"When is the appointment? I'll be there, of course."

"Thank you," she said, and gave him the details. "I'm frightened, Jim."

"So am I."

"You always think I'm strong no matter what, but I'm not. *Really* not."

"Isn't it strange," he said, "how well we function regardless? There's something really horrible about how efficient we all can be when we're so cracked inside."

"There is. There really is. It's that way for everybody, that's the thing—and I think that's what makes us all afraid of each other."

"I think it does too. Are you afraid of me?"

"Very."

"I'm afraid of you, too, Elizabeth. I'm afraid of Eddie. Which is the worst thing of all. My father was never afraid of me."

"I'm a little afraid of him too."

"It must be so horrible, for a child, to be feared by his parents."

They didn't try to comfort each other. There was no comfort for this. They let the moment slowly pass.

"I worry about you, too, Jim—do you know that?"

"I would never have guessed."

"I do. I'm allowed, aren't I? If I'm not I should be. You

looked—*terrible* yesterday. Your eyes. And calling from the zoo. How *are* you?"

"I don't know how I am, actually."

"Well—who does?" She smiled a small smile. He guessed her thought: that she wasn't going to be able to depend on him.

"Just what you needed, right?" he said.

She shrugged. "I guess I ought to go."

She slipped her feet back into her sandals and stood up. He stood. In his bare feet and her sandals she came up to his chin. They walked to the door. Looked into each other's gray eyes.

"This is the first time—" she began.

"—that you've been back in this house. I know. And the first time—"

"—we've talked."

"In months."

"Maybe years."

"Was it that bad? I suppose it was. I talk to you a lot actually." He was surprised he'd said that.

"Do I talk back?"

"Sometimes."

"Hearing voices?"

"You might say that. You?" he asked.

"I talk to you some, but—you don't talk back much, you never did."

"Eddie—does he speak about me?"

"He's angry at all of us, Jim."

"All of us?"

She made a gesture that took in the lights of the hills and the sky. "All of us. But yes, especially you. Especially me, too, but it's easier with he and I, we can get through some of it fighting over little things, the garbage, the dishes. You didn't fight with him much—he's probably angry at *that* too."

They stood at the front door. The hills glittered with lights in the desert breeze. She touched his arm, by way of goodbye. He touched her shoulder.

He stood at the door as she walked the stone path to the gate, and startled him with: "Look!"

She was pointing to the possums, the mama possum with

her babies, one of them albino, clinging to her back and around her neck. James and Elizabeth stood still and the mama possum stood still. Then the animal felt safe and continued on her way. They watched her go.

"She's headed for the Outside Cat's food," Elizabeth said.

"She'll be disappointed; I forgot to feed him tonight."

"He does fine on the mice and birds when he has to."

"He seems to."

They didn't know what to say or do. They gave each other a look that said as much, and she turned from him and went to her car. He went to the gate and watched her walk to her car, to be sure she was safe. She got in and drove off. Neither waved. The stones of the path and the grass felt cool under his bare feet. He stood where they had stood and looked where they had looked, toward the lights of Pasadena and Glendale. Those lights were supposed to mean that the world was a certain way, and he had tried for a long time to pretend he believed them, that the world *was* as it advertised itself. Well—that pretense had fallen at long last. The lights in the hills—*they* seemed the pretense now.

"I'm neither happy nor afraid, Mother, at this moment. Is it alright, then, to pray for my son?"

James Abbey stood in his yard and tried to pray. The evening air had that touch of coolness that makes Los Angeles so pleasant at night, even in the hot months. The low continuous hum of the freeways nearby blended in a kind of harmony with the incessant, pulsating chirps of the crickets, together forming an absorbant sound that rendered most other noises featureless. Abbey moved his lips but could make no sound himself—moved his lips not trying to form words, but as though hoping the movement would call words to his mouth.

The creatures noticed him—the owl high in the tree, to whom he was not important, and the Outside Cat, to whom he was. The cat sat watching from a shadow close by, though the man was unaware.

"God—"

He said the word with a low, choked rasp. It lodged in his throat, he couldn't get it all the way out. More a moan than a word.

"Eddie—" he said more clearly.

And that was all the prayer he could pray. And even those two words cost him much, made him a little dizzy. And yet he knew it *was* a prayer, this opening of each word, each name, to the other. This joining of the two words. With no request. No begging. Just the joining. A prayer stripped clean.

Thus he prayed his first prayer since he was seventeen.

A
SINGING

The gerenuks were quieter. It was a quieter time. One of those afternoons that calms L.A. now and again, when gray clouds from the sea drift inland a few miles, enough to shield the city from the sun. Often their shade lasts only through morning, but sometimes the sea's clouds remain, sometimes for days, granting a restful feeling in a city where it is possible to take for granted the irritation of constant brightness. On these cloud-covered afternoons fewer people went to places such as zoos, so, with a respite from the crush of humanity, the gerenuks were calm.

The man James Abbey was thinking that had he drawn the gerenuks since his visit a mere two days ago, he would have gotten them wrong. He had a flair for drawing, a nice feel for line—just a feel, nothing like the talent of Elizabeth, but he would sometimes sketch for relaxation. It was a gentle activity for his hands, compared to the harsh precision they were used to. So had he drawn the gerenuks from memory he would have gotten the tininess of their hooves, their tense incredibly thin legs, then the graceful swoop of the flank line into the torso, and their bodies' compact sensuality, their sleek fur and delicate shadings; but from there he would have gone wrong. Their necks were as long as he remembered, fully as long as their legs, and as graceful, as delicate; and, true, the pounce of a lion or a cheetah could snap them—yet the erect way the gerenuks stood, with neck so straight, gave the quiet, tender beasts an air of sweet dignity. Yes, they were vulnerable to virtually any predator. The mottled markings on their backs suggested camouflage even from threats above (leopards in the trees, or the eagles of the Ngong hills). But somehow even their vulnerability was contained in the sweetness of their dignity. Again he felt great wonder that a force as massive and irresistible as God could create anything like the delicacy and vulnerability of the gerenuk. And as he stood there, having walked through the zoo gate into the territory and container of what he had named his madness, he felt the gerenuk as not a creation so much as an expression.

"It's a different idea, isn't it?" he said softly.

His eyes moved over the gerenuks in a mesmerized way, and he felt that his look touched them, actually touched them—that through his look as through an invisible beam he knew the texture of their fine close fur, the suppleness of their muscles, the softness; and that they, on their part, felt his look as the gentlest of touches, a touch they would not flinch from.

"What was I just thinking of?" he said in an almost conversational voice. "Oh."

That the gerenuk was not so much a creation of God as an expression of God. Does an artist, for instance, create or express? It is *not* the same idea, James Abbey thought. There is a separation between the creator and the created: what a creator creates will go its own way and break the link with its origin—like a child when it becomes an adult. But there is no separation between the expresser and the expressed: the expressed thing, the expression, is a word in the process of being said, a cry in the process of being screamed, a song in the process of being sung; hence while the expression exists it is not finished, completed, created, but still in the process of creation—the word I am speaking, the thought it is expressing, is alive in my mouth, there is no breakage of the link between us. So if a gerenuk is a song of God's, then while a gerenuk lives, that song is still being sung, still alive in the mouth and breath of God. As I am. As you are. Not created things sent off into oblivion alone, but words formed of God's breathing. Even I. Even you. Even the gerenuk.

In the beginning was the Word. And the Word was with God, and the Word was God.

Finally, after half a century, he understood that.

And the light shineth in darkness; and the darkness comprehended it not.

"*James?*"

I am coming.

"*James?*"

Yes, I am coming.

He walked several yards with long strides, then stopped as abruptly as a puppet. With puppetlike, jerky movements he searched his pockets for a map. He had a map, in fact he had two—two copies of the same map, the pocket map of the zoo that one is given at the gate. He hadn't even noticed taking them, nor putting them in his left back pocket, much less how he'd received two. He started to throw one away (there was a trash can within reach) but thought about *which* one to throw away, couldn't decide, so kept both.

All right, he thought, I know the word "compulsive," this thing of the maps is a kind of . . . and his thought trailed off. He was interested in getting to the tigers without passing the chimpanzees again. He determined the way from one map and then carefully threw the other out, placing it rather than dropping it in the trash can.

The coolness on his cheeks: that was the drying of tears. In the last few minutes he had wept without knowing, as last night he had smiled without knowing.

"*James?*"

He turned, went the way he'd come, stepping slowly, the way one walks after an accident. If I am an expression, rather than a creation, then God is *right here* always. And everything, even the most horrible thing . . . He looked at the gerenuk as he passed them, and one looked at him, a female whose neck made the sweetest turn as she watched him go. He wished he could get closer to her, to see into her eyes.

He made his way past the rock hyrax, the black rhino, and the bongo; the heartbreaking elephants; the mountain tapir; the hippos, and that one with the goo still oozing from its eyes. At the hippos he ran out of luck. For right across from the hippos were the gelada baboons, their faces so intent, but intent with boredom—a discordant sort of expression. The thick gorgeous manes of the males, the short-haired females looking like wise old ladies who hadn't yet had enough of sex, and the strange hairless shining red areas on the chests of both genders, and how they sat still among each other and paid no attention to the people. It would be good to sit among them.

"It's not time for that," James Abbey said softly.

The sign said that in the wild (where there will soon be none) it is the nature of gelada baboons to travel in groups of as many as four hundred. Abbey walked the length of the enclosure, where these five creatures sat, and tried to imagine the hundreds that should have been beside them, and what with the foliage and how the path curved, not until it was too late did he see that the gelada baboons were adjacent to the chimpanzees—he had come upon the chimps this time from the opposite direction.

He'd had no warning, for the beasts were quiet today. But there: two were kissing, on the lips, a he and a she. Very fondly. Just like anybody. And now they're smiling at each other—those *are* smiles, unmistakably, the gentle, private smiles of intimates. And now . . . she bent her head and kissed his shoulder. What gesture could be more human? So human and, for Abbey, deeply shocking. These chimpanzees shined with love for each other, anyone could see that. The one percent difference between their DNA and ours, whatever it effected, had nothing to do with love. Those two beings were in love, and even he, Abbey, who knew so little about love, could attest to it. Love is not a *human* quality, then.

This, for some reason, made his eyes shine.

And he remembered that a human being could get a successful blood transfusion from a chimpanzee (it had been done), and that chimps could catch all our diseases. They can learn the sign language of the deaf, make up their own words, and teach their vocabularies to each other. "But can they hear voices like me and Eddie?"

Shut up, shut up, shut up, people will notice—he said to himself, clenching his jaw.

But no one noticed. Or they pretended not to. Except one who said:

"Hi!"

A very little boy, a white boy in a cherry-red cap, beamed up at him and said again: "Hi!"

"Hello."

The boy's parents were right behind him, smiling at Abbey, the shining smiles of two intelligent people who were having one of the happiest moments of their lives. Abbey saw that clearly. Saw that this was the child's first trip to the zoo, and it was one of the best days that ever was or ever would be for these three, child and father and mother.

"Hi!" the little boy said again, with his radiant and indiscriminate smile.

"Hello!" Abbey said again, louder.

And the boy pointed to the chimpanzees and said:

"There!"

"Yes," said Abbey.

"There!"

"Oh, yes."

And the mother and father laughed and Abbey sort of laughed, and they passed him with their boy, passed in time not to see Abbey's face contort to suppress his sudden bottomless sob. He could not suppress it. And he did not look around to see if they'd noticed.

"I have been visited by angels," he whispered. "I wonder if they know they're angels." And I wonder, he continued silently, how long they will remain angels. Another twenty minutes? Another year? The man James Abbey looked back at the chimpanzees, the he and the she sitting in contentment side by side. He would swear that they were smiling. Angels everywhere.

Well, that was natural at the end of the world.

He stood at the tiger enclosure waiting for instructions. He was certain they would come, though he wasn't certain what he'd do with them. All the second tiger had given him, as yet, were instructions (*Remain, Return*) or the invitation of calling his name.

"I already know my name, thank you," he said softly. "I'd much prefer instructions."

But he couldn't see the second tiger. The beast must have been deep in the cave. The first tiger, however—and James Abbey knew the difference, though he couldn't have said how—was doing something he thought very odd. The beast was pacing. Far back in the enclosure the Bengal paced back and forth at the rear wall as though in a cage, and using only as much space as a cage would allow. A stream of water flowed into the moat from a pipe high on the wall and made a soothing sound that dimmed the construction work banging and clanging somewhere near—work which suddenly stopped, and there was only the water rushing, and the wind in the leaves. In this lull the tiger paused, looked up, then continued pacing, while it glanced now and again toward the top of the wall. It expected or wanted something, obviously, but what?

The children were as excitable today as Sunday, but there were so few of them that their cries and calls were more like birdsong than cacophony. "*Tey*-gre" and "tee-*gee*-ra," the Latino children said, after they had spotted the pacing beast against the far wall. They left, and then an Anglo child of seven or so came with his parents, and asked, in that oddly formal voice children use to ask a troubling question, "Why do the tigers like to live there?"

The mother didn't like the question. You could hear in her voice that she didn't enjoy saying what she said: that the tigers didn't like it, but that they were here for the zoo.

"Is this the zoo?" the boy asked. He was told yes. "He doesn't like to live in that place. Why does he?"

" 'Cause that's his *job*," the mother said. The father said nothing. The family left. But Abbey heard in her voice that the mother knew precisely what she'd just told her son. It impressed him, her resolve to answer the boy honestly. For that boy would be changed by this day, and the way he

looked at his parents when they went off to their "jobs"—
that would change. How long ago had these three been like
the other three he'd just seen? Abbey felt badly for them,
and in a sad reverie of empathy he no longer watched the
tiger, he merely stared down into the moat, until he heard
the singing.

Oh Danny boy, the pipes the pipes are calling . . . A caressing, cracked voice, breathy, holding to the tune gently.
A young woman. *From glen to glen, and down the mountain side* . . . He was afraid to look up, afraid to look anywhere. *The summer's gone, and all the roses falling* . . . His
eyes were closed now. Though standing perfectly still and
straight, he felt lost in a swoon. *It's you, it's you must go,
and I must bide* . . . The voice hesitated longer than the
pause in the song, but when he thought she had stopped
she sang, *But come ye back* . . . She skipped the rest, went
to *Oh Danny boy, oh Danny boy* . . . Her voice softened to
silence, never singing the last line. He sang it within: *I love
you so.*

He knew he had to look at the young woman, but he
wondered if he actually was turning toward her as slowly
as he felt the movement, it seemed to take so long.

Her green eyes looked directly into his.

"Are you gonna cry again?" she said.

"Excuse me?"

"I saw you when you were standing over by the
watchamacallits."

"Gerenuks."

He was so startled at her frankness! He felt as though he'd
been slapped, but not in anger. A stinging, playful slap.

"I noticed you 'cause you were alone," she said. "I don't
mean like the photographers, who aren't *really* alone, because they're with their hobby. Or like the sketchers, who
get assigned here, you know, for some class, like. You were
alone. I kind of resented it, you know? 'Cause I like to have
this place to myself, being The Alone Person here. Is this
gonna become a hangout for people, or what? I mean, one
or two weirdos is OK, but, you know, like, *one* more and
I'm outa here. I mean, they'll start building condos an' shit."

He had to say something in order to breathe.

"Am I—a weirdo?"

"You? *No.* There's *lots* of old guys hanging around reindeer crying."

"They're not—reindeer," he said. Am I old? he thought. "They're nothing at all like reindeer."

"Fair enough. They're not. OK."

She was twenty-odd, twenty-three perhaps. Green eyes. Severely cut, dark hair, tinted with henna. It was a Russian kind of look, Eastern Europe, somewhere like that—full lips, strong nose, oval face. The flesh under the eyes was both dark and red. She was too young for that. It was easy to diagnose her sleeplessness, bad food, alcohol probably, probably tobacco too, and, given her generation, some drugs. He couldn't tell about her body; her clothes were dark and baggy, meant to hide her contours. And she wore—and Abbey felt this detail in his chest—the same sort of dark black thick-soled boots that Eddie had worn Sunday. So she was somehow of the people whom Eddie wanted to be. Or, if she was not, then at least they'd had some impact on her.

"Why are you looking at me like that?" she said.

"I'm sorry."

"You're not gonna call the guy on me, are you?"

"The guy?"

"The attendant—what-you-call-'em, the zoo guy."

"Why would I do that?"

"It happened. Somebody thought I was crazy. 'Cause I was singing. Bet they wouldn't've thought so if I'd been dressed like money."

"Does singing make you crazy?"

"*Anything* makes you crazy. But I'm not. And I'm a *member.* That surprises them."

"A member?"

"Of the zoo. I've never been a member of anything, but I'm a member of this zoo. To be a member means you belong, right? So I belong here, so I can sing here."

"Makes perfect sense," he smiled.

"Oh. You smile. Well, well. Are you a member?"

He thought of all the professional organizations and political committees he had ever been a member of.

"No. I'm not a member."

"Oh."

This made her pull back for some reason, so he said quickly, surprising himself, "I may become one, though. I will, actually."

"Well, you should. It's good for the zoo."

"I suppose it is."

"Costs a lot, though. Costs *thirty-five* dollars. Do you know how long I have to stand at a cash register for thirty-five dollars take-home? I figured it out, about twelve hours."

In the same amount of time James Abbey could make thousands.

"So I had to think about it, you know," she went on, " 'cause I only work thirty or so hours a week—they keep us officially part-time so they don't have to pay any benefits, you know?"

He didn't know what to say.

"But you have money, don't you. Good clothes. So you should *really* become a member, you should become one of those fancy members—they have titles for them, but I don't know them."

He looked away from her, into the tiger enclosure.

"There's a second tiger, isn't there?" he said.

"There sure is."

"Does it ever come out?"

"Why should it? Where would it go? New Jersey? Hang out at the mall? There's nowhere it can go."

"I meant—out of the cave back there."

"Oh. Sure it does." Then, darkly: "Don't think I'm stupid."

Abbey thought, instead: I'm out of my depth. He said, "Why would I think that?"

" 'Cause I answered a question you didn't ask. That's just a mistake. It doesn't mean I'm stupid."

"You're right. And I don't."

"OK."

They watched the Bengal pace at the far wall.

"Why do you think," she said, "he keeps looking up at the top of the wall?"

The Bengal stopped suddenly, stared straight at them,

gave out a brief throaty growl. They couldn't help looking at each other with startled eyes.

"What'd *we* do!" she said, and they shared a puzzled smile. Again the breeze lulled, and again the tiger paused and looked around. "He's thinking *all* the time, isn't he?"

"Do you sing to all the animals?"

"Only the ones I really like."

He whispered, not knowing he was whispering: "Why?"

She turned full toward him. And leaning as she was against the fence, her dark bulky clothes, her thick ugly boots, her face so young and weary, her eyes so green, he saw the grace of her that her clothing hid and was meant to hide—how lightly she leaned, how poised was her balance. He realized he liked her enormously. She was quite young enough to be his daughter; it wouldn't have occurred to him to imagine anything sexual with her. But he was overwhelmed with fondness.

"Was that," he asked, "a silly question?"

"Pretty silly." She smiled at him truly for the first time. All the weariness left her face. He smiled back. And they turned again, as though moving to the same music, toward the tiger.

"Look," she said.

"I see him."

The second tiger stirred within the shadow of its cave. He moved into the light at its entrance. When James Abbey had asked the young woman if there was a second tiger, he had, again, surprised himself. He had seen the animal two days before, and had heard others talking about the animal. He'd mentioned the beast to her because he needed to. A need that spoke of its own volition. And now, seeing the second tiger while standing by her side, he felt, for the first time in so long, accompanied.

The tiger reclined with its head and paws in the open, its body extending back into the featureless shadows of its cave, so that it seemed that halfway down its back the body somehow disappeared. They stood together simply looking, till the first tiger broke its strict pacing and walked the paths the tigers had worn in the grass of the enclosure. In its movement there remained something preoccupied, disturbed.

"Thinking all the time," she said again.

Then the beast went back to its pacing place.

"That's the damnedest thing, what she's doing," said the young woman. "I followed you, you know."

"You what?"

"I didn't *mean* anything by it. Don't look so confused. Look—when you've been to the zoo a *lot*, you know? When you really come a *lot*—you've got to find a way to walk around that isn't yours. 'Cause you use up all *your* ways pretty fast, you know, a couple-a months, and then this place just becomes, like, a *habit*, you know, and *habits* . . ." Her voice trailed off in such a way as to let him know exactly what she thought of habits. "So I pick a person, and take *their* walk—doesn't do *them* any harm, right? It's not like I'm a stalker or something. I just pick an interesting person and lay back behind them and take their walk."

"And old guys crying at reindeers are pretty interesting, you think?"

"Gerenuks."

"Very good."

"You're not *that* old—are you?"

"Fifty."

"Jeeze!"

He couldn't help laughing and, like anything unused for a long time, his laughter creaked and cracked. They laughed together.

"Jeeze, huh?" he finally said.

"Jeeze is right. But you're not retired or anything?"

"No."

"Well, what're you doing here, don't you work for a living?"

"Don't you?"

"Swing shift. Gotta go soon. Don't you? Work?"

"Sure."

"You don't want to tell me?"

"I don't mind." But his pause showed them both that he did, and it confused him.

"Let's put it this way," she said. "Yesterday, at this very time, you were doing what?"

"I was sticking a small knife into someone."

"*Good*bye."

And she turned and walked away so swiftly it was as though she'd never been there.

A
MEETING

It was as though the world had emptied of whatever made it a world. The colors, the sounds, the Bengal pacing its far wall, were the same, exactly the same, but something that had unified them and given them dimension had suddenly been stripped. They had no sheen, no depth, and seemed curiously unconnected to one another. The people who had come and gone and come, while he and the girl had been together, and whom they had not noticed, now seemed denuded even of the purpose they had before: that of proceeding from animal to animal, and stopping a moment at each before moving on, in order to make the zoo possible.

The man James Abbey would not (because he could not) have thought that for a few moments, with a stranger, he had been *in* the world for the first time in many years, and the manner of her departure had cast him out of it again. Though he had received many shocks these last few days, this one was extraordinary among them. He could not let himself think what his panic felt, which was simply: I cannot bear to enter this un-world again, and yet here I am.

He looked down at his hands where they rested on the guardrail, and they appeared still, though he felt tremors in his fingers. And in his arms, and in his calves. Is this how one comes to an end, he thought, in a stillness in which everything trembles?

The second tiger seemed not to have moved since he'd last looked. Alone in existence, to his eyes, it had dimension, its great head poised toward him, its body disappearing in shadow.

James Abbey whispered, "What am I to do? Please. Please."

"*Remain.*"

But at this word Abbey wanted to run, run, and run and catch up to her and beg her forgiveness for frightening her. That—and that was all. No spark of desire, nothing of the kind, shadowed his heart. He wanted only, and so deeply, to take the fear from the frankness of their contact.

The Bengal paced, and the Spanish children said "tee-gi-ra," and James Abbey stood for he did not know how long. Until the second tiger released him from its instruction, he would remain, no matter what the consequences.

"Don't turn around, OK?"

He made a small sound that wasn't a word.

"You *scared* me," she said from right behind him. "You don't *know* how I hate being scared. Especially here."

"I'm sorry," he managed to say. "I'm a doctor. A surgeon. It's just how I—think about it. Knives."

"Maybe I believe that and maybe I don't."

He had no way of knowing if she was actually behind him. No way at all. He very nearly couldn't stand that.

"Why did you come back?" he said.

"To say goodbye."

"What's your name?"

"No way. No way I tell *anybody* my name at the zoo. Especially you."

"You're a member," he said, "they have it written down somewhere."

"But they don't connect it to anything. I don't even connect it to anything."

"My name is James Abbey. James Abbey."

"I just came to say goodbye."

He didn't know what to do.

" 'Bye," she said.

He had the strongest sense that she was standing still as he—if, that is, she was there at all. It never occurred to him to turn around. Somehow there were rules in this. They weren't the rules of the world that called itself "the world," but they were rules nonetheless, and all the more stringent for being the only means of order in a condition that (like any world, actually) had no reference but itself. So he didn't turn around.

But he said, "People who say 'goodbye' generally—go somewhere."

"That's what you think."

Then after a little she said, still behind him: "We're *meeting*, aren't we. This is a meeting. We've met now."

"Yes. I think we have. We've met."

"We probably won't forget each other."

"Probably."

"So we've met."

"Now what?" he asked.

She stepped beside him, leaned on the rail, as she had been. Tears of relief came to his eyes. Her eyes were shining, clear, green.

"I gotta go to work soon," she said as though nothing had interrupted them. "You're a doctor, huh?"

"A surgeon."

"Big bucks."

"Pretty big, yeah."

"I hope we never see each other again."

"Why?"

" 'Cause. It's too weird. Even for me. Talking to a guy like you. Tell you what! I'll flip you for who gets the zoo. Tails you stay away, heads I stay away."

"How about, I come Mondays, Wednesdays, and Saturdays, and you come Tuesdays, Thursdays, and Sundays."

"That leaves Fridays," she said.

"Nobody comes Fridays. Fridays we'll both know the zoo is empty, as far as we're concerned." He felt as though someone else was speaking, the words came so easily.

"Deal."

They smiled at each other—each thinking that the other's smile looked terribly tired.

"I gotta go," she said. "Nice meeting you. Kinda."

"It was nice meeting you."

"That other tiger hasn't moved at all, this whole time," the young woman said.

"I keep feeling it's looking at me. Can't shake that feeling." James Abbey wasn't aware of it, but he was beginning to imitate the girl's speech rhythms.

"Why shake it?" she said.

"I don't know. No reason, I suppose."

She stood straight and extended her hand. He took her hand. It was a strong, warm hand. Her fingers weren't tapered or aristocratic, like his; they were much thicker at the base than at the tip, and the nails were bitten just a little on each finger, giving them a blunt, almost clumsy appearance. But his knowing hands could feel the strength and physical confidence in hers.

"Mondays, Wednesdays, and Saturdays," she said. "Those are your days, remember."

Their hands lingered with each other then broke away.

" 'Bye."

She walked a couple of steps backwards, taking her leave of him like a lady, and with a small half-smile she turned and walked off, a slightly pigeon-toed walk, in worn thick boots, her bulky clothes like a cloud around her body.

How long had he been at the tiger enclosure? At least an hour. Surely the "zoo guys," as the girl had called them, noticed, and were keeping an eye on him. He would if he had their job. Yet still it didn't feel time to leave.

Or rather: He didn't know how to leave.

Anywhere else a reason would be enough; here, what was needed was a sign, a signal.

The second tiger would give it when he—she? the voice was not specific—was good and ready. This he had complete faith in, with one part of himself. But other parts of him were terrified by that very faith. Thus he stood at the railing of the tiger enclosure in a state of terrified faith.

"*Follow her.*"

But she's long gone.

"*Follow.*"

Something cold took him then. Horribly cold.

He said firmly to the tiger: No.

He looked intently at the beast to get his thought across: Is this how I become a serial killer? Is this the knife trying to wield me as I have wielded the knife?

"I need help," he whispered.

"*I am your help,*" the tiger said.

Noooooooo, he said, within, in a moan.

"*I am your help. Take the help that's offered, or be lost.*"

"Speaking in complete sentences now, are we?"

"Excuse me?" a mother beside him said. She was holding her daughter up over the rail to see the tigers.

He blushed: "Just thinking—out loud."

"I do that all the time," she said in a sprightly way and walked on, talking to her daughter.

How is it that strangers forgave him so easily, yet he felt so unforgiven?

"*Follow.*"

Dr. James Abbey, not wearing a hat today, but looking quite substantial and respectable, turned from the tigers and walked in the direction the young woman had walked, aware again of his surroundings, aware that a few people were about, that the breeze was cool, that the light was clear, and he heard again the murmur of the freeway, the children's high voices, and the clatter of construction. But he repeated to himself a sentence not of a world dominated by freeways and construction work: Take the help that's offered or be lost.

The device on his belt beeped its shrill signal.

"Talk about hearing voices."

He almost didn't have the will to shut the beeper off. His vacation didn't technically start until tomorrow. He was still on call. He couldn't help it, he had to laugh (twice in one day!): his impulse was to go back and explain to the tiger, See, I'm a doctor, and this is a beeper, and when it beeps I *have to* go, call in, see what's going on, offer my services, it's my job, I took an *oath*, for crissakes, so I can't follow that young woman right now, I'm sorry very much.

The muscles in his legs wanted to turn around and go to the tiger, the muscles in his mouth wanted to speak, but he didn't permit them; instead, he checked his map for the nearest phone. He would have to walk between the giraffes and the chimpanzees. A walk he was not capable of.

Ah, he was wrong, there was a phone nearer, by the maned wolf and the tapir, the ocelot and the Galápagos tortoise, a creature which would, if fed properly, be alive long after James Abbey was dead. But so would the baby chimps—chimps live to be fifty or so, those baby chimps would probably still be alive when he was dead. And the elephants were Asians—they live to be eighty! (African elephants, he remembered, for some reason only live to be sixty.) There's a baby gorilla, too, and it will probably live another forty or fifty years. The girl could well be dead by then, as well as he. And Elizabeth. And Eddie.

There was something he had to do?

Make a call. Near the tortoise.

He worked into the night. Difficult work. For the first time since he was a student he was frightened of making the first incision.

A
PROBING

"I was thinking, Elizabeth—I was thinking . . . Why did you need a stranger, the counselor, the marriage counselor, to confess to me about—your lover, the 'other man,' what's-his-name. What *is* his name?"

"You don't care about his name."

"Why did you, though—need the . . ."

"I don't want to get into that right now," Elizabeth said.

"I was thinking . . . why not just tell me at home? I'm not a violent person. I don't even remember the last time I yelled."

"Neither do I."

"And then I thought: to have a witness. You needed a witness. And either I wasn't enough of one—"

"You weren't *there*—"

"—or I was too much involved with it all to serve as a witness. Or both."

"Involved?"

"Please."

"Please? Excuse me, James, are you trying to get a reaction out of me? Are you trying to *reach* me? Because it seems like I spent a lot of time trying, and I mean *trying*, to reach you. And now am I supposed to respond just because you've—I don't know *what* 'you've,' you've *something*. Well, I don't know what you expect now, Doctor, but as far as it concerns me I'm pretty determined you don't get it."

Her eyes were bright with tears. Something she had waited for, for so long, had come, but far beyond the time when she could meet it.

They were in the sitting room of Dr. Benjamin, the therapist she had chosen for Eddie. It was a modest room with subdued colors and comfortable chairs, and a selection of magazines designed, perhaps unconsciously, not to appeal to anyone the doctor would feel uncomfortable treating. Abbey had found himself doing the same thing, and afterwards had left the selection of reading matter entirely up to his receptionist. There were two Georgia O'Keeffe prints on the walls—of flowers, not of skulls, though the absence of the skull paintings made him think of them, and he wondered if that happened to others. He wondered if other clients (odd word, he didn't feel like a "client") had the same thoughts. There was also one of those prints he was seeing everywhere, at his accountant's and his M.D.'s and now here: Pueblo Indians in profile, wearing long capes, sitting next to pottery—striking eyes, chiseled faces. And all who purchased these prints for their waiting rooms, Abbey thought, were sure they'd committed an individual act. So strange.

"Where did you go?" Elizabeth said. "Weren't we just having a conversation?"

"Thought you didn't want to have it."

"So you immediately disappear? And *don't* say 'I'm right here,' I've heard that before and you're *not*." She took a deep breath. "Jim, Jim, Jim—appearances to the contrary, I'm not really angry at you today."

He simply nodded.

"I'm *annoyed*, maybe, but not angry," she said, trying to smile. "It's just I'm so—frightened of what's going on in there. I wish to God I knew what they were talking about."

There wasn't even a murmur through the door from the room where Dr. Benjamin was talking with Eddie. About a half hour ago Eddie had laughed, and both his father and mother had jumped as though a gun had gone off. But now Elizabeth and James seemed alone in the building.

"Do you know how many times, lately, you've gotten angry at me and then said you weren't?"

"I suppose I have," she said. "Don't expect an apology."

"Aside from being sorry for everything, I'm not very sorry for anything."

"I know what you mean."

He went on with what he'd first tried to say. "The therapists are *witnesses*, aren't they? Whatever else they are. It wasn't enough for you to tell me; you needed to tell me in front of—it's a legal phrase, 'a competent witness.' "

"I don't know what you're getting at. It's not the way I think. They're healers. Or they should be. That's why we're here, right?"

"I'm a healer."

"It's very different."

"I'm not really a *healer*, though, am I? I'm really more of a—mechanic. Or—my healing is about mechanics, the mechanics of the body, and theirs is about witnessing." He was groping, his mind couldn't let go of it. "That witnessing can heal. Yes. I'm not saying that's *all* it is, it's just . . . ," and his voice trailed off.

She said, this time truly with no anger, "Jim, if you're going to talk to yourself, talk to *yourself*, alright?"

"Sorry."

And there came a moment that James Abbey would remember all the rest of what was to be a comparatively short life. It was the moment just after the door of Dr. Benjamin's office opened, when James and Elizabeth stood with one shared movement as Eddie and Dr. Benjamin came out the door and were face to face with them; and their eyes devoured Eddie's face as Eddie's eyes avoided theirs, while the therapist greeted them, and their tinny replies of polite hello, and the doctor showing them into the door out of which Eddie had just come; and then, in the office, closing the door behind them. Now the door was closed again, Eddie on one side again, they on the other again. Abbey would always remember their opposite and oddly formal passages through the same door with this stranger.

Dr. Benjamin was a round, baby-faced man with a large middle. He had sandy hair and light eyes of indeterminate color. His look was steady, a little playful, and a little hard. As a judge of bedside manners, Abbey admired the therapist's presence. It was easy and open without losing any authority—whereas the therapist who'd done the marriage counseling had been earnest and sincere to the point of suffocation. Abbey couldn't help but think of this man as some sort of enemy, but a good enemy, an intruder of substance. He liked especially the man's peasant hands, the thick small fingers, the bulbous end of the blunt thumbs. He wondered if Sam, as Dr. Benjamin asked to be called, remembered where his hands came from, and the centuries of labor that had shaped them.

Elizabeth had worn jeans and jogging shoes and a nondescript blouse—the uniform of a certain kind of mom. James was casual too, but his expert pressing of shirt and slacks made him look formal, as usual. They looked, in fact, the two of them, exactly the way affluent white parents are supposed to look, and, sitting in that office, they both and at the same time understood why they'd dressed this way and both were embarrassed. They'd been trying to signal the therapist that they were *good* parents. How many times had Dr. Benjamin seen the same uniform on parents making their first visit?

The therapist, for his part, wasn't a man who could keep a crease. His clothes, though fresh, looked slept in, and he didn't seem to mind.

They said some inconsequential things, the therapist trying to loosen the artificiality of the parents' voices, and when that didn't work and Dr. Benjamin was convinced these were formidable people whose defenses would not gently be breached, he wasted no more time but looked up brightly, in a glance that took in both, and said:

"So! Which one of you knows what this kid's talking about?"

"Excuse me?" Abbey said.

"Which one of *you* has heard voices?"

It was as though the room were an elevator, and, with barely a tremor, it had plunged twenty floors.

"Both?" Benjamin went on. "Neither? You might not remember. That's not uncommon."

Abbey wanted to know how Elizabeth looked, but he couldn't turn his eyes toward her. His heart was pounding, and he monitored his body as it did all the things a body does when it's suddenly in fear but cannot show it. He knew very well that Benjamin, who had gone high high up in his estimation, had the skills to see exactly what he was going through.

Elizabeth, for her part, was short of breath, but her eyes were fierce: angry at Benjamin, then in an instant believing him, then turned intently on her ex-husband, but then—her eyes went vague suddenly with the thought: "Is it *possible* that it's something I don't remember?"

"Look," Dr. Benjamin said, "you're highly intelligent people. If you weren't I'd wait a month to work up to that question, but the atmosphere in this room is not going to be terribly different in a month; and it's clear that you can understand, intellectually, anything *I* can say to you; so I'd hate to ask this question in a month and have you think, *then*, that you'd spent precious time wasting your money on a quack. This is one of the big questions I'd be building up to; why not ask it now?"

The parents still could not talk.

"See, my bet is, that if he's hearing voices, one or both of you did—or even *does*. And if you remember what that was like, it could be very helpful to your son."

"This is—upsetting me very much," Elizabeth said. She was used to baring herself in therapy.

"It's upsetting both of you," Dr. Benjamin said straight at James.

James felt he had to say something. "Is this—Jungian, or—"

"Does it matter? We've got voices here. The kid does. If he's all alone in that, maybe he's nuts. If not, maybe not. If one of you negotiated it, maybe he can. It would at least be something for him to know, wouldn't it? 'Cause that's a very scared boy. A very *lonely* boy. I'm less concerned about the voices than about the loneliness.

"That's my appraisal. One visit. Acme Shrinks, Inc. Fastest in the world, or at least fastest on the block. Fire me, you don't like it. Go to someone who'll fill him up with drugs. Don't get me wrong, some of those drugs are marvelous, and the minute I think he needs them *I'll* send him to someone who'll prescribe them. The voices will stop. But the loneliness will still be there. And what will the loneliness do next? Because it does things. It *wants* things. What?"

Elizabeth wondered, aloud, about the word "loneliness." She told Dr. Benjamin that Eddie had friends and spent time with them. He said, "There's a certain kind of loneliness—kids who are lonely like that, who have *friends* who are lonely like that, they don't get rid of this loneliness with each other. They *enshrine* the loneliness with each other. When it gets *very* extreme—and I'm not trying to frighten you, this isn't where I think Eddie is; he's nowhere near this; but—when it gets very extreme you get these strings of suicides. Almost always among people who were friends. So—there's friends and there's friends."

He added quickly: "Again: I don't think we're anywhere near that with Eddie. Your kid has a kind of feisty edge to him that's very alive; it's not the terrible inner—what's the word?—paralysis, that you see in some. Eddie's voices, you know—this may be a *good* thing. It may be that part of his subconscious, his psyche, whatever word you want to use—part of it is coming alive in a new way, a good way. It happens."

They just stared at him.

"So these are my thoughts, this is where I'm coming from—do I still have a job?"

It was clear that he did, not because they were convinced, nor because they approved, but because the presence of the man and the depth of his decency were irresistible to them.

But James Abbey wanted badly to be back at the zoo. Restraining his agitation was almost more than he could bear.

As they spoke he made what he assumed were intelligent, or at least adequate, responses—though he never assumed, for a moment, that Dr. Benjamin didn't see through them, through him, didn't *know* who the voices came from. But he also knew that it wouldn't be forced, at least not yet. This was being left entirely up to him.

Who was this Dr. Benjamin, how did he learn what he knew, and how had James Abbey come to him? These were the questions that fevered him as he sat there. Eddie had heard voices and had finally spoken to his mother and his mother had spoken to a friend whose name Abbey could not remember, and the friend had recommended Dr. Benjamin, and Elizabeth had asked Abbey to attend, and these were the mechanisms by which he, Abbey, sat in this office. And a coyote came in the yard and he had thought of taking Eddie to the zoo and Eddie hadn't wanted to go and he felt the need to go alone to a place he would not otherwise have gone, in order to right the lie he'd told Eddie; and then there were the gerenuk and then there were the chimpanzees and then the second tiger spoke; and then, yesterday, the girl with green eyes. Eddie the essential, unifying element in each series of events. Without Eddie he wouldn't be here. Without Eddie he wouldn't have gone to the zoo. Where he heard the voices. And Eddie is hearing voices. And he'd said his first prayer in so long. And that was about Eddie. And Elizabeth had had that conversation with him, and that was because of Eddie. Eddie, Eddie, Eddie. Who was echoing who?

"Excuse me," he said suddenly.

Elizabeth and Dr. Benjamin hadn't time to say anything as he got up and walked out the door without explanation.

The boy didn't look up until he realized that his father had come out of the office alone. Then when his father sat carefully down in the chair next to him, the boy couldn't help but look at him.

The boy's face was sullen, tense. He was appalled and ashamed, and above all frightened, that a confidence to his mother had turned into what he would have called "such a *big deal*." In his thick black boots and black denims, with his hair sticking up in little spikes, he had crossed over into the world of the adults: he was wearing a disguise. As his mother had worn a disguise to this appointment, as his father wore a disguise to work. And he was sullen in proportion to the inadequacy of that disguise. In this sense, father, mother, and son, were sharing, that morning, exactly the same dilemma. On the one hand this made it impossible to speak, and on the other it lessened the need for speech.

Abbey sensed this, but vaguely; the boy's grasp of what they shared was the equal of his father's, but even farther below the reach of words. But man and boy were in the same state and couldn't help, in that silence, feeling something shared. In this sense they kept each other company.

The boy, however, needed more than company. He needed a father. And the man, on his part, needed to *be* a father. So it was terribly painful to both that there was no suggestion of the quality of "father" in that room.

They sat together a while in this absence of a father. The boy broke their silence.

"So do I have to come back and see this asshole again?"

"You like him," Abbey said quietly, because he knew it to be true.

"You don't know what I like."

"For the most part I don't, but I'm sure you like him."

"Do you like him?"

"Yes, actually. In a way."

I want to tell you, son. I want to tell you everything. If I can't tell you, who can I tell? I'm not even sure, like the good doctor in there, that it would do you much good; no, I want to tell you just because it's part of who we are, you and I— and, for all we know, her too. She married me, didn't she? She had you, didn't she? Is it all fucking nothing, just terror laid upon terror, like the war? Or is there some kind of grace to it? That's a Catholic word, and I forget that you are not, technically, a Catholic, Eddie. Grace—grace and terror can exist in the same moment, they don't preclude each other. That is the secret of Holy Mother Church. And it is my secret. Or I want it to be. I want to learn that secret, enter it rather than just know it. Don't I, Father?

He had the sense there was a priest in the room. As in the confessional, where the sense of the priest was so strong, but you couldn't see him.

He looked at Eddie.

You are at the heart of my life, son. How is it that each of us hears voices, yet is unable to speak?

These thoughts radiated from the man's silence. They were not unlike what came from the boy's silence, but the boy had no words, not even to himself. He had only what felt like a viscous black river, like an oil slick, flowing slowly through his mind where the words should be.

Dr. Benjamin was quite surprised to see the father and the son sitting beside each other in a silence that stuck to one's skin. Until that moment he felt that he was fairly on top of the situation. But when James Abbey looked up at him, with his eyes so bright and piercing, Benjamin first felt startled, then near to frightened—a feeling he wasn't used to in his own office.

As for Elizabeth: she felt a kind of thrill, seeing them that way, and was shocked to feel it.

If I am an expression rather than a creation—and if this moment, in this room, this moment that seems to be lasting more than a moment, the way the moments of a skid go on so long before the crash: if this moment is an expression, rather than a creation, because we are each, in this room, expressions—then God is right here, always. I have opened the gates of the zoo. The animals see that the gates have been opened, and they look toward that openedness in the quiet way that they have, wild things can be *so* quiet, and they do not move as yet. ("Where they gonna go? Hang out at the mall?") How odd that in an instant this moment will collapse before the social conventions, the chitchat and the gestures, and this family be ushered safely out of this waiting room, and that *that* is, must be, an expression also? What could God be thinking of?

PART TWO

THE GATES OF THE ZOO

I dreamt last night that my young love
  came in—
So softly she entered that her feet made
  no din—
And she came close beside me and this
  she did say—

an old Irish song

A
TAKING PART

He would have to make his confession. The question was
how. The question was when. And: before which witnesses?
And: how was all this to be decided? Must he decide it himself, or should he wait for the proper time; would, in other
words, a sign be given to him, reveal itself to him, if he was
patient?

He felt he was asking the first intelligent questions of his
life.

They're all eating it at once, the females and the male,
while it's still alive—the wildebeest on its side, kicking still,
groaning, its horned and horselike head rising a little and
then sinking for the last time among the compact chomping
heads of the lionesses; the wildebeest's great gray body torn,
where you could see it, but now it can no longer be seen,
only a mass of writhing lions crawling all over it, ever so
much in their movements like great furred maggots. And
when one lion would rear its face from the feast, its fur
soaked red with blood, its cat eyes glowed horribly white.
White, because the film had been made at night, and the
lights of the camera crew and the quality of the night film
drained the spectacle of color but for the bright red muz-
zles of the lions.

All the books say lion males eat first, but in none of this footage were the males shown any special favor. The books say the females hunt, but males and females together had taken down this kill. He'd seen them.

A break for a commercial. Several commercials. The Wall Street Journal. NyQuil. Coffee-Mate. Dean Witter. A Nissan dealership. Then the jackals surprise the warthog and her four piglets. She tries to fight them while keeping her young practically under her, but there are three jackals; every time she faces one, another grabs a piglet, and one by one her young are killed in front of her. And now it's Cracker Barrel Cheese, and a Pontiac dealership, and the L.A. Times Classified. And why do lions hate the cheetah so? Cheetahs don't threaten lions in any way, they are no match for them, and the prey cheetahs hunt are much smaller than lions require, yet lions will seek out a cheetah's lair and kill her cubs—kill her cubs but won't *eat* her cubs, how strange, the only big cat that kills for a reason other than eating or defense: lions. The scientists speculate, but admit they don't know why. And now a row of lionesses by a lake, lapping the water in the shine of a spotlight, all their eyes glaring in the expressionless stare of reflected light. And now it's an atomic submarine, there's to be a special about atomic submarines at eight o'clock tomorrow night.

James Abbey sat in the dark waiting for the tigers. But first it must be cheetahs again. The lions have killed all her cubs while she was away. She finds them in the high grass one by one. The last she takes in her mouth, walks awhile, and lays down the dead child, and crouches by it for hours. A storm comes on. She stays by the little dead one in the rain.

We are partakers, James Abbey said within. There is a great love that we and the chimpanzees partake of. There is a great grief that we and the cheetahs partake of. There is a great killing that we and the lions partake of.

And look how gracefully the vultures glide, and how slowly the huge ugly beaked birds drift down the air, to be transformed, as they touch the earth, into the grotesque: how many there are, all over the carcass of the chital, all their beating gray wings, their caws, their cackles, and the narrator says these birds will gorge themselves until their stomachs become so heavy they cannot fly. What a great gorging we and the vultures partake of. And what an uncanny gliding.

Pine-Sol. Cracker Barrel cheese again. Colgate. A denture adhesive. And there was a branch of his own profession: medical imaging. Some sort of sonar lab. A female technician in her smock attaching a heavy woman to a device. "Non-invasive," the commercial said.

And then the nipple of the tiger. An erect ready nipple only a little longer than Elizabeth's. He was so surprised! Of course they were mammals, and that means mammary glands, and that means nipples, but a dog's nipples, or a house cat's, or any number of other creatures whose nipples he'd seen or at least made assumptions about—they didn't look like Elizabeth's. It was only a brief shot, but it stayed with him so strongly, it was so familiar a detail.

A silly Freudian detail, if you ask me, James Abbey said to himself. Dr. Benjamin would perhaps, and Elizabeth would certainly, make something of it. But I make this of it: We are partakers.

And that girl in the zoo, what would she think?

Now, at three months, the tiger's cubs are sustained by her milk but also "receive" (was how the narrator put it?) regurgitated flesh. She vomits her love for her young, and they eat, or "receive," her vomit. Too bad humans don't do it. The shrinks would have quite a time writing books about it.

Am I crazy, Dr. Benjamin? Alright, I am. For now. But—I can't think of a reason not to be. I honestly cannot.

LensCrafters. American Express. Charles Schwab. Zankou Chicken. People who need glasses, have good credit, money to put in IRAs, and go to restaurants. People with dentures, who eat sliced cheese, need non-invasive diagnoses, buy new cars, read *The Wall Street Journal*, and use NyQuil—some of whom may be interested in atomic submarines. Well, he had an American Express card, good credit, ate sliced cheese when it was put before him, went to restaurants, bought new cars. So whoever did the demographics knew he'd be here, in the dark, in front of his TV, late at night, with the others, watching the animals.

Watching the tiger in the ruins. An ancient castle and fort upon a great cliff in a jungle place. Ranthambhore. "Tigers, like leopards, seem drawn to the ruins of buildings such as forts and temples," the narrator said. Abbey remembered, from his books as a child, that this point was often made about these beasts—these, and the monkeys. People, too, normal folk, consider it a good idea, a fine vacation, to spend a great deal of money and travel long distances to view a ruin. And if they saw a tiger, or a leopard, or even monkeys, upon that ruin, they would feel they'd gotten their money's worth indeed, would speak of it, brag of it, and their colleagues and neighbors would agree that, yes, they'd gotten their money's worth. What a great ruin we partake of with the tigers, with the leopards.

"Get off it, Jimmy, get off it," Abbey mimicked his father's voice, but in the instant of mimicking he felt the ruin of his father inside him, a ruin he visited when he ironed or when, as now, a snatch of his father's speech said itself through him. "I'm crazy, Pop."

His father didn't seem to mind.

The tiger in the sun atop the ruined wall seemed, to James Abbey, the most serene and powerful and most watchful creature he had ever seen. There is a great watching—"Get off it, get off it!"—we partake of.

Get off it, yes, but there *is*.

A tiger "completes," was the word used, only one in twenty attempts at a kill.

"Tigers have to work *hard*." A tigress feeding two or three cubs must be one of the hardest-working creatures on the planet, how many times must she attempt to kill in order to feed them all day after day? There is a great labor of sustenance we partake of, all of us, there *is*, oh, oh. Denture adhesive. Atomic subs. *The Wall Street Journal*. "One day, a day such as this, when her young are about two years old, the tigress will walk away." They will call to her, her cubs, but she will not come back. There is a great leaving we partake of.

Such great things we all partake of. Leaving and gliding and working and killing and gorging and love and grief. The greatness of them, the expanse of them, that each has so much for all we creatures. And madness, Doctor? There *is* a great madness we partake of, and I am at it, *I* am not mad, I am partaking.

Who is to say this is not so? Not you, Doctor, and not the girl in the zoo.

Eddie? You are partaking.

I must tell you something, Eddie.

And James Abbey rushed to the door as if his son would be there when he opened it and he could tell him.

The cool of the desert evening was gentle in the air as Abbey stood at his door. He was seen, but did not see. Various creatures, the owl foremost among them, acknowledged and then as quickly ignored his presence. The flickering moonlike light of the television screen, as it came through the open door, had more to do with their lives, changed the look of their world. They adjusted instantly and went on as they'd been.

In the time it took for Abbey's eyes to adjust from the brightness of the screen to the glowing darkness of an L.A. night—in that time, he collected himself. Had he really expected Eddie to be there? Not really. But his body had not been able to contain the gesture.

What other gestures, unable to be contained, waited within him?

The question asked itself silently, and it wordlessly spilled over his entire consciousness, and through every muscle, exhausting him with a suddenness that shocked him as a physician. What is the physiology of feeling, in an instant, that one can hardly stand?

And asking himself that, he went back inside, and, without closing the door behind him or shutting the television, he lay or rather sprawled on the couch, asleep even before his body sank its full weight into the pillows.

A SUMMONS

The telephone, the open door, a man in a chef's hat on the television screen, and the light, the sheen of the light outdoors after it's turned hot—it must be nearly noon. His eyes were open but his body was still in its sleep; though he felt the urgency of the telephone he could barely move toward it. When the caller, a woman, addressed him as "Dr. Abbey," it was hard to focus his voice with proper authority: "This is he."

It was Eddie's school. Eddie was ill. Mrs. Cairn-Abbey was unavailable. Yes, of course, he would come.

But as he splashed water on himself, gulped instant coffee, and tried to make himself look like Dr. Abbey, he could not, as they'd said in the service, "get the lead out." His body was leaden, it would not wake. He tried to wake himself with, "I'm going to see my son, I'm going to be alone with my son," but the words seemed unreal.

Why are the offices of nurses in schools so small? And why do they all look the same? It wasn't so very different in this pricey Pasadena private school from Brooklyn's P.S. 123 long ago. A narrow room made smaller by shelves and cabinets stuffed with packages and small bottles. A cluttered desk. A cot. The cot here was much finer, was all. James Abbey had lain back then in the nurse's office on an army cot with an army blanket over him, facing the wall, trembling with fever. Now the cot was plush, his son lay on a down quilt, but he too had his face to the wall.

The nurse said, "Your father is here."

They felt the boy reply though the boy said nothing. His silence was harsh.

"Eddie?"

"Where's my mother?"

The boy didn't turn his head.

"Don't know. On errands, I suppose. You'll have to put up with me."

The nurse, a slim young woman, was embarrassed.

"I'm not going back to the old house."

"We both have keys to your house."

"*You* have a key?"

"For emergencies—at least events—like this."

The boy turned toward the man.

"I didn't know you had a key."

Abbey sat down on the cot beside the boy, felt his forehead, took his pulse. Heartbeat a little fast, a little jumpy. Nothing unusual, though. Temperature seemed normal. But there were dark, deep shadows under Eddie's eyes. And the boy was very pale. Fatigue seemed to have drained the child of everything but anger and fear. It was a shocking face.

Abbey's own fatigue still weighed upon him. He was still having to push himself to make the simplest gestures. But a good look at his son's face quickened him.

The nurse had explained Eddie's symptoms. He would start to nod asleep, then wake with a kind of frightened grunt. And he was not paying attention to anything in class—causing no "disturbances," but staring off, or answering questions with respectful words but a sullen anger that clearly had nothing to do with his teacher. As far as she could tell he wasn't on drugs, but of course that was hard to know without tests. His eyes, however, seemed normal, though very tired. He seemed, she concluded, disturbed about something, and exhausted. The odd thing was that while he had begun to nod off to sleep several times while sitting up, when he lay down again he became fully awake.

The nurse offered no diagnosis, but rather looked at James Abbey with that concerned yet accusatory air which school officials reserve for parents whose children are having trouble at home.

No, there's more here, Abbey thought. Watching this exchange between us, it's probably crossed her mind that I'm abusing my son in some way. In fact, it would be irresponsible of her not to consider that. Yes, she's wondering if I've molested or beaten my son. I think I'm going to be sick.

"Where's the bathroom, please?"

Elizabeth's garden shone as bright in the sun as it had a few brief days ago. The man and boy passed its brightness slowly, both tense, both exhausted, each afraid of the other.

Inside, the boy said a simple sentence in the tone of a brutal insult: "I'm going upstairs."

"I'm coming with you."

Again the boy was surprised.

The boy's room was—a boy's room. A clutter of posters, cassettes, Nintendos, videos, gadgets, model dinosaurs, toy soldiers, little cars, little animals, games, photos of family, especially an arrangement of photos of himself (obviously arranged by his mother) at every stage of his life except the present. It was the paraphernalia of a boy who had not given up one age to go to another, but it was impossible to tell how much this was the boy's inclination or his mother's. Some of the little animals, cars, and such, were from when he was very young; other things, like the dinosaur models and Nintendos, dated from all through his early grades; and now they'd been joined by harsh punk images on CDs and on posters and scrawled across his notebooks. It was James Abbey's understanding, inasmuch as he followed (or rather, noticed) such things, that punk had peaked a long time ago; but not for this boy. The most surprising image, along with all the childish things and, with the punk, the almost-as-childish violence, was, on the closet door, a nearly life-size poster of Marilyn Monroe. What could this woman, who died twenty years before this boy was born, mean to him?

Abbey had a vague recollection of the film the poster advertised, something about her being a singer in a cheap joint, and there was something about a cowboy. She stood in some flimsy garment, bust puffed out, net stockings, and a look of—expectancy, a kind of pouting expectancy, as though you were supposed to do something for her. If you looked only at her face, it would be hard to conclude that what she was expecting had anything to do with sex.

There were also, on the walls, many pictures of animals. Cut from nature magazines. Giraffes, bears, colorful insects. Hippos. Eagles. Cheetahs. And there was the tiger. Above the bed. A full page from a magazine. Just the head. And, because it was just the head, it was one of the more dominant images in the room. Had they sat together, some day or other, last month or last year or the year before, the boy and his mother, reading together a story about a tiger or an article in a magazine, and had the boy wanted the picture or had they cut it out together or had it been more her idea, something to do, something decorative?

Nevertheless there it was above the bed. He couldn't remember if it had been in the boy's room on Cerro Gordo. Couldn't remember his room there, except that it had been a younger version of the same clutter. My boy sleeps with tigers and soldiers and skinheads and Marilyn Monroe.

"Dad?"

"What?"

"Right—what?"

"Oh. I'm going to make you some warm milk with some honey, and give you something—something mild. You need to sleep."

"No, I don't. I *really* don't."

And the boy sat in the small chair by the window, a chair several sizes too small for him, from another era of his life, and he turned his back on his father and stared into the street.

"I'll get it," his father said.

"You're wasting your time."

"It's mine to waste."

In her medicine cabinet he found the medication he was looking for and carefully sliced it in half. He saw also the tube of spermicidal jelly for her diaphragm. He hadn't seen that in so long. Odd that she left it in plain sight, but no— she and the boy used different bathrooms. He felt like an intruder, and yet he had a right, even a duty, to be doing what he was doing. Did she see men, a man, in this house? With the boy here? Well, it depended on the man and on how it was handled, didn't it, and it was none of his business at any rate. Perhaps she saw her lover when the boy slept over elsewhere. None of his business.

All that touching. All that going from somewhere in your body to somewhere in another's. What a great touching we partake of, we and the cheetahs and the centipedes. And my wife. He had forsaken that partaking for so long. And it wasn't that he missed it now, not really, nor that he felt jealousy, not at all—it was that he felt a stranger to the touching. How had he become *such* a stranger to a thing so great of God that all who live must touch *to* live? Oh. Oh.

"The knife is not enough," he said.

And didn't even know what a step had just been taken.

But that, which he did not know had happened, turned into something he could hear: a laugh. A laugh at the sudden certainty that somewhere his son's room hid a cache of dirty pictures. Women with legs spread, their vulvas oiled and shiny, touching themselves, their air-brushed bosoms, their tinted behinds. And the touching that had begun, no doubt, the boy touching himself. And the voices that had been touching the boy—from within? Who could say?

These moments of James Abbey's were experienced in the aroma of the sweet hot milk that he had set on the sink before he'd opened the medicine cabinet.

As he closed the medicine cabinet there was his face in the mirror. It surprised him. He hadn't noticed it before. The strain. And the strange light.

"Hello, I think."

And he realized he didn't feel tired anymore.

"What *is* the physiology of that?" he said aloud as he left the room, walking carefully so as not to spill the milk.

The boy hadn't moved from the chair that was too small for him. He stared out the window, his back to the door.

"I'm not taking anything," he said. "You can't make me."

"As a statement of fact, that's not quite true."

Eddie, who thought he'd been as surprised by his father as he was likely to be, turned to the man in even greater surprise. And as he turned his head quickly away again, his father saw the briefest smile—not of derision, nor of defiance, just: a smile, suppressed as quickly as it came. The son probably wasn't even aware of it. What *is* the physiology of this, Abbey said again as a joke to himself.

"What are you talking about?" the boy said without looking at the man.

"In the war I had to make strong grown men, out of their minds with horror, take things they didn't want to take."

The boy turned to him again.

"You were in Vietnam?"

"You didn't know?"

"How can I know stuff you don't talk about?"

"Drink your milk while it's still warm."

The boy looked down when he took the glass, but he took the glass. Then sipped.

"It's good, isn't it?" the man said.

"It's OK."

"Here." The man held out the halved pill.

"I really don't want to, *OK?*" The boy's eyes brimmed. "It makes me feel weird to have to do that."

"You need to sleep, kid. I'll make a deal. If I ask you to take it later, you take it later?"

"Maybe."

" 'Maybe' isn't a deal."

"OK. OK."

This is the second deal I've made with a young person this week. What is going on?

"I wasn't in—" his voice trailed. He didn't like to say the

word *Vietnam.* "—In the—in the war that you see in the movies. I almost never left the hospital. There wasn't time."

"Like *M.A.S.H.?*"

"Nothing—in the least—like *M.A.S.H.*" The words carried a quiet ferocity which the boy knew was not directed at him; and which the boy, in spite of himself, respected. Abbey added gently: "Finish your milk."

The boy did.

"Where the hell is Mom?"

"She doesn't expect you back till, when, another two or three hours?"

"I left messages, she checks messages."

"There'll be a reason."

"She's OK, isn't she?"

He hesitated just for a moment before he said, "Sure."

"How do you know?"

"Eddie, you're very tired. This is the kind of thing that starts to happen when you're very tired. Normal stuff, like an adult being on errands and out of touch for two-three hours, becomes frightening. I don't sleep much myself, I know what I'm talking about."

"You grown-ups all think you know what you're talking about. If you know what you're fucking *talking* about then how come the fucking *world* is the way it is?"

The words came up so fiercely, from such a depth, with his face scrunched up not to cry when he said them—and having said them, the boy turned again to the street.

The boy's hair—some of the spikes had been flattened on the cot in the nurse's office. The black T-shirt with the rock-group logo smelled slightly of boy-sweat—he'd probably had it on for a couple of days. The pants were slept-in. The thick black shoes looked incongruous on his thin frame. And he sat there in that moment quite literally, and without any irony, with the weight of the world on his shoulders.

I'm not afraid of him today, James Abbey thought with his own surprise. I've been afraid of him all my life and I'm not afraid of him today. I don't know how it is that we're going through the same things, but we are. I feel that nothing in him is strange to me.

Is *that* love?

Oh, God—is *that* love?

And his eyes rested on the photograph of the tiger. There is a great chaos in the world, and all creatures are feeding on it, partaking of it, and no one knows why. Something *not* chaos, something not rigid enough to be called order yet orderly enough to suggest harmony—such harmony exists, study a tidepool or the stars and it will show itself. Only for some reason now we have had to turn from it—but our chaotic turn away from one harmony, is *that* part of a larger harmony? That would mean our chaos is not what it seems, is not chaos at all, or—

"Thinking of a speech?"

"What?"

"When I say what I said the grown-ups make speeches."

"Did Dr. Benjamin make a speech?"

"No, actually."

He says "actually" like his mother, Abbey thought. I, too, now say "actually" like his mother.

"I guess I was thinking of a speech, but I don't think I was going to make one. I'm a little confused about—some things these days. Do you ever have phrases that go over and over again in your mind? Or words that turn up in sentences where they might not really belong, or you don't think they belong? That's happening with me a little."

His son looked at him with a suddenly very focused interest. Abbey himself didn't realize what he'd said till after he'd said it. It had been said so easily, without thought really. He had *almost* told him.

The boy's eyes were extraordinary, their brightness made brighter yet by the deep shadows of sleeplessness beneath them.

Neither spoke. Both were frightened. Life had snuck up on them suddenly and had given them, together, a moment that each needed but that neither knew what to do with. Nothing in their lives had prepared them for this.

It was the father's duty to speak. That much was clear.

"That happens—to me. These days," he said.

The son said nothing. The father said:

"Your—your voices. They say—what?"

"They say my name," the son said quickly. No subdued

speech like before. Each sound of each word was precise in his mouth.

"How? How do they say your name?"

"Some of them don't like me."

"Because they say your name harshly—or curtly—or?"

The memory of how the voices said his name when he was a child came back to James Abbey so clearly: "James? JAMES! Jaaaaaaayyyyy-aaaaaaayyyymmmmes. Jimmy! *James?* James."

"All kinds of ways," the boy said, "but—like they're impatient, like they're angry a lot."

"With hate?"

"I don't *know.* I guess—no." Abbey realized the boy had likely never heard hate, not real hate, not in the flesh. The boy's voice trailed off: "I don't know, I . . ."

"Your mother and I, and your friends, I imagine, have said your name with impatience, or harshly, or even angrily— but that doesn't mean we don't like you or love you."

"You copped that from Dr. B," the boy flared. This idea hurt him deeply, for a reason Abbey could not understand.

"Dr. Benjamin, you mean?"

"Yeah. He said that."

Good for him, Abbey thought. And said: "No. Promise."

"Really?"

"I *promise*, Ed."

I've never called him that before, he thought.

He's never called me that before, the boy thought.

"Some of them, Dad—are lovely. Real lovely." And the boy's eyes teared again.

The word "lovely" had disturbed Elizabeth, and Abbey could understand why, but it didn't disturb him. He thought it was a word that went well in the zoo. Perhaps he should take his family to the zoo and they would be spoken to too, and they would understand everything.

The boy saw his father's eyes change with his thought and it made him uneasy.

Not now, James. Not now, Abbey told himself.

This is not the zoo.

The gates of the zoo are everywhere.

"Dad?"

"Lovely, you say."

The moment was passing. He could feel it passing and he didn't know how to catch it. The boy could feel this too, and it made him panicky.

"I don't know," the boy said, his voice subdued again.

"Ed? Eddie?"

"What?"

It was receding from them, the moment that had come to them, and there seemed nothing they could do.

With defeat in his voice, a sound that saddened his son to the depths of his soul, James Abbey said: "You ready to sleep now? Your part of the deal?"

"I guess I should, right?"

"You need to sleep."

"I wish—Mom was here."

"I'll be here."

"You will?"

"Of course."

"You'll stay until Mom comes?"

"Of course. Eddie . . ." But he could say nothing.

"I'm gonna hear them," the boy said. "I always hear them—as I'm falling asleep, and then—I wasn't scared at first, 'cause, like, I thought it was a dream, but it *wasn't*."

The boy turned away to control himself. The man felt in his arms the holding of the boy, though he was across the room. It had been so long. But stiffly he walked to the boy, and knelt beside him, and put his arms around him. The boy did not stiffen, as the man had expected, but relaxed into his arms, still staring out the window. The man's arms relaxed in response, and the two remained that way for some moments.

The man spoke to the boy without speaking to him, as though the words could come through his arms: I do not know if I am insane, so I do not know if you are insane. So what can I tell you? I know I have crossed over a certain line, perhaps many lines, but I have no idea how right or wrong I've gone. Until I do, what can I say to you? Speaking might be worse. Might frighten you so terribly. And I couldn't bear that. So I cannot speak. And yet, we did not keep silent. Oh, son. We are at the zoo, I think.

"You're going to be alright, son."

"You don't really know that." There was no anger in the boy's voice. Just fatigue. "Nobody really knows that."

"You'll see," his father said.

The son had stated a fact, absolutely true. Both knew its truth. The father had denied that truth, gently, as it had to be denied for either father or son to move from that spot, that position—for the day to go on at all. The boy expected this denial that he would not believe but that he could not do without. If it hadn't come he might have gone mad with terror right there. And yet the boy knew, and he knew his father knew, that what he'd said was absolutely true.

Thus they had become accomplices. Which is to say, finally, after all these years: father and son. The truth of the moment had drawn them closer than the mere truth or lie of their words ever could. And this knowledge was passed from flesh to flesh though there was not the slightest movement.

When Elizabeth saw James' car in the driveway she went numb. She didn't anticipate or imagine or think, but walked quickly and efficiently across the grass (as she never did in heels, which is what she was wearing), up the steps and in through the door that had been left open. It was terrible to stand in the living room and see and hear no one. *That* made her afraid. She had an image of James dead in the bathroom. Yet, though he might be capable of killing himself (she had always feared this), it wouldn't be like him to make a spectacle of it. Still. His eyes lately. Who knew anything?

Her heels clicked sharply on the parquet floor. She thought: That sounds like death. I don't know why but it does.

She slipped off her shoes. Her stockinged feet made a whispering sound as she climbed the shiny stairs.

At the top of the stairs she couldn't help but look into her son's room: Eddie curled asleep on his bed in his clothes—lately he wouldn't take off his clothes to go to sleep. And asleep on the floor beside the bed: James. It was an odd position: one leg crooked up, the other bent, one hand supporting his head, the elbow sticking up in the air. He'll probably be cramped head to foot when he wakes, she thought. She went softly downstairs, dazed with relief.

She knew what must have happened, and confirmed her suspicions quickly. The answering machine had been broken for days. Messages recorded, but you couldn't play them back. She'd been meaning to get it fixed, but there'd been messages from galleries and from her agent that she needed to get this week, about the new show, and she hadn't wanted to be without the machine. She'd been simply taking the message cassette out and playing it back on the stereo; but of course she couldn't call in for messages until it was repaired. So she'd never gotten the messages from the school. The rest was obvious to her.

The house felt so strange, with the two of them up there asleep. The huge Inside Cat was also asleep, in the crook of the sofa. So, though the bright day lit the rooms through many windows, and the air was alive, the house seemed enclosed, somehow, by the sleep of her men—the sound of cars passing in the street, and of children playing noisily a few front yards away, seemed strangely muffled. And she too felt enclosed, yet it didn't feel confining. For as she took off her expensive business-meeting outfit and hung it carefully, and peeled off her panty hose, and felt the bedroom rug under her bare feet—a feeling she always enjoyed when she'd been wearing heels for hours—she knew a strange elation. Things were as they should be for this small time.

They were together, the three of them, the family, peacefully.

But she needed to *do* something within the gift of this moment—that was her nature. She fetched her sketch pad and her charcoal, and sat at the top of the stairs where she could see her boy and man asleep, and slowly made drawings. She worked well, for a couple of hours. Charcoal was just right to catch their strange positions.

Abbey woke early that evening on the floor of his son's room in a great deal of pain. It was hard to move his left leg, hard to move his right arm, and his neck had a bad crick. He had fallen asleep so soundly he had not moved. He had dreamed, but couldn't recall.

He straightened out his body, and lay still in the dimming room. It had been, it seemed, so very long since he'd woken in a room in which another also slept. He had forgotten the sweet company of it. Yes, it had sometimes been oppressive, it had sometimes been many things, but it had also been this, and he had forgotten.

He wondered if the physiology of dreams was at all like the physiology of hearing voices. Some studies showed the brain more active during dreams than during any waking activity. Nobody knew why. They were trying to find out, and he wished them well. They would come up, eventually, with a conclusion, and fifty years or so later others would come up with a very different conclusion, and he wished them *all* well. And if he said to someone in authority that he believed the tiger spoke, he could be put away, lose his license to practice, lose everything. And if his son had been in public school and had been needy and naive enough to tell a counselor about his voices, it would have been written down in a file that would have followed him everywhere all his life.

Why am I obsessing on this suddenly? Because I am afraid, in the most practical sense, for myself and my son, if this goes past our little circle. Dr. Benjamin? My instinct is to trust him. I only wish I trusted my instincts a little more.

Maybe this fear is healthy? Survival instinct kicking in— or at least making itself heard?

By turning his head slightly he could see the animal photos on the wall: the head of the tiger barely visible in the fading light, like the second tiger when it sat far back in its cave.

I don't want to get up. But I hear Elizabeth downstairs. I suppose it's time. But I don't want to leave this day with my son. This is my beloved son in whom I am well pleased.

She was in the kitchen making tea and heating some sourdough rolls to have with her salad. Her black, gray-streaked hair was pulled back, she wore a blue cotton housedress, and nothing on her feet. She'd scrubbed off the makeup of the business meeting, and the calm she had felt in her home during these last hours had freshened her. Her face had the clear loveliness that had once been natural to it.

It wouldn't have been so clear if she'd indulged in illusions or fantasies. She did not imagine that a life could be lived with James again. But something had changed between the boy and his father. She didn't understand it, but as she drew them it was revealed in the sketches. Something that the charcoal made of their lines, how the line of one related to the line of the other, though one was on the bed and one was on the floor. She didn't intellectualize this. There was simply a goodness in it. And, as much as she felt left out of it, it made for a great relief. Whatever was going on, however hurtful, was at least not evil. The sketches said that, and she always believed her work.

She had not realized how afraid she'd been that this thing of the voices with Eddie, and the changes apparent in Jim, might be evil.

I'm a good Catholic girl after all, she told herself, and those nuns did their job well. It's ridiculous, of course. If I *knew* I was thinking it, I *wouldn't* have thought it, I'd have realized it for what it was and passed it by. But I didn't know what I was really thinking.

She poured her tea, buttered her rolls, and sat to her meal.

She heard his footsteps behind her and didn't turn. She felt him stop in the kitchen door.

"Hello, Jim," she said without looking around.

"Hi."

Now she turned. His face, too, was freshened.

"Looks like you two had quite a day," she said. She told him about the answering machine as she made him some tea.

"I figured it was something like that." He told her about the medication, and that the boy could well sleep into the next afternoon.

And, for the second time now, they felt an odd respite in each other's presence.

"How are you?" she said.

"I wish I knew. But it was good to be with Eddie. I think it was good for him too. Don't ask me to explain that, I wouldn't know how."

"Or worse, you'd try," she said.

"Is there some of that salad left?"

"Yes. Do you want some hot rolls too?"

"Hot rolls would be lovely." Eddie's word, he thought.

They ate quietly. When he left she watched him from the open door. Three sets of gray eyes, he thought, as he started the car.

A
HABITAT

He'd hated to leave. He had wanted to go back upstairs and sleep on the floor by Eddie's bed. Or at least to sleep on the couch. Elizabeth might even have permitted it, had he asked. But the thought of the morning, the awkwardness of Elizabeth and him navigating morning coffee, not knowing if a step had been taken or not—Eddie perhaps waking early despite the drugs (you could never tell) and seeing his father and mother together again in the kitchen at the start of a day, and the expectations that might arouse in the boy— it was too much for Abbey, he felt too fragile to set all that in motion. Still, he'd hated to leave, and didn't relish facing the empty Cerro Gordo house at this late and terribly quiet hour.

He drove slowly, on what are called in Los Angeles "surface streets," meaning they are not freeways; drove slowly and not directly, following a kind of zigzag route from Elizabeth's expensive old-money neighborhood in Pasadena through residential streets of steadily falling property values—streets laid out in the confusing curving patterns determined by the hills, and everywhere there was gang graffiti, and all the vegetation had gone dry and brown where no one could afford the water. He drove the long way, Eagle Rock, Glendale, Silver Lake. The streetlights gave the old neighborhoods a sheen not unlike a black-and-white movie, as though L.A. was either bright and colorless or dark and colorless, always a place of lights and darks rather than color. The thick greens of the richer areas (the only attempt at color) looked like dressing on a film set, especially once you knew that only one tree hereabouts was native to the land.

Habitats. The zoo was no more artificial, in that sense, than any other part of L.A. It's a desert place; left to its own devices it could support only a tiny fraction of its present population, so all these neighborhoods are artificial. Zoos within zoos like mirrors reflecting mirrors. Wasn't his own house a habitat, constructed for the same purpose as the zoo's habitats, to house creatures alien to the place, house them so someone could make some money—and wasn't the money, in turn, only an excuse, as the ticket admission to the zoo was an excuse: an excuse to engage in activities only half meant (if that); activities done only because no one knew what else to do? The animals at the zoo knew they were confined; his own species only sometimes suspected the fact. "We are too busy *being* confined to be conscious of the confinement," he said aloud. What an odd way for all things to be possible.

He thought of Brooklyn and of himself at Eddie's age. The tenements. The neighborhood. Palmetto Street. Myrtle Avenue. Knickerbocker Avenue. Decatur Street. One dull brick building affixed to the other, not even an alley between most of them, street after street of such sameness. Even as a little boy, much younger than Eddie, he didn't trust what the city called itself. Didn't trust the street signs even. If his mother sent him on an errand, he paid no attention to the signs, but would count off two corners left and one corner right, or whatever it was, counting the corners and blocks carefully, then counting in reverse as he returned, determined by some inchoate conviction not to take the city at its word.

Perhaps because he'd always felt lost. A "latchkey" child, they'd call him now—both parents working (or whatever his father did during the days). From very early, yes, much younger than Eddie, his mother would be furious at any sign of dependence in, as she'd say, "my one son." Beginning in first grade he made his own lunches to go to school, while she stood over him making sure it was done right. By second grade, she had no need to stand over him. A bus ride cost a dime then, and if he had to go to the dentist, or some such thing, he was given five dimes: a dime for the bus, another for the change to the subway, two dimes more for getting back, and an extra dime for a phone call (calls also cost a dime then) if he got hopelessly lost. He was not quite eight the first time he'd done it. And he'd got hopelessly lost, but was terrified to use the dime, hear her disapproval, her resentment at being interrupted at work. Instead of calling he followed her instructions: "Don't get off the bus, if you're on the train don't leave the station, you don't have the money to get back. Ride to the end of the line and ride *back* to where you got lost, and on the way *ask the man*."

He couldn't imagine telling Eddie something like that.

"The man," of course, meant the man in uniform, but even this the boy James Abbey found confusing. Policemen had uniforms, and priests—they were the major figures. So did bus drivers and subway workers. But to James the doctors who made house calls wore uniforms too: suits and ties that he never saw on his father, nor on the workingmen of the streets where he lived (except sometimes at church). Once he got so lost that he took the train all the way into Lower Manhattan, where there were many suits and ties, and he remained disoriented by the experience for days. Who were *those* men? What went on there?

Years after he thought it might have been better to have failed his mother's tests, but he hadn't failed them—or rather, he'd hidden his failures, hidden his terror. Had never, actually or metaphorically, used the extra dime. He'd simply been too afraid to. But his fear had been taken for independence.

Over and over, as he grew older, others would mistake the way he met his fear for independence.

So his boyhood was a strange mixture: practical things, like errands, lunches, getting to and from here and there, dental appointments, and such, were left completely to him; things of taste and style—what to watch, what to read, whether to have a pet, what music to play on the radio—his mother reserved that part of his life for herself, while his father looked on and sometimes sang. So for the boy James Abbey, his real freedom existed in chores and in the routine and errands of the day. This was the time he had himself *to* himself, and he learned to stay quiet, stay away from others, and cherish that time.

He was, by environment, a street kid, but learned the ways of the street without being of the street. Learned and performed the style, the walk, and the talk, but in a subdued way. Most kids wanted to be with other kids; he wanted to be alone. He was persecuted for this, but as a matter of routine—there was no special animosity in how the others treated him. These were the days before the inundation of drugs, the days before children carried guns. The Irish kids fought the Italian kids, the white kids fought the black kids, the Puerto Ricans fought everybody, and everybody beat up on the Jews, and it went on and on with a lot of yelling and a lot of scars but it was headlines if someone was actually killed or even hospitalized. What you *really* paid for on the street, and from your own kind too, was being *smart*. He couldn't help it if by the third grade he read as well as a high school senior; couldn't help it if he could do the math in his head, and fast; couldn't help it and didn't know how to hide it. And this was the sin the street couldn't forgive, for it meant that you were leaving, that you *could* leave, and others quickly hated you for that.

Fortunately, around the time that he was Eddie's age, it got around that young James Abbey was going to be a priest. It didn't get around by accident. It was his mother's campaign. She talked to his teachers, his teachers would mention it in class—a Catholic school, of course. It both marked and protected the boy. The other kids would joke about it, but they sort of respected it, so *they* now set him apart as he had set himself apart. And it softened their hatred because they knew that, as a priest, he wouldn't *really* be leaving.

And of course there was God. Votive candles in each of the four rooms of their tenement apartment, on every bureau, even on the icebox—candles and holy pictures. Like living in a chapel. Not much was actually said, directly, about God; religious talk between his parents was more about the issues and concerns of the Church. But it was as though his mother and even his father said what they said so as to be overheard by God.

He never intended to become a priest, not for one moment (at least not consciously), but it was a convenient role they'd given him and sometime in high school he'd accepted it because it served him: the street-kid priest who would one day be a bishop, he was so serious and intelligent—a marked boy. The truth was that he, too, felt he was marked, but he couldn't have said by what.

It wasn't such a large step from the priesthood to medicine. Only three sorts of prestigious people had ever entered their apartment: the parish priest visiting his mother; doctors on house calls; and, when his father had been very drunk and had fought with a neighbor, one policeman. Becoming a policeman was out of the question, Abbey hadn't the temperament. He never intended to be a priest. So he became attracted to medicine. ("Common" labor was out of the question; his mother would never forgive it.)

Why not choose some other goal for his intelligence? Teacher, lawyer, businessman, whatever? Because he had an odd kind of loyalty. Didn't even know he had it. He wanted to leave the world he knew, but he wanted to leave it through something *of* that world, not something alien to it. The only businessmen in the world of his boyhood were shopkeepers (there were no department stores in such areas yet) and tailors, shoemakers, and such—again, not his temperament. There were teachers in the schools, but you had to be too outgoing to be a teacher, so this was also not his temperament. Doctors, however, were useful and savvy; and each had, and could keep, his own style—something that *was* true in those days of neighborhood practitioners and house calls. He knew medicine was something he could learn. He could be useful, then, and still (as he imagined doctors to be) a bit apart. Abbey could not know, so young, that what he believed to be his passion to be a doctor was more a passion to leave his people in a blameless manner, in a way that they would have to agree was honorable.

By the time he was ready for college it was the early six-
ties, the "poverty programs" were on the rise, and the actual mechanics of getting into pre-med weren't difficult for
a gifted young man, even one from the streets of Brooklyn,
especially with the strong recommendations from the Church
which his mother had somehow procured. She was bitter
that he wouldn't become a priest, but determined that whatever he became would carry a Church stamp. The rest had
come rather easily, once the essentials had been set in motion. A Catholic university. The choice of surgery—his aver-
sion to the knives decided that, gave him something in
himself to wrestle that the other disciplines didn't offer (always a need of his). The political passions of the era among
young students. Meeting the equally serious, equally stric-
tured Elizabeth, and the playful letting go of strictures which
they mistook for love. Vietnam—because he wanted desperately to be of service (he felt guilty for not becoming a
priest, though he couldn't admit that), and he wanted to
learn. Marriage when he returned. The life since. And it all
somehow went back to Brooklyn, the habitats, one dull
brick building affixed to the next, street after street of sameness, peopled by feisty, broken, yet unbreakable creatures
who spoke a vivid tongue and took no shit from each other
in proportion to all they had to take from the more powerful world.

The man James Abbey drove the streets of Echo Park. He
could have lived in Brentwood or Santa Monica or the Pal-
isades, but the plain truth was that he hadn't the heart. It
was all too far away—as when he got lost in Lower Manhattan when a boy, and couldn't imagine *who* these people
were, or *what* was important to them. He had never felt at
home even in Brooklyn, but in his odd way he had remained
loyal to it, and because his loyalty was not really conscious
it was strong as steel.

Perhaps that was why he'd felt such familiarity with that
girl in the zoo yesterday. The way she talked, the way she
carried herself, she could have come from one of his old
streets.

And how many people on his old streets, or on these
streets, or on any streets, heard the voices? His son was

growing up in a foreign country, as far as Abbey was concerned, but the voices had reached the boy even there. It occurred to Abbey, and it was the strangest of feelings, that in their whole lives the voices were what he might understand most about his son—what they might most understand about each other.

A
HEADLINE

The giraffe was suddenly black.

It had not been black a moment ago. There'd been only its blackish tint, the slightest sheen of its fur. But then the graceful creature took two steps and was black. And stood in its blackness, gleaming in the sun. Then another step, and it was not black.

Abbey's face would have surprised him could he have seen it: it was beatific. He wasn't seeing the beauty, he was joining the beauty. A joy of joining, one with the light and the movement and the beast, swept his being for several heartbeats.

His mind caught up in seconds, but, in a way, too late. He had been so transported by the beast's transformation (so moved, as they say, out of himself) that when the moment passed he had no means of remembering it. All that remained was a kind of thrill at the subtle change of light and angle that had made the giraffe suddenly black then suddenly not. The sensation of *being* the light, rather than merely watching it, left no trace that he would have recognized as memory.

The man James Abbey had come close to such moments with the gerenuks several times (creatures he loved far more than the giraffes, though "love" is not a word he would have used), but at those times pain had been his vehicle of transportment. Therefore he had not, as they say, forgotten himself; for pain was necessary to him, so to speak, *in order* to keep track of his self. Pain was so much the medium of his life, the air he breathed, that he felt it as he felt the air—it would be cold or sweet or muggy or dirty, but it was his life, his air, and he breathed it without thought.

Yet now "the gates of the zoo," as he'd called them in his recent state of mind, had opened so wide that a moment of delight and surprise had reached to his depths without need of the propellant of pain. Hence that moment had not been confined by the demands of pain. But by the same token it could not be recorded by his intellect, which had been trained by pain. This was a world so new to him that he didn't even know he was in it. Didn't know that his face, for that moment, was angelic.

It may be that it is not given to us to know when we are angels. We may only be given to know when others are. This may be one of the reasons we need each other so. For that is what James Abbey felt during his next moments: a sweet yearning, so unlike any need or loneliness he'd ever known that, beyond its sweetness, he could not recognize it for what it was: the yearning of the soul to be seen, and exchange the gift of seeing.

In his moment of joy and then his sweetness of yearning, it had been enough and more than enough just: to live. A first in his life. And this had lasted how long? Eight seconds? Twelve?

A giraffe stepped, and stood, and stepped, as light played upon its body. For James Abbey to be in so pure a state for those few moments, and yet not to know he was, made now for a vague uneasiness that moved beneath the beauty. None of the mental faculties he was accustomed to using had been involved in those moments, and it was as though they were restless at having been so suddenly but so completely abandoned, even for so short a span.

Now he did not watch but gazed at the giraffe. His eyes took in nothing specific. The colors of sunshine and shadow, leaves and grass and fur, and the forms and colors of the people and their clothing on this rather quiet zoo day; and, when he turned a little, the chimpanzees across the way, doing nothing much, picking at each other's fur—all these images made one swaying pattern in his field of vision, none more or less in focus than another. Then he saw a gerenuk in the enclosure with the giraffes! It had been at the far curve of the wall and he hadn't noticed it before. And it snapped his vision back to how humans normally, consciously see: one thing at a time. So that now all that was left of the moments he had known was a sweetness he couldn't quite place. His normal faculties (which had been able to keep track of even the strangest things that had happened till now) were vaguely aware that a little time had just passed which they could not quite account for, and that it had something to do with the giraffe changing color when the light hit it oddly.

The gerenuk had, as they say, brought Abbey back to himself—in that he began thinking, as his eyes settled upon it, that the male gerenuk (which this was) did not do for him what the female gerenuk did. Is it jealousy? he thought, having a joke on himself. Actually the male is very different from the female. Far less delicate. His upper legs are wider; his neck, graceful though it is, is maybe three times as thick; and his face is fuller. He *is* beautiful, but with his wives and daughters you get the sense that they are utterly involved in every detail around them; while this male is clearly alert, he does not have that air of total, even desperate, receptivity. Why is he with the giraffes today anyway? Something to do with rutting season? No matter. But they are pretty together, the gerenuk and the giraffes in the same field of vision.

It's good not to feel afraid of the chimpanzees for a change. I wonder why. There's still just one percent difference between their DNA and mine. Maybe I'm getting used to it. One percent makes such a difference. One percent of any being, any situation, can change; thus anything, anything at all, is possible. But that doesn't frighten me so today.

I wish the giraffe would step back through that odd little corridor of light.

SCIENTISTS PROVE HUMANS ARE FOOD FOR GOD—the tabloid's headline caught him before he realized it was she. He had gotten thirsty for hot tea and had drifted toward the small fast-food cafeteria from which you could see down the hill past the row of souvenir shops to the entrance gate of the zoo. She was sitting in the shadow at one of the yellow metal tables beside the cafeteria, thoroughly engrossed in her newspaper. She did not look up, didn't see him as he stepped into the cafeteria. He was glad. Her presence confused him. He ordered his tea, Lipton in a paper cup, and sat with it at a booth where he could see her through the window from the side. HUMANS ARE FOOD FOR GOD indeed. She read so intently. Her hennaed hair, black with reddish streaks, was pulled back tight on her skull—it showed off her strong forehead and nose, and the fullness of her lips, and the fine line of her chin. Unexpectedly fine. He worried about the reddish sacks under her eyes. Kidney, liver, pancreas, strained. Whatever life she led, it was wearing her down. But her eyes were so clear, so green. Even from this vantage, yards away, their glint caught you. In another time, with other fashions, she might have been a great beauty. In this time, when beauty itself was suspect, she did all she could to blunt it—so much so that he hadn't really noticed the first time. Now he saw again the thick black boots, the bitten nails, the bulky clothes. No way to guess what sort of body she had. But she had a swaying kind of grace in what she'd chosen to wear today. A full skirt, gypsy-like, the hem of which broke on the incongruous boots. Its color and pattern were indefinite, shades and lines vaguely suggested within a dark blue-black hue. Her blouse was a deep red that absorbed light without reflecting any. It was a billowy garment, impossible to tell the contours beneath it, and seemed the kind of thing somebody older would wear, though he couldn't have said why. Rings on her fingers. Rings on fingers with bitten nails. He didn't understand that. The remains of a burger, soda, and fries, spread out around her as she read. SCIENTISTS PROVE and STARLET'S GHOST TESTI-FIES and LOSE 20 PDS THE FIRST WEEK.

She's too intelligent for that trash, Abbey thought, but her interest doesn't look idle or amused, she's reading too intently. Look at her, set against the world, or what the people think of as "the world." Where do you go if you're somebody like her? "Where do you go if you're somebody like *you?*" he said to himself.

To the zoo, obviously.

And she turned her head. No reason to. She just did. And her green eyes met his gray eyes. Arched her eyebrows. Grunted a little laugh. Beckoned with her forefinger.

He took his tea and went to her.

"I thought we had a deal," she said.

"May I sit down?"

"You're very polite, aren't you?"

"Am I? I suppose I am."

"What about our deal?"

"I didn't mean to violate it. I—honestly don't know what day it is."

"It's one-a mine, is what. You're in *great* shape, aren't you?"

"Great shape."

"OK. Sit down."

"Thank you."

" 'Thank you,' he says. You kind of mean it, too."

"I kind of do."

"You're not gonna cry again?"

"I don't think so." But he thought he might, he was so very grateful to be in her company again. The depth of his gratitude astonished him.

"Lee," she said, holding out her hand.

"Hello, Lee."

Her hand was almost as strong as his, and rough with work. Not that she exerted her strength, but it was present in her touch.

"You have good hands," she said as she let his go.

"Thank you."

" 'Thank you'! Hey, thanks yourself. For the gerenuks. I never *got* 'em before, you know. Shit, they almost made *me* cry—and I'm tough."

"Are you?"

"Don't you think so?"

"No."

"Shit. Why?"

"Just because nobody is."

"Oh, man," she said, "I know some people who are."

"I cut people open for a living, Lee. It changes your view about that sort of thing."

"Well—there's more to life than that, you know."

"OK. You're tough."

"Anyway, thanks for the gerenuks."

Please forgive me, he thought. Please let me sit here with you. You have to. A tiger told me to follow you.

"So can I call you 'Doc'?"

"I guess so." Like the grunts in that war. "Sure."

" 'Cause 'James' and 'Jim' aren't exactly zoo names, you know?"

"No, I don't know. I'll bet lots of Jameses and Jims have come here. Thousands."

"Millions, even. It's *still* not a zoo name."

Tigers have been known to say my name.

" 'Doc' is fine."

They were both surprised to be sitting together—surprised most of all at how satisfying it was for each of them. But they were equally at a loss as to what, now, to do or say. The tabloid lay face up on the picnic table. SCIENTISTS PROVE HUMANS ARE FOOD FOR GOD, and, STARLET'S GHOST TESTIFIES AT OWN MURDER TRIAL. Everyone James Abbey knew would be embarrassed to be seen reading it, even on a checkout line. She noticed him looking at it.

"I'm done with it, you want it?"

"No, thanks."

"I guess I'll just leave it here, then. Somebody might want it."

She began to rearrange things in her enormous black handbag. It had a long strap, and would hang at her hip like a satchel.

"Are you leaving?" he asked.

"I don't know *what* I'm doing. Are *you* leaving?"

"No. I'd like to show you something. May I?"

" 'May I,' he says. What was that kid's game? You're supposed to say 'May I,' and when you don't, and the leader catches you, they say, 'You didn't say May I' and you have to start again. Something like that." She arched her dark eyebrows in a mimic of sophistication and said, "You may."

As they stood, and she collected the used wrappers of her food for the trash bin, she suddenly froze, as though she were pretending to be a manikin, and then broke the pose with a little laugh—a giggle, really.

"What?" he said.

"The weird thing is I know you're not coming on to me. Why do I know that?"

"Because I'm not, may be why. I'm old enough to be your father."

"That never stopped my father, don't see why it should stop you."

She threw the trash into the bin and slung her bag over her shoulder.

"You shocked?" she said. "Don't you watch TV? It's all over TV now, so how important can it be? You know?" Then: "It's funny, I said that to my shrink—at the Free Clinic, once a month—and she said, 'Great, first silence about abuse made for denial, now talking about it makes for denial! What's a poor therapist to do?' It was so funny. That's when I decided I liked her. She'd think this is improvement, I think—me being, you know, just friendly and all, kind of. But I don't see her for another few weeks and by then I'll probably forget to tell her."

Then she said, "Where are we going?"

"Do I have to say in advance?"

"You're so *shy!*" she said, and laughed.

They walked in step past the alligator and the penguins, the wallaby and the euro, and the gorillas, and the black rhino, and the nyala.

"You know, we're not the only zoo freaks," she was saying. "We're just not as well disguised as most of them. Some of these mothers come here *nearly every day*. I watch 'em. It's got nothing to do with the kids, the kids by now are bored stiff, and the moms don't even get it, they're still saying 'Look at this and this,' and getting impatient, but *they're* the ones who are staring. You wanna just shake some people. 'Cause, like, we *know* we're zoo freaks, but to be one and not know it—that's *too* weird.

"See, there's all these people—like you—look perfectly normal, right? Weird as *shit*. I don't know whether to laugh or cry. I mean, I'm just tryin' to grow up, you know?

"*Some* of these mothers, they look like they wanna feed their kids to the lions. I follow 'em, you know, like I told you last time, I take their walks, and I watch 'em, and, man . . ." Her voice trailed. "A guy jumped into the lion place, you hear about it?"

"I heard."

"Do you know that lion ate *forty pounds* of that guy before they could get him away from her? And they moved pretty quick, I hear. Forty pounds! And that's a lion that was born in captivity. The guy had a crucifix in his hand when he jumped in."

"That I didn't know."

"Yeah. A crucifix. You're a Catholic, I can tell. Me, too."

James stopped walking.

"Are we here?" Lee said.

"We're here."

He had been thinking as she'd talked that now, truly, he was flying blind, and it gave him a kind of vertigo that was not unpleasant. The delight he felt at being in her company included and overwhelmed his confusion. Why was he doing what he was about to do? Something not quite a memory, just out of reach, made for this impulse—an impulse made, in turn, permissible by Lee's frankness. For it seemed that whatever she thought, she would say—couldn't help but say. He was only aware of trying to meet, and in a way repay, her frankness, her company, for which he was so grateful.

She followed YOU, remember. She spoke to YOU, remember.

A strange voice had said that. Not the tiger's. Not any voice he'd ever heard.

"Hello in there?" Lee said.

"Sorry. That seems to be happening these days. Please don't be offended."

" 'Offended,' he says. You're really something." Then: "What are you looking at?" For he was craning his head at different angles, looking into the air.

"Trying to see how the light is now. Come here."

And he gently took her arm and led her a few steps, and she let herself be led.

"Watch that one," he said, pointing to the giraffe with the blackish tint.

"Just watch him?"

"Yes. Wait, maybe over here." And he moved her further. "No, here. Here."

"The zoo guys are gonna think we're nuts."

"Just watch."

"OK. You're *sure* you don't want me to move again?"

"Just *watch*."

"Just a few steps over there," she laughed, "you're sure? 'Just watch,' I know. I'm watching."

And they watched, him behind her, with his head bent to her height, looking over her shoulder.

"I'm watching, Doc, but I'm telling ya, the zoo guys—oh my god! *Oh*."

Abbey hadn't seen it. His angle of vision, just inches to the right of hers, wasn't placed for it. But she'd seen.

"Oh. And—where'd it go?"

"It changed again?"

"Zap. You didn't see?"

"Different angles."

"Oh, Doc, I'm glad you were here. If I'd seen that solo I'd wonder about certain controlled substances, you know?" Then she turned her head away from him and said sharply, "Shut up, shut up, shut up!"

"What?"

"Not you, me. I talk things away. I talk too much. And then things spill all over and I don't have them anymore.

And they're *so* hard to get back. Shut up, shut up. Walk with me while I shut up."

He took her arm and put it in the crook of his own, as though he were escorting her at a formal function, and they walked.

"It's when I'm around other people, anyone, I can't shut up sometimes."

"Shut up," he said gently.

And they smiled at each other with such faces as they had never seen on themselves, ever, nor on anyone in any time they each, with their different measurements of time, remembered. Then she looked ahead in the direction they were walking, to be with herself, to keep in her awareness the suddenly black giraffe and the face of the man as she'd just seen it and the face she felt upon herself, and all the words stilled in her but, My god, I'm happy, how *weird*. While for him the moments that he'd known and lost, when alone, rose now to where he could know them again, and he was amazed. And those well-disciplined faculties that had not participated in either moment began to clamor, This sort of thing doesn't happen, and he said to them, Shut up, shut up, shut up.

"We gotta go back," she said.

They had strolled, silently, arm in arm, on a curving road up the long hillside that was the zoo, past the kudu, that superb antelope with its huge eyes (a large elegant female watched them as they passed); past the ostrich, and the giant eland. They'd stopped at the zebras. Two of the creatures stood together as horses do, end to front, very still. The two zebras and the two people stood equally still.

"We gotta, Doc."

"Sure, if you like."

And they walked the way they'd come.

"Any special reason?" he said.

" 'Do I have to say in advance?' " she mimicked.

They squeezed each other's arms in the same moment and walked on.

Each would remember the zoo that day as being virtually empty, but it wasn't. It was a normal weekday. Groups of children of various ages, from classes and day cares, scrambled about noisily. There were various assortments of parents and kids, and the photographers, the sketchers, the old people, the couples—of which they were now one. Though neither would have put it that way.

They made their way back to the giraffes. The black-hued stood with another adult, side to side, and then stepped away, across the enclosure, to where the giraffe child, so perfectly the miniature of its kind, stood nibbling leaves from a branch that hung over the wall. The male gerenuk, with its short curved horns, stood not far from them, gazing at nothing.

Lee stood there holding Abbey's arm now with both her hands, and softly sang to the giraffes, *Down in the valley, the valley so low* . . . Her throaty, breathy voice, like a song whispered. *Hang your head over, hear the wind blow* . . . Abbey was so proud of her, and surprised at the feeling. *Hear the wind blow, dear, hear the wind blow* . . .

She let the song end there. Looked up at him. "Gotta give something back, you know?"

"I think so."

"Then I don't feel so bad about, you know—the zoo. 'Cause zoos, I mean, when you *think* about it—it's terrible."

"Yes. But—you don't sing the whole song?"

"I sing what I sing," she said, as though that explained it. "Hey—I can't seem to leggo your arm."

"Good."

"This is *weird*, Doc."

"Maybe."

" 'Maybe,' he says."

They strolled now just to stroll, as though in a kind of dream. They didn't let go of each other. They knew it was getting late. How soon would it be before closing? Once they disentangled themselves to go to rest rooms, and when they came out, first he then her, the awkwardness with which they linked arms again was in proportion to how very much they wanted to. They stopped at the red-cheeked gibbon, the gaur, the Indian rhinos. The peacocks were in full feather, and everywhere. They commented on none of them, there was no need, they seemed in such agreement about the place. Hungrily and silently they absorbed each other's presence.

Now they were at the tigers. The first lay resting in the sun. The second seemed not to have moved since the day they'd met.

Without thinking about it at all he said, "That tiger told me to follow you the other day."

"Yo! *Tiger!* Neat idea!"

They laughed together with shining eyes.

"I mean it, Lee. That tiger back there speaks to me sometimes. I mean: really."

"I'm jealous. He doesn't speak to *me*. Or is it a she?"

"I'm not kidding."

"Who says you were?"

And she tugged his arm to walk on, and they walked, Abbey almost giddy with what had just been said. They walked past the orangutan and the spectacled bear ("That's a dumb thing to call a bear") to the snow leopard.

"That's my favorite," she said.

"I never looked at it before."

It would be small beside the tiger, but it was marvelous, with its thick long fur, ghostly grays and whites, and a full tail that seemed longer than the body and head. Huge paws, good for walking on the surface of deep snow. And you could see straight into her eyes behind the glass, and they were solemn. The most solemn eyes, he thought, he had ever seen.

"Read the thing," she said. "Nobody ever even *photographed* one till 1974! I was, like, three years old, and there was still this totally mysterious animal. *In my lifetime.* They're from China and Tibet, those, like, holy kind of places. Almost all gone now. Look at her."

Abbey was still in a floating sort of state because he'd said something about the tiger's voice, and because of her response. Now both to Lee and Eddie he'd said something about his secret, and hadn't realized till he heard the words leave his mouth. What will happen to us all?

"Earth to Doc, Earth to Doc, come in, Doc?"

"Doc to Earth."

"What do you think of her?"

"I want to know what you're going to sing to her."

"You like that, huh?"

"Yes."

Lee got quiet and looked away. The snow leopard lay curled but awake behind its glass—it was a totally sealed space, far too small. The thick glass reflected their images, and they looked through their reflections at the beast. He felt a change in Lee's grip on his arm—how seriously she took the singing, how truly she tried to give something. It would be easy to think her effort ridiculous and pathetic. In a way he had been trained to think exactly that. And now he thought: Life is singing to life, what could be ridiculous or pathetic about that?

Softly she began, *Deep blue sea, baby, deep blue sea* . . . She sang so sadly this time. *Deep blue sea, baby, deep blue sea* . . . *It was Billie what got drownded in the* . . . And she let the line hang there, then continued even more softly . . . *deep blue sea*. Took a breath, and very sweetly began the next verse. *Lower him down with a golden chain* . . . *Lower him down with a golden chain* . . . And stopped.

"That was—lovely," Abbey said. "Where do you know all those old old songs from?"

"Mom thought she was a folksinger. Gigged around some, coffeehouses and like that. She used to sing them to me when I was a kid. I know, like, hundreds. They all feel like lullabies to me. Hey?"

"What?"

"You're not gonna come on to me, right?"

"No. No, I'm not."

" 'Cause if you did, I probably would. I mean, I usually do. That's, like, partly what the shrink's about, and everything. 'Cause, like, they don't call stuff *fucked*-up for nothing, you know?"

"I get the message."

"Does that mean I have to let go of your arm?"

"I don't want you to."

"Good. I've *said* this is weird, right?"

"Several times."

"Well—I've been right every time."

There is a great singing in the world, and she is a partaker of that singing, and she has allowed me to join that partaking.

And the strange close voice, which he had forgotten about already (he was learning today that extraordinary things happen which don't fasten themselves to memory until they are—what? supplemented?—so how much does one lose of one's life?) . . . that voice repeated:

She followed YOU, remember. She spoke to YOU, remember.

And this gave him a curious sense of responsibility for her.

"It's OK I said that, about coming on?"

"Yes."

"You don't feel rejected or anything?"

"No." And he stopped and turned to her and looked into her eyes: "No."

"Hey, you."

"What?"

"Thanks for the giraffe."

A
ROOM

There were crimes nearby. The sirens signaled them, and the police helicopter circling in the night sky mapped their circumference. James Abbey stood at his open door and watched the beam of light from the helicopter several blocks away. Could it possibly involve her? Was she in danger?

Silly question. Of course she was in danger. My God. Next to no money. No health insurance. (If she became ill my hospital wouldn't admit her.) A life that was devouring her body. No education, or no evidence of one. No recourse.

I will alert the authorities. I will write my congressperson. That's what I've done about the Gulf War and the environment and AIDS research and many things. So. Dear Sir or Madam. I would like to introduce you to a citizen of your country. She sings to tigers, and is kind, and has little, next to nothing, and she talks funny. I would like to know if she is included in your definition of your country. For that matter, I would like to know if I am. Tigers speak to me, and I met with the young woman above at their suggestion. Also, I seem to have passed a strangeness on to my son. I am beginning to wonder if this strangeness might be valuable. I would like your congressional opinion about these matters, and would especially like to know if you think about us at all, and if we are included. Your prompt attention to this letter would be appreciated. Respectfully yours, etc.

P.S. Someone is shooting at the helicopter.

He listened to the gunfire and looked at the moon. It was full, casting an enamel-like sheen you see only in desert air, an air that made every light glitter harshly on the hills. The helicopter rose suddenly, veered sharply, its lights blinking red—he saw the sparks of a round hitting the frame, but the chopper seemed stable and was quickly out of range. He noticed his skin was clammy. He wondered how many others in range of this little firefight were having the same reaction.

Well, we always knew that that war would follow us home.

Suddenly the gunfire ceased. Sirens again. He said aloud, "It's probably already on the evening news. Just like the war."

And if I had met a Lee instead of an Elizabeth back then? I wouldn't have been able to see her. She could have been right in front of my eyes and I wouldn't have been able to see her.

I don't mean to slight you, Elizabeth. We thought we were two of a kind when we met. I can't remember *what* kind, but I remember that's what we thought. We were right in front of each other's eyes and we didn't see each other either.

That gunfire would have been a big deal ten years ago. It's just TV news now. Probably won't even get into the paper.

It was because he was looking at the moon, where it hung now over the branches of the tall tree in the yard—it was because of this that he saw the raccoon. At first he thought it was a boy. A boy huddled hugging his knees on a thick branch midway up the tree. Then it moved, startling him. It is a fearful thing to see a boy move like that in a tree until you realize it is a raccoon. He saw only its shadow, and moon sheen on its fur; then the eyes glittered, and it was invisible against the leaves and twisting branches.

James Abbey vaguely remembered Elizabeth telling Eddie, when he was small, that there were raccoons and skunks and such about, and occasionally they would see them, get excited about them, the mother and the boy, but none of this had registered very deeply with him. Yes, now he heard her clearly, telling Eddie they were all over these hills, they and the possums and coyotes, and that they raided the garbage cans and pet dishes and were very clever and came in the dark and no one saw them, yes, and she gave them names and told stories about them. "Mom stuff," she used to call it. He remembered, now, that the "mom stuff" had irritated him and he'd tried not to overhear, to leave the living room or kitchen unobtrusively, to be occupied with something else. And, as he remembered, he knew it wasn't the stories that irritated, it was the magic circle that the telling of them seemed to draw around the woman and the boy, which he seemed able neither to enter nor to imitate by drawing one of his own. Standing in the moonlight now, knowing that the raccoon was probably watching him from the tree, and amid the background of cricket song that sang itself lightly everywhere, he felt a dull bitterness at himself. How could he lose so much, and lose it so quietly he hadn't even known? He could imagine a man who might look at that magic circle and be made happy by its beauty whether he was in it or not—and his happiness at its beauty might make that circle widen, not to include him, but to recognize him, and to draw strength from his appreciation, and *that* would have been palpable, and *that* would not have left him feeling so alone. He could imagine such a man, now. It seemed not that difficult to be such a man, not *many* steps from being the other, if he'd but known the steps were there to take. It had to do with magic, too, he knew that now, and he knew why he knew it.

" 'Magic' isn't the right word," he said aloud as he went inside.

I don't know many of the right words, he thought in the dark. As had been his habit, he'd turned off all the lights in the house when night settled, but the glow of the moon through the windows was bright enough to cast shadows. In the living room, dark shadow leaves moved gently on the sofa. Will the shadow of the raccoon pass across these cushions if I wait long enough? What is there to do but wait, and try to wait well, when you don't know the right words?

He stood awhile, a short time or a long time, he couldn't have said; and as the moon rose higher the shadows of the leaves changed on the sofa, lengthened, seemed almost imperceptibly to crawl. But not the shadow of the raccoon. I am just as glad, he thought; I don't want the power to summon things, I wouldn't know what to do with it. (She followed me. She spoke to me.) There's already enough I don't know what to do with.

Finally he sat in the moonlight on the sofa. Looked down at his hands, silvery in the glow. He had not realized how light his hands had felt these last few days. They had not held a knife in a week.

Had it been a week? Almost.

What will happen to me? That's a fair question, isn't it?

"*No.*"

It was that same strong close voice that had spoken earlier at the zoo—the different voice.

"What do you *mean* it's not a fair question!" James Abbey burst out.

And then he laughed, and his laugh matched the light.

I know exactly what you mean, wise guy, whoever you are. You mean it's not a *pertinent* question, "What will happen to me?"

Abbey felt approval in the room.

I was happy today.

"*You were happy today,*" the voice repeated.

For that matter, I was happy yesterday, with my son. That was a happiness, too.

"*Yes.*"

"I KNOW that, I don't need you to tell me." And I will not join the line of idiots who demand of happiness always one more thing. One more proof. One more question. One more day.

And in that place, within, where he had seen the black giraffe, far below words there cohered an understanding. If it had come with words they might have been: Demanding more of happiness is a way of not trusting happiness—a way of stopping it. Because happiness exists only when you follow the giraffe into the light, it exists only on its own terms. Like the animals it shies from us when we move toward it. It appears almost by accident and returns only when trusted. And, when trusted, like the animals when they trust us, it comes again and again to us. And in no other way.

As with the first time he saw the black giraffe, the man James Abbey did not know he was thinking this, so he would not, could not, remember it. Only if something revived it would he remember—something even more than the voice which now said:

"*Yes.*"

"Yes WHAT?" Abbey said, almost laughing.

"*Yes.*"

It was *yes* to something Abbey didn't know had gone on within him. Abbey was only aware that the word created a deeper stillness in the already very still moonlit room.

How could Abbey both feel such a stillness and yet not be ready for it—was a question that lived suddenly and, like the understanding he would not remember, wordlessly in his trembling. For he was trembling now, little spasms in the muscles of his thighs, and panic gripped him and rose to his mouth in small giggles, horrible sounds, and then a kind of laughter, but it wasn't laughter, and he asked of the voice, "WHO the *fuck* ARE you? Who the fuck ARE you? Who the FUCK?"

And the moon shadows of the leaves danced crazily upon him as he shook and said over and over "Who the *FUCK?*" until he couldn't anymore.

Until, while catching his breath, he heard:

"*I am close.*"

And the shadow of the raccoon passed at his feet.

The shadow passed so quickly he doubted he had seen it, but then with a kind of terror he knew he had.

"It means nothing. It's a coincidence. I am mad, we know that, I've accepted it. Soon I will be destroyed. There is something to say to my son before I am finished. The rest means nothing. The shadow of a raccoon, nothing."

They've been here all this time, in that tree, and I've never seen one before. Even when Elizabeth and Eddie called, that time, I remember now, "Come quick, Daddy, a raccoon," I didn't go, "I'm busy," I said. And I was. I was busy not seeing raccoons. So it's always been there and the shadows have passed here before in this light and Elizabeth probably saw them and Eddie too, but had given up on calling out to me by then, and I was bound to see them too if I sat here long enough in the dark, it means nothing.

What was I thinking of before?

I can't remember.

The zoo has a couple of raccoons in a glass enclosure. Coyotes too. How terrible for them. Their kind roam free all over the hills of the city, through all the neighborhoods settled in the hills, near-to-invisibly but freely. The zoo is in the hills, raccoons must now and again get in, forage in the trash. How very strange for the zoo to keep raccoons. Perhaps I should write a letter to them.

He was angry and upset. There was no reason to keep raccoons in a zoo.

He stood up, agitated, not knowing what to do with himself. The sweetness that had lingered for hours after he'd parted with Lee at the zoo gate—it was long gone now, but this was the first time he'd missed it, and he walked a few paces in one direction and a few paces in another as though trying to follow it.

And he said aloud, as though trying to prove something to the strange light in the room, "I *was* happy today. I was *happy*. And I was happy yesterday with my son."

And he went in the dark into a room he had not entered for over a year.

Eddie's old room. It was empty except for a small wooden table stained with paint and glue, written upon with pencil and markers, carved into—where Eddie had made his models and drawn his drawings and done his little projects with his mother. I guess I made a few models with him, too. A long time ago. I guess.

In the bright moonlight he could see little wedges of paper on the walls, stuck with tape—all that was left of the posters and drawings that had been taken down. The bed had been here, the bureau there. Now even the shelves had been removed. (Elizabeth was a one for shelves, as his mother would have put it.) The wall was pitted with nail holes where the shelves had been. He scanned the floor hoping to find a toy soldier or a small rubber animal that had been neglected, but there were none. The faint boy-smell the room had kept grew fainter with the door open.

"I was happy today and yesterday," he said softly to the room. "I was more than happy." He said it again louder, a serrated plea in his voice: "I was more than happy."

He went to Eddie's window and looked out in the moonlight where Elizabeth's garden had been, and the small studio they'd built for her close by the high plank fence overgrown with shrubs. Nothing moved out there.

I am crossing many lines and very soon I may be destroyed, that much is clear. But if I survive I will take these days with me, I will not leave them behind.

He could not know that this thought had come to him from an understanding moment which he could not remember.

There is a great happiness in the world, and we partake so little of it.

James Abbey did not think that, as he had not thought before. But that wordless thought or movement within him is what took him from Eddie's room to go and feed the cat—an impulse which, he could not know why, made him feel lighter, and a little silly, and a little dazed.

"Feast tonight, Outside Cat. Forgot to buy you food again. Tuna last night, ground chuck tonight. As a nurse in a far-off country used to say, 'You're shittin' in high cotton.' So where the hell are you?"

The Outside Cat's plates were beside the kitchen door to the backyard. The man James Abbey sat on the step of the door.

"Pssssst. Pssssst. Hey, Cat. Psssst."

The cat was suddenly there, gray, tense, always very nervous. She looked Abbey up and down, then went to the dish and devoured the meat.

"You're not gonna leave any for Mama possum, are you? Of course you're not." He reached out and stroked the cat, who let herself be stroked. "You're born with an instinct to kill, you know that?" He was repeating what he'd learned in one of those cable documentaries he'd become obsessed with. "You're born with an instinct to kill, but tigers aren't. They're born with an instinct to chase but not to kill, even for food. If the cubs are chasing a little fawn, say—if the fawn sits still suddenly, the cubs don't know what to do with it. They sniff it, mostly. Never occurs to them to bite it or scratch it, even if they're hungry. It takes a mama tiger almost two years to teach her children that they have to kill, and how to do it. Cats *do* change. What do you think of that?

"Not like you, huh, vicious little bastard."

He scratched the cat roughly behind its ears. The cat purred and sat to be scratched some more.

"Here's something you'll be interested in, Mr. Outside. Lions and tigers have almost identical skeletons. Even experts often can't tell them apart. So, say there were no people around right now, say we didn't evolve for another million years, and by that time all the lions and tigers were gone. When we dug up the fossils, we'd think there'd been one cat from Siberia through China and India, Southeast Asia, the Mideast, down to the tip of Africa. One basic cat with slight differences in size depending on the locale. There'd be *no* way to know about the tiger's stripes. NO way to know about the lion's mane. *No way.* We wouldn't know that lions hunt in packs and that tigers hunt alone. We wouldn't know that lions hunt down and kill other cats, like leopards and cheetahs, but that tigers leave leopards and such mostly alone even though the smaller cats are no match for them. Nor would we know that, with lions, the cubs eat last, after *all* the grown-ups have eaten, and if there's not enough food the grown-up lions let their little ones starve to *death*. But the tiger—the tiger lets her cubs eat first, lets the children eat until they're full, even if they leave nothing for their mother.

"If we just had the skeletons, Mr. Outside, we wouldn't know any of this. That's not the bad part. The bad part is we'd pretend to know. We'd draw pictures of the Great Asian-African Cat, no stripes, no mane, and we'd make up all sorts of stories about them and call our stories 'theories' and put them in textbooks and museum exhibits and have people memorize them. But we wouldn't know about the cubs. Not a thing. I mean, Mr. Outside, and I hope you're listening closely, we'd never guess, we'd never know, when it comes right down to it, what shits lions are, and how noble is the tiger."

The Outside Cat continued purring.

"These seem to me very significant facts, Friend Outside, and I would appreciate a more elaborate response." Then: "I was happy today. Today and yesterday. More than happy. I was."

AN
ABSENCE

He stood at the enclosure of the raccoons. It was in a small
building, arranged in a curve to create a grotto effect, with
the beasts behind glass. The glass (or whatever variant it
was, to withstand both animals and people) probably made
it harder for the raccoons to smell their own kind who
roamed free so nearby—just beyond that hedge, likely. The
coyotes were in the same building, also behind glass, beyond smell, in these hills where coyotes hunt at night. Now
and again the hillside homeowners of Los Angeles and Glendale and Pasadena, whose pets were eaten by coyotes, clam-
ored for the beasts to be destroyed. People had come to
Abbey's door with petitions (which, he was thankful now,
he'd never signed). Each time the authorities would patiently
explain that the Hollywood Hills, and all the hills from Mal-
ibu to Riverside, were rife with rodents, and that without
the coyotes there would be a surge of rodents throughout
the cities of Southern California, and that these rodents
sometimes carried bubonic plague, and what would the
homeowners prefer? How strange that even the plague sim-
mered in these desert hills. And these two captive coyotes,
though behind glass, still must hear their kind yapping after plague-ridden prey in the dark.

The puma, or mountain lion, was nearby. Such a lithe
creature, so alert. The sign said it could jump a span of forty

feet on level ground. They had once roamed from Alaska into Central America, and all east and west across the continent, and now this one sat upright in a space less than she could leap, sat on her haunches staring past glass at land her kind still hunted only forty years ago. The man James Abbey felt a sense of purpose in her stare, and he left that purpose to itself, and went on to the jaguar. The sign said that the last California jaguar was killed in Palm Springs in 1860, but that there were jaguars in Arizona and Texas as late as the 1940s. Now they were found only in Central and South America, and were rare there. Here was a black and a spotted jaguar—their great heads, their air of strength, pound for pound the mightiest cat.

So still. Not bored. Still. Not like the tiger with its air of watchfulness. Just—still, as though nothing that crossed their vision could be of importance. They partook of the great stillness that is there to sit within if we choose. Abbey felt himself becoming smaller in the jaguar's stare, till he barely existed at all.

It frightened him. He left quickly. He filled his fear with ideas. Thinking it was different for the tiger, for the rhino, for the gerenuk, for all those creatures who must know, in their cells, that wherever *this* is, it is not their place, it was never their home. But the puma, the jaguar, the coyote, the raccoon, knew just as certainly that this *is* their home, which has become a prison.

Gotta give something back, Lee had said. I don't know what I have to give. If I have something, I don't know what it is.

And the longing to give something back, to give *something*, in return for their beauty, in return for all beauty—this swept him.

What can I give you, marvelous maned wolf, with your silky wavy red-black fur and your long legs and the ladylike way you step?

I have seen people dying of the longing to give something back, but they didn't know it, and I didn't know it. With my knife I have postponed their dying a little. I have seen so much death and never understood before that so much of the terror of death is terror of dying without having given. Without even finding what one has to give.

Like Eddie's terror. Not that the voices are calling, but that he has no answer.

We are father and son in dread, Eddie. I have had no answer either.

I wonder if the voices I heard before sleep when a boy, exactly like yours, Eddie, calling my name—I wonder if that's why they finally stopped? They got tired of calling out to someone who would not answer.

Where is Lee?

They had picked a time and an animal at which to meet. One o'clock at the bison. It was an enormous beast. It stood at least six feet. A beast of great migrations, many thousands in a herd roaming hundreds of miles in a season. Indians and the early whites told of herds so large they took two days to pass. Now: this solitary animal, in an enclosure about thirty yards wide and maybe twenty deep. There is nothing for it to partake of but a solitude I can't conceive. It is one thing for a snow leopard, say, which lives alone in the wild, to be alone in the zoo; but for one whose home is to be in the company of hundreds of its kind? I am beginning to think of the zoo as a center, a node, out of which radiates the unthinkable solitude of the bison, the unwavering watchfulness of the tiger, the sweet dignity of the giraffe, the playful tenderness of the chimpanzee, the delicacy of the gerenuk, the stillness of the jaguar—radiating out in waves upon the city, like fountains of spirit, from which all drink without knowing, and to which people take their children not to see but to drink, to drink from this stream to replenish what is being lost: solitude and watchfulness, tenderness, dignity and delicacy, stillness and sweetness—here, where the world is ending, they are in plenty.

It is not enough, of course. What could be?

But at this moment it is enough for *that* boy. Look at him, pressing his face to the glass in front of the meerkat. The little house cat-size rodent, with its long nose and sly eyes, was granted the ability to stand up straight and survey the world from the position of a human being. It is disconcerting to watch a ratlike thing do this. But the little blond boy, of about four, was delighted, delighted, delighted; the meerkat would run a few steps and stand, the boy would run a few steps with it and press his face to the glass again and the two little beasts would stare at each other, and the boy would laugh and make this little squeaking sound, and the two would do their dance again. The sign said that this meerkat had been separated from the others, and was in his own enclosure, because the other meerkats had "rejected" him. Abbey wondered what kind of meerkat you had to be, to be rejected by meerkats and play games with a boy. The boy's mother watched from a few feet away in a kind of Heaven, yes. She was slight and pretty, sandy-blond, wore glasses, and, here at the end of the world, the meerkat had taken her and her son out of this existence and into another, and Abbey turned from them before the moment passed so that, in him, it would always be there, that moment.

One o'clock at the solitude. That's what she'd meant when she'd picked the bison. Did that mean she *intended* not to come?

Where is she? She is not irresponsible. Somehow I know that. When she picks a time she tries to be prompt, I know that. It would be too frightening for her not to be. She would need all those small ways of knowing she could depend upon herself, upon her own word—it would frighten her to be late because it would make her feel undependable, to herself, and that is her deepest fear and torment. I know this. Where is she?

Where is Heaven?

Where is Paradise?

The boy and his mother and the meerkat found it.

That it passes so quickly . . . well, maybe it doesn't pass. Maybe we are the ones who pass.

It is possible I cannot bear that.

It was now nearly two o'clock at the solitude. He had waited, and walked, and come back, and waited.

Twice.

Something slipped in James Abbey now. Something that had held all this time now slipped, and he felt the slippage, and he careened toward his destruction.

Where. Is. She.

Happiness is terribly dangerous. That is why people avoid it so cleverly. A gate opens, and then? Madness, of a kind, had saved James Abbey from nothingness. But what could save him from the consequences of happiness?

The snake had two heads.

Abbey did not know such things existed except in Lee's tabloids. Yet it was so.

"It's not . . . *fair,*" Abbey whispered. "It's not fair that I—should see this."

A San Diego Gopher Snake, the sign said. Then, in a parenthesis, as though the sign too were whispering: "(Two-Headed.)"

One head was where it should be, at the tip of the snake. The other was about two inches down the spine from the first, and pointed to the left: There was a bulge or bump before the—what? ancillary?—head. At first Abbey assumed that the second head was lifeless, or at least not a *real* head, with all the inner workings of a head, because the first head had its eyes open and the second did not. But when the second head opened its eyes, and a tiny tongue flicked from its mouth, and the tongue of the first head also flicked, and the snake moved, its two heads bobbing, tongues darting, eyes blinking—something within Abbey blinked back with *his* second head. Or so it felt.

And Abbey made a gurgling sound in his throat. A sound he'd only heard from people dying. And he felt a tiny blinking deep inside his brain.

So that dream he'd had, when he'd been afraid to look into his head for fear he'd find flies? Not flies. A San Diego Gopher Snake. (Two-Headed.)

Let's count the eyes here now, let's get this straight. Four eyes on the snake, blinking. Two eyes on my face, blinking. And two blinking—somewhere else.

"And round about the throne," he whispered, "were beasts full of eyes, and they were full of eyes within." Revelations, Mama, as you read it to me, in that little tenement, where water beaded on the wallpaper, and I recited it back to you, and you were pleased. The strange thing is that the brain is a physical entity that, unlike any other physical entity we know about, does things that are not physical. Creates images. But *is* it just an image, the eyes I feel blinking inside me don't feel like an image, let me tell you, there is a second head in my head, I am full of eyes within.

"Look at that man, Mommy," a girl said.

"*Don't* look at him," the mother said.

Abbey had bent toward the glass and bumped his forehead on it, his face not six inches from the snake heads. He looked hard at each of those eyes. Each eye tiny, each eye shiny.

In the womb the embryo is gilled, then froggish. Abbey had held in the palm of his hand the reptilian thing taken (he had taken it) from a human woman. Had peeled back its eyelid, thinking he was being merely "clinical," clinical scientific curiosity. Had that eye been alive, it would have looked very like one of this snake's four eyes.

Very like my eyes once, when I was a reptile in my mother's body.

But the mother and the girl could not see what James Abbey stared at in his open palm.

"Is there no strangeness anywhere?" he said aloud. "Is the wildness of oneness so complete?" He looked toward the mother and daughter. "*That* is exhausting," he said to them. And looked away from them. And didn't see them leave.

I have met the two-headed snake and found its commonality with myself and I can turn from it now. I have gone from creature to creature and have never found a stranger.

Nor found anything that does not seek the shade of mercy. What else could you be seeking, San Diego Gopher Snake (Two-Headed), both heads bobbing, tongues darting, eyes blinking, two heads up and down as you move over the sandy surface of this enclosure; you have need of nothing, you're fed, you have nothing to hunt, no enemy to flee, nothing to explore, for who knows this small window box better than you; yet you go from here to there to there, you cannot stop, you're seeking, you cannot be stopped from it, the shade of mercy or something else, how would I know, I'm just a knife man, but there is a great seeking in the world that we partake of with you and the tarantula, tarantulas live to be *twenty years old*, twenty years of such single-minded seeking, and the cockroach and . . . there are no strangers.

That's the most exhausting thought I've ever had. I think I'll sit down a bit. Right here. Yes. It'll be good to just rest for a time.

No. I'll just see the rest of the reptile house. Then sit down.

And he walked slowly past the boas, rattlers, a cobra, a viper, gecko, adder, skink, iguana. The black mamba of Africa, twelve feet long, deadly, but so small around. And look at it propelling itself straight up the glass, two feet straight up! Its underside flattened against the glass, each scale distinct, and it remains there, defying gravity, as if this snake were the stem of a vine. It is fed regularly, its needs are cared for, why does it do this? And James Abbey felt the vertigo of the irresistible propulsion that all life feels so deeply it can be said to *be* life.

Where is Lee?

Even the stillness we partake of is a means toward movement, a propellant from here to there, we move into stillness and then are still in order for something to move, even if the movement is further into stillness.

Where is she?

What do you think, Doctor, what's your diagnosis, am I living in the Book of Revelation, surviving it verse by verse, "and I beheld another beast coming up out of the earth." Albino rattlers. Two very long snakes curled together in a heap of snakeness. The ugliest whiteness. The whiteness of maggots. They are, yes, like two incredibly long, very wise, very white maggots.

There is always one more thing to see.

And any of the one-more-things may be one more than you can bear.

And you may come to the end of the world.

And have nothing left but what you cannot bear.

What song would she sing to this whiteness? For she would have a song to sing, she would stand here for as long as it took for the apt song to rise to her mouth, she is like that, it is her way of being *responsible*. I know I am only a parenthesis in her story, like the parenthesis on the sign, *(Two-Headed)*, my story is not her story, I know that, she has one all her own I cannot imagine, and I suspect even if she told it to me I wouldn't imagine it very well. But something brought us together, she did, she followed me, she must have sought—what? I think I'll rest now.

He sat on the floor with his back to the wall under the enclosure of the albino rattlers. People, mostly mothers with children, passed him quickly. Now two zoo attendants approached him, a man and a woman. They looked worried. They had the clear but somehow vacant faces of most of the zoo attendants, preoccupied expressions he didn't understand.

"Are you alright, sir?" the young woman asked.

"Dizzy."

"We can help you. You can lie down in the office."

"I'd much rather sit here for just a while."

The man said. "We'd really prefer you came with us, sir."

"I'm all right, honestly. I'm a doctor."

They said nothing.

"Could you help me up?"

They assisted him to his feet. He liked the feeling of being raised from the ground.

"I'll be fine now."

"You're sure," the woman said.

"Really, it's just something I ate. Fast food at the zoo." He tried to smile but it didn't come off. "Tell you what, you help me to that bench over there, if you could, and I'll just sit awhile. We doctors never admit we're ill. You come back and check on me in a bit if you like, and if I'm still woozy I promise I'll admit it."

He tried his smile a second time, his most charming, reassuring, bedside-manner smile. To the young man and woman it looked wan and desperate, the smile of a cancer patient. But because of the smile they at least believed he was physically ill.

They helped him to the bench. He liked the pressure of their hands on his arms, helping him. And it made him miss, terribly, the feel of Lee, yesterday, as she held his arm with both her hands.

"Thank you, you're very kind," he said.

"It's alright, sir," the young woman said.

"Thank you," he said again.

I am dizzy, he said to them in his mind as he watched them go, because every creature in the world, every tree, the molecules of every rock, are *always* moving, move *all* the time, the movement of life is staggering, the heart of the white rattlesnake never stops beating until it dies and then it decomposes, still moving, and the world is coming to an end, *moving* to an end, their world, our world, as my "dizziness" made you move from one place to another, and now you two are moving elsewhere, as our civilization is moving elsewhere, but do you know where *she* moves?

The tiger will know. The second tiger. Who has been monumentally silent lately, I might add. *Not* holding up its end of the conversation.

And he sought out the second tiger, passing the gaur, the siamang, the white-cheeked gibbon, the Celebes crested macaque, until he stood at the tiger enclosure.

The first tiger paced its wall as before.

The second tiger was absent.

Not merely out of sight, but absent. He was certain she wasn't in the recesses of the cave, nor anywhere near.

Was, in fact, Lee the second tiger?

Both, in fact, were absent.

"You know better," he said softly.

Fine. I know better. They were both here at the same

time, I saw them at the same time, they are different creatures. They are nonetheless both absent. Don't look now,
but this is Hell. You have died from the world and gone to
Hell. Not so bad, as Hells go. Pretty cushy, in fact, for Hell.

My mistake. It's not Hell at all, *actually*, as Elizabeth would
say. Paradise. It's Paradise. What is more frightening than
Hell? Paradise. What is Paradise? All Things Are Possible.

James Abbey felt as though the plates of his skull were
about to split. It was not pain. It was a feeling of expansion
within that flesh might not contain.

I will try to explain to you, Lady Tiger—and if I am
preaching to the converted, forgive me, it's—

Those who have the privilege of being victims of evil
need not know themselves, or need not know *much* of themselves, no more than the perpetrators of evil need to know
much of themselves—evil reduces choices, that is the purpose of evil. *Almost* its definition. What a relaxation it would
be, now, for me, to be the object of evil, the victim of a mug-
ger or Nazi. Our choices are truncated in evil's presence,
our responses *so* confined. Whereas with joy—"good," by
the way, Lady Tiger, is not the opposite of evil, joy is the opposite of evil—happiness, if you like . . . I was happy . . . in
joy our choices, I say, may appear to be few, but one's *responses* are anything but confined, they're inspired, ex-
panded . . . I learned it all from a black giraffe . . . but with
evil, *so* confined, I was saying, are our responses, that evil
often confers simplicity. That is its gift. And people need
simplicity so badly, as a refuge from Paradise, that they will
always generate evil.

And if they can't find any evil, they'll make do with pain.

"God," Abbey said clearly, loudly.

People looked at him.

"God gave the capacity of evil unto man so that hu-
mankind could find refuge from Paradise. All Things Are
Possible *is* Paradise. Is all around us. Moving. Every moment. Every possibility. And it is more than can be borne
by most, I am witness to that, and my *knife* is witness."

He clutched the fence of the tiger enclosure, and did not
notice anyone hearing him, nor that people were stepping
away from him. He was staring such that everything in his

line of vision flattened onto one plane like a painting, and the pacing tiger walked across that painting as Abbey went on in a clear biblical voice.

"God has sent us the lesser forms of love for the same reason. Refuge from Paradise.

"My God, my Creator!"

The few still in his vicinity stood some yards away from him, watching him.

"You sent my marriage," and he laughed a rasping laugh, "sent my marriage unto me, and unto my wife, as a refuge from a Paradise we could not have borne, not in deed nor thought, and I have waited too long to thank you. As to the higher forms of love—of which, I admit, I know little, but I have my suspicions: God sends them unto us for the *opposite* reason: to condemn us to Paradise.

"For when the more, shall we say, elevated or passionate or even *holy* lovers, when they say such things as . . . what *do* such people say, I should know, I once read books— when they say things like, like, *the gods gave us rights to each other, my beloved*—Paradise is awakened by the challenge and then, no matter how they try to run from those words later—and they will try, for *they* are not gods, and how many are ready for All Things Are Possible?— Oh, when they try to run, what they have said will follow them across the universe with little bits of Paradise still clinging to the words, and I know this once because once I loved God."

At those words Abbey almost swooned. Only because he was holding the rail did he keep his feet.

"I loved God and was loved by God, and for reasons I don't really understand because they weren't really reasons, I turned from that, and from the love I could have had if I'd remembered that, and . . . what I am attempting to say is this: Paradise *is* Hell—*that* is the innermost secret of the Bible, Paradise *is* Hell, when you are not worthy, or when you are not ready, and you find yourself nevertheless in Paradise, full of a joy you are not able to follow, paralyzed by All Things Are Possible, Paradise *is* Hell.

"Yesterday. The day before yesterday. Invitations to Hell.

"For I was happy. And the burden that puts upon me *is* unbearable. How can I live in Paradise? I? Me? How? And now I know that GOD DOES NOT ALLOW! GOD DOES NOT ALLOW! God does not allow anyone a permanent refuge from Paradise. One day, one day, you may stand too long at the place of the tiger, or at the place of the gerenuk, or the place of the two-headed snake where the giraffe walks into black light in the sun—or, or: even from a lesser love God may send children who are empowered, fully, for a time, to let you know without doubt that All Things Are Possible. Oh, yes. Did not God send a child, once, unto us, exactly for that reason, with that mission? And does not every child partake of that mission? And isn't that why the story is so *believable* by so many? Oh, yes. All Things Are . . .

"And it sometimes happens . . . that from Paradise will come . . . something . . . someone . . . and you will turn . . . toward . . . or away . . ."

James Abbey stood silent. Nobody was watching the animals. Everyone was watching him.

"*Run!*" the second tiger said.

Where the hell are you?

"*Now!*"

Strength came from the urgency of the voice and Abbey ran. Past the people watching him, who got out of his way quickly, past the Indian rhinoceros, through a crowd of children, up a path, down a path, this way, that, till he found himself in an area where he had never been: a long wide road, fairly steep, that curved slowly down the hillside. There were no animals here. No enclosures. Even no peacocks. Just thick brush and high trees on both sides. It must be the far west end of the zoo. Beyond this, no zoo.

Down the hill a couple walked, looking at their map, trying to figure out where they were. He could see by their faces that, like most couples he had ever seen, they were shielding each other from Paradise: as long as they remained together all things would not be possible, and that was their bond. He thought he saw this clearly when they turned around at the sound of his running. He ran past them, then slowed down.

Walking now, he was sweaty, his shirt soaked through, and he liked the smell that came from him. Somehow the exertion had brought him, as they say, back to himself. More or less.

The thought came: They are looking for me.

He found this oddly enjoyable.

They think I may be dangerous, and I am, but not in the way they fear. I have tasted of Paradise. Not because I wanted to. I *didn't* want to. But it has borne down upon me and there is no escaping it anymore. All Things Are Possible. It bears down upon everyone and we run from it as hard as we can and many manage to keep it at bay, but I have not. I am condemned, now, never . . . to settle . . . for the lesser . . . ever . . . again. And, yes, that makes me a dangerous man.

They think I have become one of the wild animals at the zoo, and I *have* become one of the wild animals at the zoo.

This is a great day.

AN
ETERNITY

"*There* you are!"

"There *you* are," he said.

"You're wearing the same clothes," she said.

"Am I?"

Her clothes were brighter, though the same in form and line: the billowy blouse was a soft and shining yellow, the wide skirt was black with a reddish tint.

"This place is *nuts* today," she said.

"I've noticed."

"And they're *looking* for a guy."

"Guess who?"

"Oh, Doc. Oh, man. You lost it?"

"Some."

"A lot?"

"A lot."

"Hey, could I hug you? I saw you and just wanted to—you know?"

"I wish you would."

Her arms went around him slowly and she pressed her whole body against him. It had been so very long since he'd felt such an embrace. His flesh was so shocked that all his muscles tensed against her, but in moments they relaxed, and he returned her hug and felt how full and sweet her body was, as she felt and was surprised by the tense strength of his, and they rocked from side to side standing there holding each other. Her scent mingled with the smell of his sweat and both of them liked the aroma they made and breathed it deep. It was the embrace of people who, after a long time, have come home.

Finally they let go and faced one another holding hands.

"Your shirt is soaked," she said.

"I was running."

"They were *after* you?"

"They were about to be."

"Jeez, Doc."

"Jeez is right."

A few people passed, paying no attention to them. Together they seemed just another oddly matched couple one sees at the zoo, like the biker couples, like the punk couples, like the heavy-metal couples, like the couple Abbey had seen once in motorized wheelchairs riding in tight formation holding hands across the space between the chairs.

He said, "Since you're wiser than I am—"

"Oh, *right.*"

"—I want you to tell me, from your great store of wisdom, why I can be one crazy out-of-control weirdo, as you would say, one moment, and then I see you—and it all—comes together in a different way, and I'm more or less OK. I don't get it."

"We're friends, Doc."

"That's a hell of an explanation."

She took his hand, and led him down the road, and as she did he wondered, What is the physiology of *this?* This sudden sanity! And, with their two strong hands joined together, she a little in the lead, taking him like a child, which she did with surprising authority, he thought:

This is a sanity that leaves nothing behind.

The birds laughed but didn't speak.

Abbey felt sane in the aviary. Enclosed and camouflaged. They stood, holding hands, and listened to the trillings, the throaty coos, the shrieks and the caws and, piercing through all that, the strange laugh-like cries, all blended together with the sound of running water, and absorbed in the thick greenhouse foliage, and the smell of guano, and the smell of flowers. It was hard to tell which creature was making what sound. And every bird was outlandish. Crazy combinations of colors. Why were jungle birds so bright? So that their mates could even *find* them in the thick growth? Certainly that meant their predators could find them too. Of what exuberance are they the expression?

He remembered a guy in the VA hospital, years after the war, who was bothered because he couldn't remember any birds. He wasn't crazy, he was just getting an old wound treated, but he got on the subject for some reason and it bothered him. "I can't remember what the fuckin' birds are, I can't remember *any* birds. It's so odd. I dug foxholes, and there were these huge earthworms, round as a quarter, even round as a half-dollar, and a foot or two long, I remember *those*. You hear a lot of stuff—you hear monkeys, you hear roars, and all kind of birds, and when you get there it's not there. Or there's all this sound, and then you call in a strike and after the explosions there's *nothing*. No sound. A guy in my outfit shot two black leopards once, they were crossing a path a few yards in front of us, I felt sick about it. But I can't remember any birds. And I'm not close to crazy." Abbey remembered the man so vividly because he himself, as he told his son, had hardly been outside the hospital, had virtually hidden there, had been in a jungle country and had never seen the jungle. Now here were the birds that man could not remember.

"What are you *thinking* about so hard?" she said. "You're just like that tiger. Thinking *all* the time, you guys *never* let up."

There were supposed to have been tigers in that country, but Abbey had never heard anyone speak of them.

"The tiger!" Lee said.

"What tiger?"

"Your tiger."

"She's not there."

"What if I know where she is?"

He didn't say anything.

"You thought I stood you up, didn't you?"

He still didn't say anything.

She said, " 'Oh ye of little faith.' *That's* from the Bible."

"It certainly is."

"Well, I was *early*, oh ye. So I strolled over to the tigers, and the one who talks to you wasn't there."

"You just accept that that tiger talks to me?"

"Sure. She wasn't there. I thought, Oh, man, Doc is gonna shit green, he *needs* that tiger."

"I do?"

"Sure. So I went to find her." She paused a beat. "Look, Doc, don't look at me like that. I mean, maybe it's just in your head, right? Who can tell? And who cares anyway? Either way, that's one important tiger, right?"

"What am I going to do with you?" he heard himself say.

"You're gonna be my friend." And Lee's eyes teared. "You don't know how bad I need a friend." And her face of confidence and sweetness and levels of energy upon levels of weariness—that face broke and she sobbed as he reached out and held her. "Oh fuck, man, is this allowed?"

"Yes."

"I'm in lousy shape, Doc."

"You could have fooled me."

"I *know*."

And she pulled back and looked at him. Her face got red when she cried. He knew the physiology of *that*.

"That," she said, "is one of the things I like about you. I fool you good. 'Stead of like, I fool you bad. You know?"

"I think so."

"Hey." And she smiled just as suddenly. "That ain't bad, 'I fool you good 'stead of fool you bad.' That could be a song."

And she dug in her immense purse and brought out a battered notebook and dug around some more for a pencil. As she wrote down the line she said, "I'll make that a song and dedicate it to you."

"You write songs?"

"Yeah, what did you think, I just do cash registers? Got a little band and everything. You oughta come hear us sometime." Then quickly, intently: "No. No. You don't come hear our band, I won't go to your hospital. *Much* better. Deal? I said, Deal?"

"Deal."

"But we *keep* this one, right?"

"OK."

"Look at that guy!"

By "guy" she meant bird. He had never seen so many colors on a living thing—greens, yellows, reds, blues, and a tuft of orange on the head. God had been drunk.

"So I was *telling* you," she said, "about the tiger. I thought, I'll ask around, and it'll only take, like, five or ten minutes, and I'll be a little late but I'll know where the tiger is, and Doc'll give me a gold star. Well, it took more like forever, because if you look too close this place is like anyplace else in that nobody who's *supposed* to know anything actually *knows* anything, and you go from here to there. But I found out."

"Can I say something?"

"Don't you wanna know about the tiger?"

"Very much. But first I want to say something. But."

"What?"

"*I don't know what it is.* That I want to say. I don't know." She laughed. He smiled.

"Is it OK to laugh?" she said.

"You were right, your newspaper was right, about food for God."

"You think?"

" 'And I saw an angel standing in the sun . . .' " He looked hard into Lee's eyes and she looked hard back into his. " 'And he cried in a loud voice, saying to all the birds that fly . . .' " He gestured toward the outlandish birds. " 'Come and gather yourselves together unto the supper of the great God; that ye may eat the flesh of kings, and the flesh of captains, and the flesh of mighty men, and the flesh of horses and of them that sit on them, and the flesh of all the free and the slaves and the small and the great.' "

"Quite a party."

"Revelation, chapter 19, verses 17 and 18. I used to have to recite Revelation for my mother, chapter and verse. The angel called to those birds about us."

"You can be a little scary, you know that?"

"You're supposed to be tough," he said gently. "Remember?"

"Hold my hand, Doc."

"I am."

"Hold the other one, too."

He did.

"What are we gonna do?" she said.

"I don't know."

"Does God talk to you, Doc?"

"Only tigers."

"That's pretty good though, isn't it? Tigers?"

"Yeah, Lee. Yeah, it is." But not, he added to himself, before I could share it with you. Before, it was a terrible burden, more than I could admit. But I won't say that to you, I'm afraid it would make you afraid.

"So I *found* the tiger," she was saying, "like I started to tell you. And—we could do that. That's not what I meant by 'what are we gonna do,' but . . ."

She let the sentence go, as she did with her songs.

He said, "Think they're still looking for me?"

"I'll bet not. The zoo guys have *lots* of other stuff to do. They probably figure you left by now. Anyway, they were looking for a wide-eyed crazy dude who's alone and talkin' weird, not a dignified gent with a sweet young thing on his arm." Then: "There's nothing to do about the rest of it, is there—Revelation, all that?"

"In a way we *are* doing something. Right now. *I* think we are."

"I do if you do," she said.

"Well—I do if you do."

"Fair enough."

And they walked as they had walked the day before, clinging to one another. Each was wholly with the other.

The tiger had been moved to a structure that was an exhibit more than an enclosure: an artificial mountainside, with a steel net hung above it to keep the tiger from escaping, within a wall in which were set large windows so that you could peer at the beast from as little as a few feet away—less, if the tiger moved closer.

The sign was explicit.

In 1920, there were 100,000 tigers in Asia. Today fewer than 500 remain. There are only 300 Sumatran tigers left in the wild. Less than 50 Chinese tigers. Probably only 200 Siberian tigers. Less than 10 Javan tigers. As for the Malayan, Vietnamese, and Cambodian tigers, because of the political unrest in this part of the world it is difficult to know how many actually survive. The Caspian tiger and the Balinese tiger are extinct. The largest population of tigers today are the Bengals of India. Approximately 2500 live in wildlife preserves, but these are threatened by the encroachment of human population upon their habitat. There are approximately 1500 tigers in zoos around the world, where, unlike other cats such as the cheetah, they reproduce well. But both in zoos, and in the severely limited area of remaining natural habitat, tigers are cut off from a wide genetic pool and this in itself may harm the species.

"James," she said.

"Lee," he said.

"Certain kinds of people become extinct too, don't they?"

"Maybe," he said.

The second tiger lay sleeping on a ledge almost within arm's reach.

"She breathes so fast," Lee said.

"She doesn't like the heat. They came from Siberia originally. About a million years have gone by and they still haven't gotten used to heat."

"Gonna take me a million years to get used to some stuff. At least. How do you *know* all the shit you know?"

"TV, books, whatever. Facts just stick with me, stick *to* me, always have."

"I feel like *I* don't know *anything*. It's like Einstein's the-

ory of relativity—it's here all the time and I *never* see it."
He bent and kissed her forehead.
"That's a *kiss*, Doc."
"It's OK."
"It better be."
And the tiger opened its eyes.

"Is he talking?"
"No."
But the tiger, so near them, had turned and raised itself slightly, its head erect, its eyes level now with theirs. Lee took a step away from Abbey, like a step in a folk dance to the side, creating a space between them. It was as though Abbey was alone with the tiger now, but also somehow guarded by Lee's presence, as his vision filled with the beast. And a line said itself within him, properly annotated as his mother had always demanded: *And I turned to see the voice that spake with me*, Revelation, 1:12. However one cannot see a voice, except perhaps in the Bible. What James Abbey saw were the tiger's eyes. He had never seen such eyes in any photograph or any film, ever. And he understood now that the tiger's eyes are not susceptible to being recorded on film. Abbey thought this was just. In twenty or eighty years, however long it will take, when the last of them is dead, or inbred so much in zoos that they're no longer what they were, people looking at the films and photographs will think they've seen the tiger's eyes, but it will not be so. The people won't know, and the tiger doesn't need them to know, that the stare of the tiger will be gone from the world utterly. This will be, not its revenge (Abbey could see it had no need of that), but simply the space it will leave. A space to be filled by what? In what way? And how will that which fills it arrive? Will it arrive as the tiger arrived (and did the tiger make the space, or did it fill a space made by something that had come and departed earlier?)—will it arrive as the tiger arrived, so slowly, through thirteen million years of cats changing as slowly as mountains, as slowly as continents, until a million years ago or so, no one really knows,

the tiger came to be as it is now? And then the last seventy years undid the sweep of thirteen million? That is what does not photograph: a million, even thirteen million, years. In those eyes. Present.

Abbey had seen the eyes of the jaguar, and they were not like this, nor the eyes of the snow leopard, the puma, and the lion. Perhaps it was the tiger's task, as the greatest of cats (for a Bengal or a Siberian is larger than the largest lion) to carry Time itself in its eyes. Perhaps that was the quality of watchfulness that had struck him so vividly.

How honored he felt, now, to be watched by this watchfulness. How privileged to be spoken to.

And all this coursed through him not as words, nor even thoughts, but as a burning glow that filled his chest, and rose and spread to flush his face, and flow down his arms, into his hands, which tingled gently now as with a strange current—this while he concentrated on nothing but returning the gaze of the tiger. Not matching it, that was not possible; but meeting it with whatever he had in him for such a meeting.

This was nothing like the moment of the black giraffe, when so much of Abbey couldn't participate. As, wordlessly but with a wondrous coherence, the gaze of the tiger enveloped and swept him, every part of James Abbey knew and saw. Yet it wasn't that the beast was looking at *him* in particular; it was that he was included in its gaze. A gaze implacable yet at rest.

. . . the black pupils, tiny, points hardly visible; while the huge irises, golden, seemed to take up the whole world, so that Abbey didn't feel five feet from the beast but face to face, aware of nothing but its eyes, and now he didn't know if they were gold or white, and now other colors shimmered in the gold, in the white, purples and iridescent reds, gleaming yellows and greens, delicate blues, eternity.

Now the tiger turned its head a bit, so that Abbey was at the periphery rather than the center of its gaze, and slowly the sense of eternity that had poured into him from the beast—slowly this sense or spell loosened its grip on the man, though at the same time it was clear to him that he would never leave these moments, not really. And it occurred to him that the world that called itself "the world" wouldn't make much of all this. It felt strange to be so in and out of life at the same time.

"Thank you," James Abbey said to the beast. I don't know what I can give, but I can at least give thanks. And no voice said to him, but he said to himself: It is the movement of thanks that makes all the difference.

He had discovered the bond he shared with the girl.

"James?" she said.

He held out his hand without looking toward her, and she took it and clasped it in both of hers. He was surprised to feel the current tingling in his fingers and in his palms still. And she felt that his hand was warmer, and somehow more alive in hers.

"Hi," he said, still looking toward the tiger.

"Where'd you go?"

"*Some*where. Did you see his eyes?"

"Her eyes."

"Whatever. It keeps changing on me."

"*Yeah*, I saw 'em. I was right here, though, and you were—elsewhere, let's say. I did good, didn't I, bringing you here?"

"You did great. Thank you, Lee."

"You gave me the giraffe, I gave you a tiger. Least I could do."

"Let's walk."

And he turned into the depth and brightness of the green of her eyes—eyes so unlike her voice. The timbre of her voice skimmed the surface of her nature when she spoke, even when her words did not; when she sang it became breathier, deeper, as though it came from somewhere else, almost from someone else. But her eyes lived differently from her voice, their green had no ending to it—not like the tiger's but in a human way, full of compassion and determination. The words came to him, felt strange within him, and he kept them to himself: I love you, Lee.

"Earth to Doc. Come in, Doc."

"Doc to Earth. I guess I 'left' again. I've been doing that a lot lately, I think I've told you."

"I like it. You'd be kinda more scary if you didn't. 'Cause you are *so* goddamn serious."

And they walked, holding hands tightly. Now Lee drifted. Abbey thought he felt the moment that the new thought, whatever it was, struck her and pained her. She began to sing in fragments: *Eyes like the morning star, cheeks like the rose* . . . There was a mourning in her voice. *Weep all ye little rains* . . . *Wail, winds, wail* . . . He stopped and looked at her, and she looked up at him as she sang, *All along, along, along* . . . She ended it there, as she often liked to, before the last line of the verse, so that the song never finished but gave the impression of having floated away from her.

"What's wrong, Lee?"

"Fuck it, it doesn't do any good."

"What doesn't?"

"Talking about it."

"What?"

"Boy-girl stuff, Doc. Garbage."

"Come on, Lee."

"Don't tell me 'come on,' OK? You got what you came for back there, and now you won't come back."

"I'm not thinking that."

"So? Used to be I was on my own here, but now if you don't come back I'll be alone here. That's different. Man, I'm alone enough."

"I said I'm not thinking that."

"Well, maybe *I* am. Maybe *I* won't come back."

"I'm out of my depth," he said. There was a catch in his chest.

She laughed harshly at herself.

"Shit, you're not even my *boyfriend* or anything, and

you're not *gonna* be, and here I am already wondering if we're 'breaking up' or something. I mean, what's *that?*"

I love you, Lee. I'll never say so, because I know what confusion it would make, and I know we can't be together, those gates aren't open. But I love you.

"Why wouldn't you come back?" he said.

" 'Cause the music goes 'round and 'round. Alright? 'Nuf said."

"Good, because I don't know *what* to say. I don't even know your last name."

"Damn right. Oh, *I* don't know. I'm just carrying on, OK?"

And she clutched his arm tighter, and he pressed her hand with his free hand, and they walked on.

"Lee?"

"Uh-oh."

"What?"

"Just your voice. 'Lee.' Uh-oh."

"Why me, Lee? Why did you follow me? Why did you talk to me? Why did you come back even though I frightened you?"

" 'Cause, like I said, the music goes 'round and 'round."

And before he could respond she said, "*Look* at those birds, they're goin' *nuts.*"

The flamingos were in some kind of panic by their pond. So lovely and dignified when they are still, so awkward and silly when they move quickly, the pink birds of Africa spread their wings like outstretched arms and held them spread as they ran full-tilt from one end of their enclosure to the other, making panicky throaty clucks. A crowd had gathered, catching the flamingos' excitement, egging them on, and an indulgence in panic passed between the birds and the people.

"I hate when things get like this here," she said, "and I hate those goddamn birds. I've seen them *fly* in movies. The zoo guys clip their *fucking wings.*"

And she yanked him away with a strength that surprised him, her anger simmering now as they walked on past the penguins ("Dullest fuckin' birds in the world") and the wallaby and the black bear.

Then she suddenly stopped and let go his hands and faced him.

"I don't think all the time like you and the tiger, OK? It doesn't do any good anyway."

"Maybe it does."

"For guys, maybe. I never saw it do a girl any good."

"Maybe it does."

She turned away from him and walked two steps. He stepped with her. She turned toward him and said very softly, "See, I love everything. It's a real pain in the ass. I mean, it's dangerous to love *anything*, and I love everything. I just do, can't help it, never could help it. And I'm not very, you know, *mature* about it. 'Cause, like, everything doesn't love me *back*, you know? I mean, I care about those flamingos, but they don't give a *shit* about me."

"You don't love the penguins."

"Yeah, I do, they just piss me off, 'cause they're so dull. Like my family. It's *such* a stupid ugly world. It's weird, like, to hate the whole fuckin' mess in *general*, but to, like, love the *details*, the—the stuff. Just: the stuff. I saw you cry, and I knew you loved everything too, you *do*, and, boy, I loved you for that. I just did. I just wanted to be near you. I'm not mature so I don't know *how* to do anything, I just do like I do."

"You do fine."

"No. I pay too much. You don't know."

"That's right, I don't." Then: "I love you, too. Five minutes ago I didn't think I could say that."

"Yeah, well—five minutes is a long time around here."

"Who does their eyelashes?!" she said. "I'd give anything for eyelashes like that."

They were watching the Asian elephants, two females standing near one another. Abbey had never noticed their eyelashes, long, curled, as though tended with the greatest skill. The elephants stood peacefully together and Lee and James stood peacefully together. There was a tall dead tree in the center of the enclosure, and one of the elephants began to rub against a bulging knot in the tree.

"She's feeling an itch just like I do," Lee said, "and scratching it just like I would."

He thought, Was it only a couple of hours ago that I saw the two-headed snake and the albino rattlers? Only a couple of hours ago that I stood at the solitude of the bison and went nearly mad for wanting her beside me as she is now? And how Paradise coursed through me, and my danger, and the tiger's eyes, and now the strange sense, conveyed by the pressure of her arm linked with mine, that I will not forget, that there *is* a sanity that leaves nothing behind, but all these swings of mood and thought, and the voices, don't they mean I am mad?

She stood a little higher on her toes and brushed her cheek against his.

"Thinking all the time," she said.

Then she kissed his cheek.

"That was a kiss, Lee."

"It's OK."

Then:

"Doc, *what* are those elephants *doing?*"

They didn't believe their eyes, nobody believed their eyes. Children screamed in glee and disgust, parents tried to drag them away, while people gawked openmouthed at each other and said things like "Do you *believe* that?" and "I guess elephants do just what they *wanna* do."

The slightly smaller elephant had been probing the other's anus with her trunk, and now had inserted her trunk into the rectum and pushed her trunk almost its whole length into the other's ass—while the slightly larger elephant, also female, stood unperturbed, as though nothing was going on. And they remained that way, one trunk inserted into the posterior of the other, the smaller female moving her trunk gently as though probing.

"*Look* at these fuckin' people," Lee whispered with glee, "they're gonna die, they're tryin' to run and stare at the same time, I fuckin' *love* it! *Go* pachyderms!"

Abbey felt the grin upon his own face, and shared Lee's evident conviction that somehow these elephants were in the process of proving that Lee-without-a-last-name and

James Abbey, M.D., were *right*. Right about what, he could not have said, but right, nonetheless, and *very* right at that.

And he noticed, among the spectators, a few others with grins very like his and Lee's, and he thought: We're not alone. And he nudged Lee to look at the other grinning people, who were noticing them as well, grinning back.

But the elephants did them one better. The smaller female pulled her trunk from the other's ass, and the tip of it was curled around a clump of undigested hay—which the elephant proceeded to eat.

"Oh, *jeez*," Lee said, closing her eyes and looking away. And Abbey laughed. Full out, from his belly, he laughed. He got the joke and soon Lee did too: even *they* were disgusted with the elephant's meal, and all the other grinning people seemed to be as well, and now no one could feel superior to anybody, as Lee started to laugh too, her frame shaking so that it hurt her. Lee and Abbey held each other, laughing, rocking back and forth, while the smaller female elephant dove her trunk back where it had been in search of another snack.

"Whataya think, Doc? Have we seen it *all?* Can we die now?"

"Not just yet. The elephants may have something else up—"

"Not 'up their sleeve,' don't say that, I'll brain you, man, that ain't no *sleeve*. What's wrong, Doc?"

He'd let go her arm to clutch his stomach with both hands, as though what had been laughter (and was now a sound she'd never heard) had wrenched organs inside. A cough, a gurgle, a guffaw, all tore his throat at once. Lee had never heard anyone die, but Abbey had heard many die, so he knew this sound and now his legs and arms trembled as his stomach heaved and Lee, with all her strength, grabbed him from behind and held him from falling while she said over and over, "It's OK, honey, it's OK, sweetie, OK? It's OK, honey, baby, sweetie, OK?"

He hadn't eaten in two days, there was nothing to vomit but a greenish-yellow bile, and as he spit it out he was amazed that some part of him retained the presence of mind to realize that the people standing around looking at him

now wouldn't think he was crazy, they'd think he was re-
acting to the elephants, but he felt new words rising in him
and if he said them they *would* think him mad, and the same
part of him that had kept its awareness through all these
days, that part managed to make words pass through the
other sounds and fluids that crowded his mouth, "Get me
out of here, get me away from here," and she said, "Sure,
baby, come on, honey, sweetie, OK? I got you, you're alright, OK? Sure, sweet, this way, OK, baby, sweetie?"

And as she walked him away, past the Nubian ibex, the
rams and ewes paying no attention, he said, "What do I
know about Paradise?", and they passed the black rhino, "The
tiger will never speak again, not to me," and Lee said, "You
don't know that," and she held him, half holding him up, as
they passed the gorilla, with its air of baffled strength, and
he said, "It's hard to say 'eternity,' " and she, "Oh, sweetie,
you sweet man, did you know you're a sweet man?" and he,
coughing, "It's hard to say 'eternity,' " and she, singing a little, "*Eternity, said Frankie Lee, with a voice as cold as ice*,"
and now he laughed again, a helpless laugh, as they stood
together and she clutched his arm and he clutched hers, and
she looked at him, nervous, scared of the sincerity of his
helplessness, and then he stopped, and he said, with what
voice he had left, "Look where we are?"

They were at the enclosure of the solitary bison, where
they'd agreed to meet hours before.

Now, quietly and simply, he said, "Here we are in Eternity, Lee."

"Where else *would* we be?"

She meant it as a joke, but it almost made him cry.

"Thank God for you, Lee."

"You mean that, don't you?"

"Doc means it."

"Nobody ever said that to me before."

"Nobody's ever said it to me either."

"Thank God for *you*, then. Now we both got it."

"We both got it," he said in her way. "Eternity. That's exactly it."

"Nothin' 'exact' about 'eternity,' Doc. Oh, man, I can't pretend to know what you're talking about."

"I don't know either. But I know I don't feel crazy anymore."

"Then you won't need *me* anymore." She said it so fast she surprised herself.

He looked into her green eyes and heard himself say, to their equal surprise, "You want to marry me, Lee? Will you marry me?"

"I thought you said you don't feel crazy anymore?"

"I don't."

"Don't upset me, hey? Doc? Say 'eternity' an' shit as many times you have to, but don't *upset* me. You didn't say—what you just said, right?"

"Didn't I?"

"*Right?*"

"All things are possible, aren't they?"

"How would I know? *Right?* You *never* said it?"

"OK. Right."

"You nutty motherfucker."

"I could use a cup of tea."

" 'A cup of tea,' he says."

It was almost closing time at the zoo. The sun had gone down behind the hillside, so that, while it was still well before sunset, the zoo was in shade—and where the foliage was thick and the trees hung over the walks, it was a dark shade, almost as though they were walking in a wood.

It took some moments for them to realize that there was no one else around, no one at all. Not only no people. There were no animals. They had walked up the path to say good-bye to the gerenuks, but the gerenuks were not there. A few steps on, the lioness was not there. Around the curve of the road, the giraffes were not there. Nor the chimpanzees. And not one human being. It was like being in an empty theater, or walking in an ancient ruin. When they spoke, they spoke softly.

"*What* is going *on?*" Lee said.

"Here we are in Eternity, Lee."

"We're the only goddamn people here. And *where* are the *animals?*"

"They must have taken them—in."

"*In* where?"

"See that gate at the back of the giraffe enclosure? All these places have them, but sometimes you can't see them."

"And you think at night they take them—in?"

"They must."

"Oh, *man.*" She almost sobbed. "That sucks. That's *really* lousy. They sleep in fucking *cages?* Oh, man."

"It's only sleep, Lee."

"Don't say that to me. Don't get stupid on me, right?"

"Right."

"Oh, man."

The elephants were gone, and the giant anteater, the black rhinos, the gorillas. The gates of the zoo had opened, but not in the direction James Abbey had assumed. He and Lee held hands and slowly walked.

"I wish they got to sleep in the open, James. It's awful that they don't."

"I know."

"But you know—this *is* delicious, no one but us."

"I know."

Those were the last words they would ever say to each other in the zoo. It would be many years before Lee returned, seeking the memory of the man she'd called "Doc"; and James would not come back for months and months. Now they would not say more until they had walked through the zoo gate to their cars, where they'd plan to meet at the tiger again in two days—intentions that would come to nothing.

They walked slowly, holding hands. Down around the next curve, where three pathways joined, they would see other stragglers walking toward the gates; until Lee and Abbey made that turn they were the only creatures that they saw, but for a few birds, and it seemed to them that they were walking in the Other World.

PART THREE

PARADISE

Behold, I have set before thee an open door, and no man can shut it.

Revelation, 13:8

AN
APPOINTMENT

He didn't eat again that night. With a physician's curiosity he stepped on the bathroom scale and noted that he'd lost twelve pounds since his vacation began. Examining himself in the mirror he judged that he didn't look gaunt, just strangely younger. He had no vanity about his age. On the contrary, he felt a little embarrassed at looking younger. A little disoriented. It wouldn't be good to lose any more weight, but he couldn't force himself to eat. He decided that as long as he drank plenty of water and fruit juices he'd be fine, and these days would function physically as a kind of fast. Also, black tea, so that he wouldn't get caffeine headaches. There. He felt responsible. He determined that in a couple of days he'd begin eating again, whether or not he felt like it, because it wouldn't be healthy, nor would it look professional, to lose more weight. Having made such sensible decisions, he felt satisfied.

He thought: I'm glad I asked her. When you find someone you're more alive with and at home with than you've been with anyone, you shouldn't ask a lot of dumb questions, you should marry them.

I'm an idiot. Still, I'm glad I asked her. There's a kind of peace in that.

I don't think I've ever thought of peace before. There *is* a great peace out there. I can hear sirens all night. All night.

And yet it is there. Here. Not somewhere else. Even the animals don't partake of it. Not even the tiger who contains eternity. Yet it *is* there. I'm not sure I want it, really, it would separate me too much from all that is not peaceful, the gerenuks and Lee and the two-headed snake and Eddie, these links that are so precious and so new, no, I'm not really interested in being isolated by peace, and yet it *is* there, I am sitting, at this moment, at the shore of the great peace that exists, and just a sip of it has come to me because I am willing to let all things be possible with Lee. A sip's enough for now. I must be mad. And I see no reason to be anything else.

Eden has been turned inside out. In Eden, Adam named the animals. Now the animals name you. Or brand you; it comes to the same thing. We are in the furthest reaches of Eden, we are the end of Eden, the zoo is the end of *that* story.

" 'And I saw a new heaven and a new earth,' " he said aloud, " 'for the first heaven and the first earth are done.' "

He was sitting in the kitchen, in the dark, looking out the window, naked but for the white towel on his lap.

I'll bet she's glad I asked her too.

The blue of the surgical smock is supposed to be a bland color, but in his dream it had an irritating sheen. And the masks. And the plastic covering that you put over your shoes now—an innovation he detested, it made him feel silly. With the fear of AIDS, there were plastic coverings on everything: the instruments, the machines, even the lights. Don't they know that life is porous and death can always seep through? The researchers were still going back and forth over whether AIDS came from the monkeys of West Africa. He hoped it did. For the sake of the metaphor.

When new males take over a monkey clan they kill all the children so that the females will come into estrus again immediately and have *their* children. House cats do that too. And lions, and tigers. Even in the dream he had to admit this flaw in the tiger's nobility.

He was decked out for surgery, in an operating room, but the other doctors and nurses were telling him to go through a door. He didn't like their eyes. They resented that he was going through the door, and at the same time they had no intention of going through it themselves. And he was uncertain, now, whether he was the doctor or the patient.

The door led to the room made of wood, and in the center of it was the stone slab. He didn't look at the slab, though he knew someone lay on it. He was more interested in the windows. He hadn't been able to see out them once, but now he could. He saw savannahs, a mountain in the distance, a forest to the west. The gates of the zoo had been opened. *This* is where the animals sleep. Lions and tigers rest as much as twenty hours a day . . .

. . . a part of him, within the dream, thought: How good that I still know my facts when I'm dreaming. I'm a good boy.

. . . but actually sleep little, the sleep of lions and tigers is so shallow, what with flies and such. Tigers had been observed to leap straight out of sleep and kill a monkey that had strayed too close. A giraffe (I hadn't the heart to tell this to Lee) sleeps only about a half hour a day, and that in five-minute naps. Giraffes spend almost their whole lives awake.

Is this where they will be when they are no more among us? On this savannah in the sleep of men and women? Will children, in a thousand years, dream of the cheetah, of the elephant, as children now dream of dragons? Mammals began in the time of the dinosaurs. That's why the dragon is so strong an image to us: the first mammals, the first warm-blooded creatures, the first capable of love as we know it, as we and the chimpanzee and the tiger know it, those first mammals' brains were seared so deeply by the image of the enormous dinosaurs that even millions of years of evolution later that image lived in the human dream as dragons—lived thus *before* archeologists began to unearth the fossils. So one day we will find the giraffe on the savannah of dream.

"What about me, Doc?"

He turned and looked at the slab, then quickly averted his face. Her body astonished him.

"It's OK, hey, you're a doctor. Look, I'll close my eyes, if that makes you feel better. Play dead."

Her body was so full, so perfect. He could have known this, if he'd allowed himself, he'd felt its fullness in their embrace. Her line and muscle tone had such voluptuousness and sweetness. Her nipples were erect, like the tiger's. Her breasts like what they sing of in the Song of Songs. No wonder she wore the clothes she chose. Some beauty must be secret.

For the first time in a very long time James Abbey felt desire. It came as though from far away and filled him. And made him feel helpless.

What was her diagnosis? Why is she here? What am I supposed to do? Where are my instruments?

Don't play dead, Lee. Play alive.

There was a tray with a white cloth spread upon it, incredibly clean and white. And upon the cloth was a large round stone which was, apparently, his only instrument.

He picked it up in his left hand, and it felt good to hold. He took off his gloves to feel the grain and coolness of it. This rock had existed for many eons and it would do what's right.

He woke.

His erection was painful, it was so hard and large, the strain of its hardness made him fear its sides were going to split. He made himself breathe evenly and be calm so that his erection subsided.

"Hi, Dad."

"Hello, Eddie. Where's your mother?"

"Down the hall. Ladies' room."

"How you doing?"

"OK, I guess. I just don't sleep good, you know?"

James Abbey sat next to his son in Dr. Benjamin's waiting room.

"Mom was sitting there."

"I don't think she'll mind."

"Or you guys will start one of your no-word fights. You're fighting like crazy, but you're pretending you're not."

"Did we do that a lot, Eddie?"

"Are you kidding?"

"It's good to see you."

"Thanks," the boy said.

A strange thing, Abbey thought, for Eddie to say.

"I guess we did do it a lot," Abbey said.

"You *guess?*" the boy said.

Elizabeth came in. Like Abbey, she'd been careful to dress naturally, not in the good-parent costume that had embarrassed them both last time. She had not succeeded. She looked like a grade-school teacher today, another style favored by Good Moms meeting the authorities. Abbey had also tried to look appropriate, but that was not possible because his clothes fit a man about fifteen pounds heavier. Elizabeth had to restrain herself from asking if he was ill. She didn't want to do that in front of Eddie.

James was staring, unseeing, at the Georgia O'Keeffe print. He felt Elizabeth's eyes on him and turned to her. (What is the physiology of *that?* Of feeling someone's eyes on you?) He felt a question in her, and just as he felt it Dr. Benjamin opened his door—all attention, a welcome but wary smile. Wrinkled clothes (Abbey liked him very much for this). And eyes with a strange lack of color, yet very forceful.

"Ah! My tough guys." His gesture to Eddie somehow spoke of great familiarity between them. "Toughest guy first."

Eddie's pleasure at being spoken to this way was almost too quick to catch; he displayed and retracted it almost with the same gesture as he rose and followed the therapist into his office and closed the door behind him.

Elizabeth waited a moment, then said: "Jim?"

"I know."

"Do you?"

"I've lost weight. It's alright."

"Is it? and is it alright for Eddie to see you like this?"

"What, are we going to let him believe that he's the only one here going *through* things? We're assured and adult, and he's weird? Especially when he knows that's bullshit? Why don't I pretend for him? *That'll* make me a better father."

I am such a hypocrite, he thought, while Elizabeth said, "Stop it. You're not doing me justice."

"Do me some."

"How? Do you have any suggestions?"

"I have a lot of things, these days, but, actually, not one of them is a suggestion."

"That's not news."

I'm sorry, Beth. I'm sorry. I always hide from you. Why do I always hide from you? And he heard himself say:

"I might get married."

"*What?*"

He couldn't believe he'd said what he'd said. Nevertheless, he continued.

"I might. Get married. I met someone. She said no, but— you never know."

"You're seeing somebody?"

Now Abbey, as it were, took over his own conversation, saying, "That's such an interesting phrase. Yes, that's exactly what's happening, I am *seeing* somebody. I am also *being* seen. I am also seeing myself, some. I am *seeing* Eddie, more than I ever have, anyway. I think I may even be *seeing* you. I'm also seeing—" and his words almost left his control again, he almost started speaking of the animals, but he swallowed it. "Seeing—lots of people."

"What's the line in that movie? 'I think I picked the wrong week to stop smoking.' "

"You haven't smoked in years."

"The wrong lifetime, then." Now she sat back and smiled. He was shocked that the smile was genuine, and not one of the smiles they reserved as minor weapons in their arguments. "Actually, I think I like you like this. Or I would, if I weren't also Eddie's mom."

His cheeks trembled.

"I am—his father. His—*father*, Mom. For the *first* time, the other day, I was *really*—Eddie's—father. And you *know* it—because you know such things, I know you do. The man sitting in this chair—is Eddie's father, his *real* father, not the man he and you lived with for years and was too busy to—" and it was too late, the words shot out before he could stop them—"see the raccoons."

"See the what?"

"Please, Beth." And he tried to collect himself.

"This is going to come as a shock to you—it comes as a shock to me, actually—but I love you, Jim. I still love you. I—made drawings of you and Eddie the other day, when you were asleep. Is *that* strange? Do *I* get to be strange too? And the drawings—well, you're Eddie's father, finally, yes. Congratulations, by the way."

They were quiet a moment before she added, "There aren't any bad guys here, that's the trouble. That's why our story isn't in the movies. In the movies you have to have a bad guy or they don't even *make* the movie."

"A refuge from Paradise," he mumbled.

"What?"

"As many bad guys as there are in the world, there still aren't enough to make life as simple as we want it to be."

She laughed. "That's actually pretty smart."

He said, "Thinkin' all the time."

"Now," she said, "let me go slowly this time. OK? You—may—get—*married?*"

"Not really."

"You asked somebody?"

"I shouldn't have said anything."

"No, it's OK, you're a lot of things but you're rarely entertaining, and today you're *very* entertaining. You asked somebody?"

"Beth, give me a break." He smiled at her.

"Not on your life." She smiled back.

"Eddie would like to tell you what he just told me," Dr. Benjamin said to James and Elizabeth as they took their places in his office. "I didn't ask him to. He said, 'Should I tell them?' and I said—what did I say, Eddie?"

"You said it's up to me. You said there isn't a right way and a wrong way to do these things."

"It would be wonderful if there were," Dr. Benjamin addressed them all, "we could just go by the book. The trouble is, there are lots and lots of books, each one's different, and each one thinks it's right. Eddie, it's your turn."

Eddie didn't look at anyone when he spoke. "I don't

feel—safe. When I'm alone in the house. Like—when I'm taking a shower, I'm scared somebody's gonna—*get* me, like in *Psycho*. And—I feel safer with you"—he looked at his mother—"than when I'm alone. But like, if I wake up, sort of, and you're asleep, I don't feel safe." He paused a bit to keep from sobbing. "It's such a wimpy *word*."

How like us he is, James thought. The words mean something to him. All the words. He gets that from both of us. And Abbey felt a deep kinship, for a moment, with Elizabeth.

"I don't think it's wimpy," James said.

"None of us do," Elizabeth said. She was holding on to herself as tightly as she could, within. She had not admitted this to herself before, but what he'd just said was what she'd feared most, for it was the thing she could do least about. Perhaps drugs might be a solution to Eddie's voices, but what could solve this?

Abbey was thinking: Nothing is safe in the wild. Nothing. More than half the cubs of the tiger don't live past a few months. And we are *in* the wild, we *are* the wild. A tigress slowly teaches her cubs to hunt and kill. It takes nearly two years. *The only safety is to be given sufficient skills for the dangers one will meet.* And what does that mean for this boy?

Then Abbey realized, with panicky shame, that his son had begun speaking again and he had not been listening.

". . . with Dad around," Eddie's sentence finished.

Abbey gave his son a fugitive look.

"What's wrong?" the boy said. "Did I say something wrong?"

"No," Abbey said pleadingly, "no, nothing wrong."

"Are you OK, Dad? You don't look right."

"I'm not—physically ill. Alright? Things have been a little—strange, emotionally, for me, lately."

"So maybe *you* should be the one who's the center of all the attention."

The boy gave his father a slight smile. There was a kinship in their desperation that the others were excluded from.

Dr. Benjamin intuited, as his training had taught him, the reason for Abbey's panic a moment ago. He said: "So you were saying, Eddie, that you didn't used to feel safe with your father either, but that the other night—"

"Yeah, I woke up, and I thought you guys were both downstairs, and—that was better. It was better. And when I found out Dad had left—I was—you know? So I think you two should get back together, sort of. It would be—better."

Elizabeth sat there feeling wrong. Wrong, wrong. To her soul. Shame and guilt swamped her. She didn't know where to look. She felt responsible for everyone's suffering.

James felt helpless—that feeling which, in a father, a son can least forgive.

And Dr. Benjamin wished there was a magic wand he could wave, and he hoped that these people didn't think of *him* as such an instrument.

With weariness James said, "I don't think that's going to happen, Eddie."

"Why not?"

They talked for a while, the four of them, about why not, the major and even the minor reasons, all quite reasonable. The boy said he understood them, and everyone, including the boy, knew he didn't. The hearing of the reasons was more a ritual than a conversation, and all were vaguely aware of this. Then Eddie's part of the session was over, as had been planned at the beginning, and it was time for Dr. Benjamin to speak to the parents. He told them it was good that this had come out into the open, but clearly they weren't so sure. Elizabeth asked about Eddie's voices. "That's why we're here, isn't it?" she said, and then, "Forgive me. I wasn't trying to change the subject. Does he hear the voices because he doesn't feel safe, do you think?"

"That would be a handy explanation. And it *might* be true, or it might be part of the truth, and you could find a lot of qualified people who'd tell you that, and they might be right. But I'm going to tell you: I don't think so."

"What do you think?"

Looking straight at Abbey, Dr. Benjamin said, "I don't know what to think yet. I don't yet have enough information." Then, to both of them: "But it is true the voices add to his fear. I told you last time. That's a very frightened boy."

"What do I *do?*" Elizabeth demanded. Then shot at James: "A question you might ask too, mister."

Dr. Benjamin said, "What I am going to say is going to sound—Eddie would call it 'lame.' Maybe. You're very upset, and when we're upset we try, in order to keep control, to make the situation about *us*, even when it's not. This isn't about you, it's about him. You have to face being *afraid* of Eddie being afraid. That's first for you. He feels your fear of *his* fear, and gets more frightened."

Her eyes were furious. She felt both insulted and cheated.

"It's my experience," he went on, "that when you name things and look at them without panic, the situation changes. In increments, but it does. There aren't any miracles here. Yes, the boy is frightened. For one thing, it's a terrible world out there. And he's a complex person—in the long run that should make it better, but in adolescence it often makes it worse. Somehow, in a way that's his and not necessarily yours or mine, he's going to have to learn to live with a lot of fear in his life. His parents learned, so his chances are good, I would say."

"Would you?" she said. Dr. Benjamin started to say something and she said, "Don't tell me anything else, alright? I'm not sure I see the use." And to James: "Are you going to say anything?"

But Dr. Benjamin said: "Sometimes all you can do is stop pretending and just . . . wait."

"Very wise," she said acidly. "James?"

Dr. Benjamin said, "That boy stopped hiding something today, he admitted something important, and you two had better honor that."

Elizabeth stood up quickly.

"Do you have anything for guilt, doctor? A pill? Or a sledgehammer?"

"I have this for guilt. You probably ain't gonna like it. You're trying to feel responsible for everything, you want to think your actions caused this, because *then* in some fashion that would mean you controlled it. And *therefore*, in some fashion, you might continue to control it. Do you get the connection? Between guilt and wanting to control? To keep a fantasy of control?"

"Don't condescend to me, you bastard."

"I'm sorry. You're right. I have too good a time sometimes.

But, Elizabeth, feeling guilty isn't going to give you any more control of the situation; in fact, it's just going to get in the way, make Eddie feel worse. So why bother with it? Yet how does one *not* feel guilty? Easier said than done, I know. It begins with relaxing the need to control.

"See why I like this job? I get to do the easy part, and then I get to see what people (who are perhaps braver than I) do with the hard parts."

"I'd still prefer a pill or a sledgehammer. And I accept your apology, some. I'll see you, Doctor. I think I've *had* my one-on-one, thanks."

Elizabeth left.

"You've been pretty quiet," Dr. Benjamin said to James.

"So I have."

"And you've lost weight."

"Right again."

"I have people coming in here all the time in all sorts of states. I would have to be an idiot, after all these years, not to recognize the general spectrum, let's say, of your present state of mind."

"That's been clear to me from the first."

"That I'm an idiot?"

They smiled at each other like conspirators. Dr. Benjamin made a mental note that Elizabeth needed a female therapist, because she would never feel conspiratorial with a male in authority, and there were moments when therapist and client needed to feel that they were sharing a conspiracy.

Dr. Benjamin said to James:

"So—when you gonna tell this kid about your fuckin' voices?"

Abbey said nothing. The question made him feel heavier in his chair, and yet he felt relieved it had been asked.

"He needs to know," Dr. Benjamin said. "It's a gamble, but it's not as big a gamble as not telling him. Right now he thinks he's a freak. And he's not." Then: "And by the way, he needs to see you survive. That's a *big* deal with him. So don't fuck up too much."

"That's good. I'll take that under advisement. 'Don't fuck up too much.' Right."

"Dr. Abbey, what is sanity?"

"You tell me, Dr. Benjamin."

"It's a description. That's all it is."

"*That's* all?"

"That's all. The only thing anybody can judge by is how you function. There's nothing else they can talk about. There's nothing else they can describe. Once a certain level of functioning breaks down, or you start doing terrible things to other people, they describe you as insane. But given a certain level of functioning—and in our society at present, for better or worse, that level is not too demanding—given that level, *you* get to decide whether you're wacko or not, or in touch with higher powers, or in love—whatever. Because, given a certain level of functioning, the truth is: nobody else much *cares*. You now and again hear voices. Correct?"

"Correct."

"Like the kid's?"

"Used to be like the kid's."

"And these voices, they . . ."

"They called my name in various ways and tones, exactly like his. They never said anything but my name. It was as though, when I was falling asleep, they didn't want me to—didn't want me to sleep."

"Wanted you to wake up, stay awake?"

"I suppose."

"Did you ever ask them why they wanted that?"

"It sounds pretty stupid, Dr. Benjamin, but no, I never did, it never occurred to me. And then one day—I was in my twenties—one day I realized they hadn't come in a while. And that was that."

"Would you be surprised—"

"—these days very little would surprise me—"

"—if I told you that this phenomenon, while rare, is not unheard of. I've been practicing for something like twenty-five years. And in that time—I don't know, maybe twenty people have heard exactly the same thing. As a percentage it's not a scientific sampling by any means, *and* I don't pretend to understand it *at all*, and I'm very suspicious of those who claim to—but: in my experience it hasn't been psychotic. For what that's worth. It happens."

"I know it happens. I know that." Then: "You've said that to Eddie?"

"Of course." Then Dr. Benjamin said: "But your voices now—they're—"

"—a little more dramatic."

"Are you scared?"

"Not anymore."

"These voices—they tell you to run naked in the street or chop people up into small pieces?"

"No. Nothing like that."

"And you promise to tell me if they ever should?"

Abbey hesitated. "Alright."

" 'Alright' isn't 'I promise.' "

"I promise."

"For what it's worth I don't think they *ever* would, or this would be a very different conversation. And they don't tell you you're Jesus or anything, they just—"

"They just give me some pointers. So far."

"Good advice, bad advice?"

"Pretty good. In their way."

"Could be you're just in touch with higher powers?"

"Is *that* a psychological theory?"

"The other explanation is you're nuts. Given a certain level of functioning, nobody can prove either one, so *you* get to choose. Which do you like better?"

"Do you get many malpractice suits?"

"I'm careful."

They both laughed.

"Put it this way," Dr. Benjamin said: "Either *they* tell me who I am—by 'they' I don't mean the voices, I mean *they*, the society in general—you know who *they* are, there's plenty of *them* around—"

"There seem to be."

"Either they tell me who I am or *I* tell me who I am. And the thing is, often *they* don't like me, so I *can't* let them tell me who I am. It's crazy to accept descriptions of yourself from people who don't like you."

"Is this psychology?"

"It better be. Or a lot of good people aren't going to survive. That goes for Eddie, too. Where does his description of himself come from? That's something parents need to think about."

"Who the fuck are you, Dr. Benjamin?"

"I like to think I stand for a certain level of functioning. I just figure: a hundred years ago behavior was explained by one shelf of books, now it's explained by a different shelf of books, and in a hundred years they'll explain it differently again. And not only will their new shelf of books explain it all differently, but we'll be considered not very bright for thinking the way we do, just the way we condescend to the thinking of a century ago. So—why wait a hundred years for the definitions to change? Might as well make some up yourself, since today's are going to be discarded anyway."

"It's been a very stimulating conversation, Dr. Benjamin."

"I try my best, Dr. Abbey. That'll be one hundred and thirty-five dollars, please."

They laughed again.

And what is the physiology of *this*: that my level of (let's call it) sanity changes palpably, even drastically, when I'm alone; when I'm in my house as opposed to at the zoo; when I'm with Lee; with Eddie; with Elizabeth; with Dr. Benjamin; with combinations of the above—*what* is the physiology of that? What is the *anything* of that? I change, not utterly, but significantly. I think the tightness I've felt all my life was, in part, strain at resisting those changes. Trying to be the same person at all times. And I pretty much succeeded. What a disaster. But—*what* is the physiology of these changes, if they *have* a physiology?

He's right, the shelves are swept clean of theories every few decades. Even hard, scientific data is found, later, to be fragmentary, incomplete, and old data changes, often drastically, with every new piece added. Darwin and Marx, Newton and Einstein, Plato and Descartes and Freud—would any of those gentlemen recognize their theories as they've been revised and reconsidered each era, almost each decade? The only books that have remained on the shelves

for centuries and are actually *read* are—what? The holy
books, I suppose, though how they're interpreted changes
all the time. The holy books. A few poems. A few excep-
tionally well told tales. They have been the constants—
though that doesn't mean they'll continue to be, does it? As
for the rest—it passes. So many people depend upon a certain shelf of books so completely for a time and then . . . it
all changes. Yet every generation behaves as though *their*
books are the right ones and will stay on the shelf forever.
You look at it long-term and that behavior is—unrealistic,
maybe even insane. So I shouldn't feel so bad.

"Watch where you're *going*, Dad!"

Abbey hadn't been driving well recently. Now he was so
taken with Dr. Benjamin's metaphor that he was barely driving at all, though the car was moving.

"Would you rather I drive, Jim?"

Elizabeth's car hadn't started. They'd taken a cab to Dr.
Benjamin's and Abbey was driving them home.

"Actually, that might be a good idea."

Eddie was getting used to James surprising him, but Elizabeth wasn't. As he pulled over to the curb she gave him
what her mother used to call "the family look." Abbey got
out the driver's door, Elizabeth got out the passenger's door.
Eddie watched from the back seat as his mother and father
passed each other in front of the car, and he laughed at how
their eyes never left each other. He was still laughing when
they got back in the car.

"What's so funny?" Elizabeth said as she fastened her seat
belt.

"*You* guys. The grown-ups." The boy's voice was different in timbre somehow. It was a moment in the life of the
three of them. The bare suggestion of ceremony in the way
they'd opened their doors at the same time and then crossed
in front of the car, had triggered something in the boy. He
said, with a voice that had not yet changed physically, but
that had, in this moment, changed somehow: "I'm sitting
back here having a grown-up thought. You wanna hear it?"

"Sure, kid," his father said.

"Nobody has a handle on *anything*. That's my thought."

"I thought you had that thought already," James said.

"I thought I did too, but when I used to have it I didn't believe it."

"*That's* your first grown-up thought," James said proudly.

He looked at Elizabeth, who couldn't help smiling, for she shared the pride. She said into the rearview mirror as they pulled out from the curb, "Watch it, hon, or you're going to become an intellectual like your parents. And you may not like it."

"I already *don't.*"

And the grown-ups in the front seat laughed, and the boy laughed with them in a more grown-up way than he ever had.

Eddie had gone inside. James was in the car, behind the wheel. Elizabeth stood by the car, and bent toward the driver's window.

"Married?" she said, raising her eyebrows.

"No, Elizabeth. I shouldn't have said anything."

"But you did."

"Daydreaming." He paused. "Actually—I miss my family."

"I don't think that can happen, Jim."

"I know."

"There's both too much and too little between us."

"I know."

"You weren't daydreaming, either, James Abbey. You were serious."

"I was seriously daydreaming, how's that?"

"One minute I think that something good is happening with you, and the next—I really worry. I don't know."

" 'Why do you wonder?' "

"What?"

" 'And I wondered, seeing her, with a great wonder. Then the angel said to me, Why did you wonder?' "

"And what chapter and verse is that from?"

"*All* the chapters. *All* the verses."

"I think that's my cue to say 'Have a nice day.' Take care, Jim, OK?"

"You, too."

As he drove away, he completed the verse: " 'And the angel said to me, Why did you wonder? I will tell you the mystery of the woman, and of the beast who carries her.' "

Then he said, "Revelation, chapter 17, verses 6 and 7. To be used strictly on a need-to-know basis."

A BITE

The people pressed to touch the beast, body to body, women and men, children, in bright sarongs and work clothes. Some of the children were naked. The tiger lay dead on a cart. They'd gathered around the cart, masses of people who slowly moved around the tiger in a serpentine line, and one by one they touched it. They were seeking its blessing, the narrator said. They would touch it with the fingertips of their left hand, then touch those fingers to their forehead, quickly and over and over until the press of the crowd shoved them past where they could reach the tiger.

It was a man-eater. They had determined which tiger was killing the villagers, then they had tracked it, then they had killed it. The beast was so shocked. To be shot. Its roar was more surprise than pain. And the way it thrashed as it died— not like death throes, but as though to kick and paw away the death it could not see. Then it lay still on its side with little spasms of its legs, but its shoulder muscle thumped hugely with the last beats of its heart.

When that stopped, the hunters approached slowly. The man who shot it saluted it. He was a quiet, apologetic person with a very long, old rifle. It had taken two shots.

When a man-eater is about, people simply disappear. The tiger drags the dead person off into the jungle where they're rarely recovered. Two villagers had survived: an elephant driver and a girl in her early teens. They showed the scars of teeth and claw—ripping wounds, difficult to deal with. Abbey's professionalism was aroused. He would have liked to have treated those two when their wounds were fresh. Ripping wounds were such a challenge, especially the punctures of the teeth. The tiger has the largest canine teeth of any land animal.

"The tiger threw me many times, three or four feet into the air. As I fell, I kept my head facing the ground, so that the tiger could not grab my throat and choke me. The tiger thought I was dead. He moved aside and sat watching me. Now he was waiting to carry me away." This was the elephant driver, who spent his days on a great animal's back, and had felt their ways through his legs, his crotch, his bare feet. The tiger had torn all the skin from the top of his head. A friend of his, not of his caste, an elegant Hindu woman whom he apparently worked for, said, "I've known him for so long and this man—he put up such a great fight with the tiger. And he didn't bear any grudge against the animal that attacked him."

And the footage went on and on of the villagers and the tiger. "Everyone wanted to touch it," the narrator said.

Abbey ran the tape back to what the woman said about not bearing a grudge. He watched her say it several times. Then he watched again how they would touch the tiger, then touch their foreheads. A transmission of blessing. He admired them, their ability to press against each other, body to body, and though touched on all sides they still could have this private contact with the beast, contact so important many had walked miles and miles for it.

James Abbey felt these people would understand him. They would understand Lee. Not in many things, of course; but in the things of the zoo, they would share understanding and respect and nothing would have to be explained. It calmed him to have found them.

I wonder if I'll go my whole life not turning on the lights at night? The fear has lifted. I don't know why. You'd think

it would be worse, but it's not. It's lifted like a fog thinning
and rising. There just isn't a reason to turn on the light. The
L.A. night is bright enough that one can see if all the cur-
tains are open. Perhaps if I ever want to read again, I'll turn
a light on. That's an odd way to put it. Surely I'll want to
read again?

Abbey laughed. Am I the only one in Southern California
debating on the advisability of turning on lights when it gets
dark outside? But I like this, is the point. And I've only myself to make the point to. Sanity is a description? How would
I describe this? I would say that for a million years human
beings ceased their activities when it grew dark, except on
very special occasions. This business of lights in the house
is very new. Less than a hundred years in many places. Especially outside of cities. And it's only in the last fifty years
or so that so many people live in cities. So my description
would be: this isn't aberrant behavior; I have simply chosen
to leave my time, by this rather simple device—leave the
rhythms of my time and choose a rhythm closer to Eden's,
or, not to be so biblical, closer to the rhythm of those villagers who walked their distance to touch the tiger.

It is so easy, really, to leave this city. A matter of light. An
animal's eyes. A very old song on the breath of a girl.

The phone rang.

In a few days he would again have the obligation to answer phones, but tonight he let it ring. It stopped. There
were some mechanical clicks. Then, through the small
speaker in the other room:

"Oh *shit*, a machine. Doc, are you my friend?"

He fumbled through the rooms. He was trembling. He
didn't know right from left. (What's the physiology?) Of all
the voices he had heard, this was the most unexpected. And
it continued, "Oh, man, be there, be *there*, oh man—don't
lose it on me, everybody fuckin' loses it on me."

"Everybody loses *what* on you?" He was short of breath.

"Everything, man. Everybody loses everything."

"Hello, Lee."

"Hello, Doc."

"This isn't a zoo, you know."

"Who says?"

She sounded like she'd been drinking. She said, "Hey, where do you *live*, man, your phone number's like mine, 661."

"Echo Park."

"Fuck, *I* live in Echo Park. You *really* a doctor?"

"Really."

"Then why do you live in Echo Park?"

"Because of the story of my life."

She lived not ten minutes from him. Their lives had been this close to one another since she'd moved here, just before Eddie and Elizabeth had left. The information frightened him. "Synchronicity," Elizabeth would call it, that nonthreatening word with the vaguely scientific sound. Abbey felt something both sweeter and darker. Down Cerro Gordo, right on Echo Park Boulevard, up where it crested the hill and became so narrow, past the fence made of hubcaps, to the dead-end at Landau, right, down the steep road as it narrowed, too, into a dead end. He took down the directions.

"Two wrongs don't make a right," she said, "but what do two dead ends not make?"

"What?"

"*I* don't even know what I said, it doesn't matter. It doesn't matter, Doctor. And *it doesn't matter* that it doesn't matter. It doesn't matter that it doesn't matter."

"Is that a song too?"

"You comin' over?"

He followed the directions.

I am following directions, he said to himself, up and down the steepness of these hills that conceal one street from the other, and the thickness of this foliage that conceals so many houses from each other, so that it's possible not to see our neighbors, nor the raccoons, and I saw the mama possum tonight and the albino child still clung to her, what a resourceful creature that mama possum must be. The road is so narrow here, curves sharply, only room for one car to pass at a time. It is so dark with all this foliage. You say "synchronicity" because you're afraid to say "God." You say a lot of things because you're afraid to say God. I am following directions.

At the dead end he turned right, and the road dropped steeply and narrowed more. Below in the valley the great freeways ran with light, the Golden State, the Ventura, the Pasadena, he could see them all from here, on this hillside road so narrow he wondered if his Buick would make it. Up and down the hill was a virtual forest, at least for Southern California. Many tall trees, thick growth beneath. And the lights of shacks and houses through the trees. Dead end up ahead. There was nowhere to park but to edge the car off the road as far as was safe so that it slanted down the hillside. Hard to believe such places existed in the center of millions of people, but there were many such enclaves still, though not as many as there once were. In his volunteer work with the old, and with AIDS patients too poor and sick to travel, and with illegals (he was always volunteering for one program or another, service that brought him to people's homes, for it was the house calls to his tenement that had made him want to become a doctor long ago)—in this work, which he did out of a sense of responsibility, and in which he behaved less like the savvy house-call doctors of his childhood than like the distant, preoccupied priests who visited when his mother took ill—but in this work he would come across such places as this nestle of shacks on a hill down a road that the city had not repaired in years. Of course she lived here. It was her natural habitat.

When he'd asked on the phone how she'd found him, she said, "Doctors aren't hard to find." And he was struck with the sense that tonight was a night that could not be avoided, could not be stopped. This thrilled him.

He forgot the slant of the hill, and the heavy Buick door

slipped from his grip when he opened it and slammed into a tree trunk.

There were yellow eyes. Abbey hated them. A big black dog, now growling. Dog eyes could be so dead. And this dog had a deadness to it that frightened Abbey very much. Abbey reached to close the door but the dog snapped and Abbey flinched. He moved back on the seat. The dog came closer, growling.

"Go away," Abbey said.

The dog barked. Abbey flinched at the barks.

"Go *away.*"

Abbey hated the helplessness in his voice and that the beast could hear it. The beast loved his helplessness and barked louder. Abbey wondered if he'd be eaten by the dog. Is this how I'm to be fed to God?

"Goddamnit, Leftie, God DAMN!"

He heard her, couldn't see her, and she was throwing stones. One hit the dog, who yelped, and one clanged loudly on the car. Another hit the dog, but the creature was confused; it wanted to run but was caught in the crook of the door and the only place to run was into the car at Abbey, but it was frightened now, even of Abbey. It stood snarling, cringing. And now Lee was standing over the dog, and it quelled, slinking down, looking up at her with its yellow eyes, making resentful sounds.

"I hate this fuckin' dog."

"So do I."

"Scared of dogs, huh? What a laugh." And to the dog: "*GET* the fuck out of here!"

The dog flinched and found a way to slink under the car into the underbrush. Dogs, the creatures of people for eons, do they know that the great beasts are leaving, that the tiger and the elephant and the polar bear will soon be gone, and the leopard (which loves to eat dogs, which will conquer its shyness to enter a village and even go inside houses to kill and eat a dog), the leopard will be gone, and will some weight fall upon the dogs when they, and the house cat, and the rat, and the horse, are, with us, the only mammals left?

"Hi," she said. "Don't stare like that."

"Hi," he said. "Thank you." He hated that she'd seen him so afraid.

"It's the neighbor's—the dog. Sometimes I think I'm gonna poison it, there's *nothing* good about that dog, but, then, I suppose, it doesn't hurt around here to bark at strangers—I mean, the Hillside Strangler left two bodies right down there." She pointed a short way off.

"Did he?"

"Yeah, well, you know—it's a hillside."

She wore a cotton housedress, faded blue, shapeless but for the youthful rise of her breasts, as full as in his dream. When she embraced him there was only her body under the thin cotton, and it was the body of the dream. For the first time while embracing her he became aroused and he knew she felt it and it made him shy. But she didn't seem to care, she pressed against him and buried her head in his shoulder, saying, "Oh, it's alright, it's alright now."

"What's alright?"

"Nothing."

They slowly let go of one another.

"Thanks for coming," she said. "You don't want to hear about my love life, do you?" Then suddenly her voice was very young: "Who we gonna visit? We're *visitors*. We visit guys, tiger guys, gerenuk guys. I hope I have dreams of that zoo when I'm an old lady. Have a drink with me?"

She took him by the hand and led him down the dark stone path to her little wooden house—the shack on the strangler's hillside. It had windows on all sides, which were open, old-fashioned windows with latches rather than locks. A door on the side and a door on the front, with the kind of locks anyone could open with a hairpin. As things were now in this city, such a place was as vulnerable as a tent. There were other shacks like it in a cluster. He could hear the television from the one just down the hill. A sitcom with computer laughter.

The din of the freeways in the valley directly below was so constant and loud that, instead of noise, it was like river sound or sea sound, and it made for a sense of silence.

And James Abbey was again what he was with Lee: in the presence of everything within him, even his Paradise and his fear of dogs.

This is love. It is this precisely. When I am with this person I leave nothing behind.

Again he could not get over how quickly he became a different person in her presence. *It is not just that I miss Lee. I miss* me. *I miss this person I am as I step with her. We visit* me.

There are directions. It began when I turned off all the lights in the house at night for the first time. I didn't know why I did it, but I was stopping everything, and waiting for directions. It took a long time for the coyote to come, but the coyote did come, and began all this. It did not occur to me till now that the coyote would not have come to the yard of a lit house.

It was as though he'd entered car-crash time, skid time, when you have so long to think before the impact (let them explain the physiology of *that*), the small ways she moved her fingers in his hands as she led him on the stone path, the light in her hair, the movement of blue cotton on her body, and her green eyes looking back and catching the strange light in his grays.

"What?" she said.

"That tiger's eyes went back a million years. I saw that."

"I'll bet that dog's eyes didn't go back five minutes. *That's* why you were scared." Her voice softened. "Your eyes go back a ways, too, Doc. I don't know about a million, but— a ways."

"They do?"

"What kinda company you been keepin', nobody's ever told you about your eyes?"

"You keep talking like a song."

"I'm supposed to," she smiled brightly.

She brought up his hand and kissed it quickly. She said, "I know, Doc. That was a kiss."

Whoever called such talk "sweet nothings" was wrong. They are insubstantial words, yes, but that's so they can float on the stream and catch the light. In the moments before they disappear they are everything.

"I'm better with you here," she said softly.

"You going to tell me about it?"

"Probably not. Come on in."

That's fair, he thought as he followed her in, for I haven't told you about Eddie, I haven't told you about Elizabeth and Dr. Benjamin—Dr. Benjamin, who left the oddest message on my machine today. It was waiting when I got back from taking Elizabeth and Eddie home. "I have a question for you," Dr. Benjamin had said, his voice tinny on the little speaker. "Is there a spirit world? I don't mean *is* there, I mean what do you believe? Not what do you *want* to believe, or what do you *intelligently* believe, but what is it that you can't help but believe? Remembering, of course, that nobody can prove you wrong. Maybe the voices have something to do with those beliefs. There's nothing more dangerous—'dangerous' is too strong a word—there's nothing more undermining than having beliefs you don't know you have, beliefs you don't admit you have. Aren't answering machines wonderful? That happens to be one of my beliefs, and I admit it." Then the sharp beep when the caller hangs up.

He liked it inside. It was odd how secure it felt, in spite of its vulnerability. Something about being surrounded by the foliage. And it was bigger than it looked from the outside. The rooms were small, but there was a kitchen, a living room, a bedroom, a bathroom, all crowded with her things, messy but clean. An old sofa took up much of the living room, it had a sheet over it; he could imagine how it looked under the sheet, frayed and cracked and faded. There were tapes and a tape player, a microphone stand, speakers, earphones, two guitars, a keyboard, various wires— tools of her trade. (By contrast, the basic tools of his trade could still fit in a modest black bag.) Posters and prints on the walls—people he had never heard of and didn't recognize, groups of young people calling themselves strange names. Abbey had liked rock music till the war, when the incessant playing of it on small record players in the hospitals, with the country music on the military radio station, and the pathetic renditions of American hits by Vietnamese bands in the bars, all combined to become a kind of torture to him, an inescapable wall of sound that couldn't be ignored or turned off except very late at night in the hospital, or in the operating room, and sometimes not even there, until the rock songs became all one song, a song meant to block out something it could not possibly block out, while at the same time trying to evoke something it could never fully evoke. When he'd returned to America he had, without thinking of it, banned the music from his life. Even now, when he chanced to hear it from a loud car radio or in a store, or when Eddie listened to it, he felt it was music for a war zone, that this was its inspiration and purpose. Which was natural, since the war was everywhere now. But it hurt him to see that this war-zone music was, to all intents, her *life.*

This was her life. As the thought sunk it hurt and hurt. Where would he be more out of place than where people half his age gathered for songs they didn't even know were war songs?

"Like my place?" she said.

"Cozy."

"That's one of my favorite words," she said. "That's a real compliment. Everything should be cozy. Everything."

In her bedroom there was only a mattress on the floor covered by an old quilt. Prints on the wall by Impressionists, and a movie poster—*Wings of Desire.* There were socks and underthings about. A gentle disarray, as though the rooms were in a kind of perpetual motion and nothing stayed still long enough to be tidy.

"What do you want to drink? I've got white wine which isn't too good and scotch which is very good, because I stole it from the last club my band played 'cause they stiffed us. Stole everything I could get my hands on."

She stopped short and looked at him.

"Nervous, Doc? Alone with me in my, what's the zoo call

'em, habitat? It fucking hurts me that you're nervous, man."
Her eyes teared up.

"Nervous, Lee?"

"I guess that's a 'gotchya.' I had to call you. We are *visitors*, man, and there's nothin' to visit here but *me*. In my
sleeping cage. I want you to feed me in my cage. *Grrrrrr*,"
and she showed her teeth. It was supposed to be playful but
it wasn't.

What was not to be avoided had begun. And for some
reason this made him calm. Her behavior felt somehow apt
to him, and this, in turn, calmed her.

"We could, if it was light," she said, "visit the animals
around *here*. Got hummingbirds. Got parrots—wild parrots
in the high wires, you should hear them, they *hate* us, hate
us worse than the crows, and the noisy damn crows around
here just hate everything—hard sounds those creatures
make. Or we could turn out the lights and sit out with the
bugs and wait for critters. Got possums, got skunks, got raccoons, now and then a coyote—"

"I have those too. Never saw a wild parrot though."

"Owls?"

"Don't see them, but I hear them."

"Ants."

"By the millions," he said.

"I've gotta hang my garbage from the doorknob, if it's on
the floor it's a mountain of ants."

"Spiders."

"*All* kinds."

"Eden," he said.

"The Garden?"

"It's a lie in the Bible," he said. "Nobody ever left the
place."

"It just got developed, like?"

"Right."

"Malls and shit. I get it. You gonna have scotch?"

"Before the freeways cut these hills off from the others
there were deer."

"*Yeah*, there's this old guy in a cabin down the way—"

"Old guy?"

"Even older than *you*, man, and he's lived here since, like, the thirties, and he said there were deer *all* the time, they'd come to his little porch an' he'd feed 'em. There were bobcats too. Don't tell me you're not gonna drink?"

"Scotch is OK. He must miss those deer."

"Says he dreams about them."

"Eden."

She went into the kitchen and poured Glenlivet scotch into two wineglasses. She didn't offer water or ice, and he took it as she gave it.

"You talk a lot about that stuff, 'Eden,' 'eternity,' I mean, you don't *talk* about it, you know? You just kind of *say* it. Mention it. I feel like I'm supposed to know what you're talking about, but I don't. I mean, I *do*, but I don't."

"Does that bother you?"

"Does it bother *you*, I'm asking? It's like, the way you say them, they're the words to a song. It's like you're working on a song and it comes out a little at a time like that."

"Sit by me, Lee." He was sitting on her sofa.

"I was hoping one of us would get that idea."

She sat by him, her legs curled under her, her knees touching his thigh. He sipped the scotch. It was strong and smooth. He felt the first small swallow reach delicately into him and touch him. It had been a very long time since he'd had alcohol, and days since he'd eaten a real meal. He knew the physiology of *that*.

"That's exactly it, Lee. I knew you understood, I knew that. Better than me you've understood. I'm working on a song, and it comes out a little at a time, and those are some of the words."

"Now don't confuse me, I've had more of these than you. You're not *really* working on a song, I mean, I couldn't *sing* this song—"

"You sing it all the time, you know it better than I do—"

"—but you *are* working on a song, and that's what you're really up to, but it's not a song. I think I get it."

" 'You are wise in your generation.' That's from the Bible."

"We are fucked in my generation. That's from me. Screwed to the wall. Bruce aside, we'd retreat *and* surrender, if we could find someone to surrender *to*, but there ain't no one, nobody's interested."

"Bruce?"

"Springsteen. Plays guitar." She rolled her eyes.

"I've heard of him."

"Really plugged in, aintchya, Doc?"

"Making fun of me?"

"Somebody's got to."

He put his hand on her knee where it pressed against his thigh. She covered his hand with hers.

The constant wave of freeway hum, pierced with cricket song and now and then a barking dog, filled their silence. The lumpy sofa, the strident posters; the scent of the wooded hillside, its night-blooming jasmine, cut with a fine edge of valley smog and whiffs of scotch; green eyes and gray eyes; hennaed hair and steel gray-black; the oddly black-and-white look of the room, what with the posters and the equipment and the white sheet on the couch, with her faded blue, frayed housedress, and the strain-tinted skin under her eyes; and his creased black slacks, and his old, navy-blue cotton shirt, the softest shirt against his skin; and, in the dim bedroom, lit only by the lamp from the living room, the peach sheet on the mattress, and, more dimly still, the Impressionist posters, their pale colors, Pissarro, Monet; and, the windows wide open, the slight shine on the screens and the light on the leaves of the branches close by, and how they moved slightly in the air, so that it seemed the light trembled and not the leaves—Lee and Abbey sat, breathing together, and wanting nothing more than what, in that moment, they had. Then as gently as it formed, and as gently as it held them, just that gently the moment passed.

Sooner or later life becomes a matter of being, or failing to be, loyal to the beauty one has known. Some part of them would always be there, on that couch, in that gentleness. When Abbey would think of it later it would fill him with the sanity that leaves nothing behind; and when, much later, the moment's memory would find and surprise Lee, it would help her save what could still be saved.

"If you don't love me, love whom you please . . . Hang your

head over, hear the wind blow . . . When I was little I thought my mother made up all those songs, and the prints she had on the wall—I thought she'd painted all those pictures. Even though I never saw her paint anything. I just didn't *think* of that, you know? When I got older and found out that they weren't her songs and they weren't her pictures, I felt like the world had stolen something from her. I still do."

"My father sang old songs. Old Irish songs."

"That's what we have in common, then." Her face changed. "That old zoo stole something from me yesterday. Man, I never thought it would, but it did. I mean, I'd sit outside the door on warm nights, on the straw chair there that hardly has a bottom, and I'd feel the night air, and I'd think the animals were feeling it just like me."

"It doesn't really matter about the zoos," he said. "They won't *really* preserve anything. The genetic pool is too small. After a few decades the animals may still look like what they were but they won't *be* what they were."

She leaned and kissed him lightly on his cheek.

"I don't understand that, but it sounds depressing, so I don't think I want to, at least not tonight."

"Sorry. I don't want to, either. But sometimes it just comes to me— I—"

"You're kind of obsessed with it?"

"I guess I am."

"Well, I wouldn't give two cents for a man who wasn't obsessed with *something*. Don't you like the scotch? They age this stuff twelve years. That's more than half my life."

"Don't remind me." And, to please her, he took two swallows.

The phone rang. Lee stiffened. The machine picked it up. She squeezed his hand hard as, after the clicks, a young male voice said: "Hey, Lee, baby, come on, answer up. Lee? Stop being such a *bitch*, alright? I mean, what's it *for?*" And the caller hung up.

Lee took a quick drink. For moments she couldn't look at Abbey. He felt a pang in his chest that he hadn't felt since he was younger than that boy's voice. He was amazed.

"Well, now you know all about me," she said darkly.

"What?"

"You know I'm a bitch."

"Lee—"

"A two-timin' bitch, at that. Kiss the bitch, Doc."

And she puckered her lips in an exaggerated way, and closed her eyes tight.

He raised his fingers to her lips and pressed gently, like a kiss. She relaxed her eyes but kept them closed, then relaxed her lips and kissed his fingers. She opened her eyes.

"You a two-timer, Doc?"

"I'm not even a one-timer."

"Oh boy! Can I—where the fuck is my pencil?"

She got up awkwardly. The alcohol was starting to hit her, or perhaps her unsteadiness was only that her legs had been curled under her, he couldn't tell. She looked here and there for paper, couldn't find a piece, and finally wrote the "one-timer" line on one of the posters. He got up and went to her as she did it, to see what she was writing.

"You're gonna be my greatest hit."

They stood close without touching.

She said, "The guy on the phone, he sounds like a creep, but he's not, OK?"

"OK."

"He'd shit if he saw you here. You were funny yesterday. Askin' me to marry you. Fuckin' idiot."

"Want me to ask you again?"

"Don't you dare."

He put his arms around her and held her to him, and again she embraced with all of herself, as though she couldn't hold anything back if she wanted to. He wasn't embarrassed at his arousal now. He wished they could just stand there like that for hours, and not have to make even the choice of whether or not to sit down. She said into his shoulder, sobbing now, "I can't forgive him for making me feel so unforgiving."

Then, in an utterly different voice, she said, "You're obsessed with gene pools—'Let's go swimming in my gene pool,' how's that for a come-on line, *that'll* get 'em into bed in droves, it's all yours, Doc—you're obsessed with gene pools and I'm obsessed with tabloids."

They were standing next to one of several stacks of supermarket tabloids.

She knelt down at one stack and he knelt with her.

"When I get down I read these. These guys are *really* twisted. Makes you and I look like solid citizens."

She picked one off the top and read it and cast it off, and kept doing it till the floor was strewn with luridness: "*Space Alien Meets with President*—well, man, *somebody's* gotta get *to* that guy. *First Fotos Ever of Dead Space Alien*—died of boredom meeting with presidents. *Child's Footprint Found on Moon. Return the World's Been Waiting For—Elvis Will Sing at Superbowl.* Here's my favorite: *Nest of Bugs Live in Girl's Right Eye.* Have another drink, Doc."

She took him by the hand to the couch and picked up his glass from the floor where he'd left it and handed it to him.

"A toast," she said, "to the right eye of the world."

They clinked glasses.

"You're looking at me funny, Doc. Come on. Let's have it. But not standing up."

She pulled him down onto the sofa, and snuggled against him and put her head on his chest. "This is better."

I am drifting, he thought, I am letting her do everything, because she seems to know what she wants to do, or at least she has impulses. I only knew what I wanted when we sat so still. I wanted to remember that moment always.

He kissed her hair. She clung to him like a little girl.

"Ouch, what's this?" she said.

She took his beeper off his belt.

"Two-gun Jim."

"I didn't realize I had it with me. It's a reflex."

"You got another one on the other side," and she fumbled around him, half tickling, half caressing, and he slowly caressed her back and her hair. "Guess not," she said. "One gun. So why were you looking at me funny? I like that, your hand on my hip, big strong hand. Oooooh." And she nuzzled her hip against his hand. "So why?"

"You'll get mad."

"Not tonight. Not at you."

"I was wondering about the papers. I know you don't believe them—"

"Sometimes I do."

"But they're not how the world is."

"They're how the world *feels*."

She sat up, half on his lap, holding him by the shoulders.

"Listen to *him*," she said, "listen to, 'They're not how the world is.' Read all about it! *Tiger Speaks to Surgeon! Says Follow Young Girl!* Read all about it! Most guys don't need *tigers* to tell 'em that, Doc. Oh, man. You should see your face. Gotta kiss."

And they kissed a lover's kiss. And kissed for a little while. Kissed, softly, each other's eyes and hair and forehead, and then lips again. James Abbey had forgotten. He had simply forgotten.

When the wave of kissing passed she pulled her head back and said, "That was a bunch of kisses, Doc."

"It's OK?"

"Oh, yeah." And she leaned against him like a child again. And she said to herself, as though he weren't there, "This is what it can be like. Now I know. Funny I didn't know, and thought I did. Now when it's not like this, I'll know what it's not."

To be told so offhandedly both what he was giving her, and how dispensable he was to the gift, made him feel disoriented, as though he must have heard wrong. He reached for the scotch and drank down a large swallow.

"Me too," she said, and drank from his glass.

She settled herself in a more conversational position, sitting beside him with her legs over his lap, as he was thinking: Of course, she's a child, and children are ruthless, and they don't know that they are, and she's giving me so much, I will accept whatever role is offered. I give myself to you, Lee, in whatever way you want. But I won't say that, it would frighten you far more than proposals of marriage.

"I wanna know something," she said.

"What?"

"Something no one else knows."

"About what?"

"About *you*, dummy. *No one* else. I wanna have that."

"Where's your drink?"

"Where we can't reach it and we're not moving till you tell me. Kiss the bitch, Doc."

And she kissed him again now, another wave of kissing,

but with little bites now, biting his lip, biting his tongue, he taking it up, biting her chin, biting her cheek, small nips, then licking, then kissing, gentle animals, making small sweet sounds.

They lay against each other, breathing quietly again.

"Don't call yourself a bitch, Lee," he said quietly.

"I just like the way it sounds. Good song title, good *album cover*. 'Kiss the Bitch,' man, you *are* my greatest hit, I swear. So? Something *nobody* else has on you. What's wrong, man? What'd I say?"

"Do you know what God said, Lee?"

"Uh-oh. Are we goin' bye-bye, Doc?"

"What they *said* God said. 'I know your works, that you are neither cold nor hot. You should be cold or hot. Thus because you are lukewarm I will spew you out of my mouth.' Revelation, 3:15–16. Mama always liked me to annotate when I quoted."

"Mamas are like that."

"Well, that's what the Lord does when we are fed to Him—"

"To Her—"

"—to Whomever. When He likes not the taste or the temperature, we are spewed from His mouth."

"Her mouth. I'm listening, but I'm not getting, and I want that drink after all."

She got up and got the bottle and filled their glasses.

"They had this war. You probably heard of it."

"I heard."

"It was just a big hospital for me. One endless body that was always wounded. At first you think it's a great experience because the wounds present really interesting problems, wounds are *very* unpredictable, a bad wound isn't one problem, it's fifty, and you have to attend to every one of them or it won't heal properly. I saw the wounds, I didn't see the guys, and they were usually fucked-up enough that they couldn't see me, so it all worked out. Until one day you *see*. You don't know why it's one particular day and one particular guy, but you *see*. Ask me, 'What do you see?' "

"I love you, Doc. What do you see?"

"I love you, Lee. I love you."

"What do you see?"

He sipped his scotch. He was no longer sober but he couldn't tell to what degree he was drunk. Lee was curled comfortably against him, her leg over his lap.

"What you see is this guy, now that he's lost an eye, a leg, a hand, all of the above—he's all alone. He doesn't care about the war anymore, if he ever did, and he's afraid to go home, and can't figure why it happened at all—why, on the word of some strangers, did he go hurt a bunch of other strangers, who ended up hurting him? It seems unnatural, doesn't it? But how can it *not* be natural? It *happened*, right? If it wasn't really natural, how could it ever happen? I couldn't stop asking that question. Nothing that defies the laws of nature can happen—'cause you need the laws of nature to *make* anything happen. This means that guided missiles are natural. Styrofoam is natural. I don't see any way around it. Humans are nature too, so everything we *do* is nature, God is in everything, God is in war."

"I don't think you're really answering my question, Doc."

"Give me time. And give me a kiss."

She kissed him lightly.

"All the animals, the great animals, are going, they're all going, Lee. An elephant lives about fifty years. An elephant born today, in the wild, is probably of *the last generation* of elephants. Dolphins live as long as we do. A dolphin born today, who knows what the sea will be like when it's old, which will be after you and I are dead. And what's happening to the sea and the rain forests and the animals—*that's not natural*, we say, but—the long-term behavior of nature is that it uses some element of itself, like ice or water or a meteor, to wipe out almost everything and start over. Well, what if *we're* that element? Then this is all natural. Because if it's *not* natural, how could it even happen?"

"You mean: then there's no real reason to get mad."

"That's one way of putting it."

"Well—*I'm* mad, and intend to stay mad."

"Bless you, my child. But that doesn't mean you have a good reason."

"You're mad," she said softly.

His eyes teared. "But that doesn't mean I have a good reason."

"Gotta kiss—those—tears." And she did.

"This kid I finally looked at—this terrible thing that had happened to him—in some hellish way it was natural. Which means: God doesn't give a shit about right and wrong. We do. God doesn't care about the price. *All* things are possible. That's the only thing that's important to God." He took a drink. "And when I realized that—I got too scared. Too scared. I quit. Lee, I quit. I never said that before, but it's true. Until not too long ago. And then it was like—a matter of not turning on the lights. *Not* turning them on. Like, OK, God, if that's how You want to play, that *all* things are possible, I'll play that way too. And here I am."

"James, James, James. I don't get it. But you don't get me either, and here *I* am, so that's OK."

"I don't get you?"

"Naw. Not a clue."

"Maybe a clue."

"Maybe just."

"Anyway—what I started to tell you . . . Here was this guy's leg. *He'd* been taken away but his leg was still there. And it was pretty raw where it had been connected to the rest of him. So, real quick, I took my little scalpel and cut a little piece off and put it in my mouth and tasted it and chewed it."

"Oh, *shit*, man," she put her hand to her mouth and made sounds that were part choke and part laugh, and said from behind her hand, "You *got* me, Doc, and I asked for it, and what you said *doesn't* go with scotch."

She took some deep breaths. Then offered her face to be kissed, saying, "Taste my mouth."

He kissed her.

"Terrible, isn't it?" she said.

"Pretty terrible."

"Serves you right. Read all about it! *Surgeon Eats Human Flesh Raw!* Read all about it! Man, I just *read* this shit, you *live* it. So?"

He was smiling and feeling foolish and suddenly and incredibly light.

"So?" he asked back.

"So *what* did it *taste* like?" and she laughed again, help-lessly, and tickled him, and he laughed.

"Why are we laughing?" he said through his laughter.

" 'Cause we'd *better*," she said laughing. "*So?*"

"It was lukewarm. And sour. And I spewed it out of my mouth."

"I'm kissing a cannibal."

"Cannibals eat dead people. This guy was still alive."

"Oh, *that* makes me feel better: I'm kissing a guy who eats people while they're still alive!"

"That leg wasn't his anymore. Finders keepers."

"But it was just one bite? Just once?"

"Promise."

"And you didn't swallow?"

"Honest."

"Neither did my mother. She said, 'Don't swallow, guys don't respect it.' But that's another story. You know, I'll bet *lots* of you guys do it. Doctors. I'll bet hundreds, thousands, just can't resist, gotta know what it tastes like, sneak a nip on the side. I'll bet some guys get addicted. To little secret sneaky slimy bites. And they go to little secret slimy twelve-step meetings. Maybe I love you 'cause you're crazier than *I* am."

They fell into a silence, sat and listened to the crickets, and now some frogs, and the freeway, and the loud TV nearby, broadcasting a quiz show. Dogs barking at some distance.

"Whom was it you couldn't forgive?" he asked.

"The guy on the machine."

"Why can't you forgive him?"

"Not a good idea."

"To forgive him?"

"To talk about it."

"I forgive you," he said.

"For what? What'd I do?"

"I'd forgive you for anything."

"Anything's an awful lot."

"Is it? 'Anything' is what God likes. It's amazing not to be afraid of it anymore."

"Shhhhhhhh," she whispered.

"What?"

"Shhhhhhhhhh."

She stroked his face. And she started to bite on him a little. Bit his hand. Bit his chin. Bit his earlobe. He let her. He
liked it. She bit just hard enough. Small places within him
opened at each bite. How could she, who was so lost, be
available for so much? "Speak for yourself, Doc," he said for
her to himself. It was the first time he did that, but he would
do it for the rest of his life, talk to himself in her voice, to
call up the wholeness he felt with her. While she would take
from him something she could not define and had never
known anything like: being seen as he saw her. Now and
again, for the rest of her life, she would be walking or sitting alone somewhere and suddenly feel his eyes on her, so
strongly that she'd look to see if he was near; he never
would be, but for those moments she would remember so
clearly the Lee she liked the best, the Lee that came out in
his presence at the zoo—a person within her that was like
her best friend. Many years later she would, in a sense, be-
friend herself and *be* that person. A mature woman's version, marked by all she would have done and lost by then,
but still that person, and in memory she would thank him
for being the beginning of that long befriending. But now
she bit him. A little harder. And felt a thrill when he moaned
with the bite. When he moved to bite her in turn. When he
could not help it. When he trembled. She was never going
to see him again. She was, in effect, sacrificing him. But she
loved him. She knew *that*, too. They were not quite human
beings, now. They were like creatures, perhaps leopards,
with human heads, or like humans with leopard heads. He
lifted her housedress and bit at her thighs. She opened his
shirt and bit at his chest. His erection was so painful,
cramped in his pants. Her desire gnawed so. But they made
no move to do more than bite and kiss; neither could go
further than this lovemaking in which nothing could be satisfied but everything was included. While outside the owl
made its cry. And dogs barked. And in the zoo, not three
miles from her shack, the animals slept in cramped spaces,
those that could sleep, but not the tiger, which does not

sleep at night, nor the snow leopard, nor the giraffe which sleeps hardly at all. While Lee and James bit each other's hands, bit each other's arms, and suddenly she laughed, and he laughed with her, and they held on to each other for dear life.

"I gotta pee. But I don't wanna let go." Then, as she pulled back a little: "Oh, shit, I gave you a hickey, Doc. A couple."

"You're kidding."

"Uh-uh."

"My first in about thirty-six years."

"*You're* kidding."

"No."

"Your wife was sure restrained."

"So was I. I don't think she wanted to be, though. I think I restrained her. Or she thought that's what I wanted. Or—in that way we never had any idea what the other wanted, or even *if* they wanted. Two hickeys, huh? Are they good ones?"

"Rubies. I gotta pee."

She stood up, swayed a little.

"Oooooh. Scotch."

"You OK?"

"Not as OK as I was."

She went into the bedroom, and, looking after her, he saw it lit from the bathroom. She'd left the bathroom door open. He heard what sounded like a stumble, some small things knocked over and hitting the floor. Then the strong sound of peeing in the bowl, surprisingly loud for a woman. Then sounds of retching. He got up to make sure she was alright.

Her head was bent into the toilet bowl. She was naked. Brushes, vials, combs, and tubes were all over the floor. He felt at home with her nakedness, as she felt at home naked in front of him, and he knelt behind her, and held her shoulders and patted her hair as she vomited. The smell was terrible. (It surprised him, in his profession, that he'd never gotten used to bad smells.) He'd reach over and flush the toilet when he couldn't stand it anymore, pulling her back so that the contents wouldn't splash her. When she was through with it, and still kneeling on the floor, he wrapped his arms around her from behind, held her, rocked her a little.

"That feels so good," she said wearily.

"Yes," she said.

He helped her up.

"I gotta lie down," she said. "Lie down with me."

They went to the mattress on the floor, and he steadied her as she knelt and lay down. Then he lay beside her, and pulled her toward him so that he held her and she used the crook of his arm for a pillow.

"Sorry about the hickeys," she whispered.

"I'm proud of them."

"Nobody ever helped me puke like that. You're the sweetest man."

"You've got a friend."

"I know."

"I don't mean me, I mean in the window."

"*What?*" She whipped her head around. Then relaxed.

"Oh," she said, "it's you."

A black cat sat in the window. It had eyes as green as hers.

"I figured you'd have a cat," he said.

"Had a cat. Had to give Bosco to the neighbor. But she doesn't realize what's happened yet. No, Bosco. Get outa here. Mommy's gone, you just don't know it yet."

Abbey felt so at home lying beside her, feeling her strong, lush body through his shirt and his pants. Even the vomiting smell didn't matter, as he lay there and gave in to his own fatigue and drunkenness. The cat pawed at the screen and mewed.

"Go away, Bosco," she whispered, "this isn't home anymore."

"How come?" Abbey said sleepily.

"Oh, boy," Lee said.

"What?"

"Just hold me real tight for a few minutes. Hold me. We'll hold each other."

And they held each other. And began to breathe together.

And now they were neither awake nor asleep. It felt like they were floating in the center of the world.

"Jimmy? James. Jiiiiiiii—iimmmmmmmm. JAMES! Jimmy! Jim, Jim, James-Jimmy-Jim."

"What, hon?"

"JAMES!"

As he realized what it was his heart pounded him awake. It had been almost half his life since he'd heard those voices. The pounding in his chest was so strong it woke her.

"You *OK?*"

"Hold me. Just hold me."

Hello, he said to the voices—though they were gone now. Hello. Why now? This once, or will you come again? Hello.

"James?"

But it was Lee this time.

"What?"

"The cat."

"He's still there."

"You asked about the cat. It's time to tell you. I had to give the cat to the neighbor 'cause things are about to get too crazy for a cat. We're going soon."

"Good. Where are we going?"

"You're not going. We are. My band. We're going to Austin."

"What?"

"The music scene here sucks. You try and try and nothing happens. We've tried and tried and we're *good*, and nothing. Austin's got a great music scene. A band can get *heard* there, you know? There's no money there, but we ain't makin' any money here. I want you to know even though, three weeks ago, it was my idea—the band's democratic, we voted yesterday, I voted no, 'cause-a you, really, but I lost."

"Don't go."

"Got to."

"No, you don't. You and I—"

"But that's *my* band—it's—what I do, man. It's . . . I don't know how to explain. Come to Texas and be a doctor."

"My kid's here."

"He can visit."

"I have to be where my kid lives. Don't go."

"Got to."

"You've known this all night?"

"And all day. And last night."

"You're quite a girl."

"You mad?"

"I hope so. But I don't think so."

"You got no right to be mad."

"That's true. That's probably true."

The trust of their bodies, the comfort of their touch, did not abate or change at all. Both felt this, and neither was surprised. And he understood why the voices had come back: they did not want him to fall asleep, they did not want anything to be wasted.

Elation. Elation went through him at what he'd just thought. The voices do not want anything to be wasted.

The voices do not want anything to be wasted.

Lee raised her face above his.

"Kiss the bitch. Please. Kiss the pukey bitch."

He kissed her in his elation. Not one taste in her mouth was wasted. She felt and could not understand his elation; she'd expected, wanted, a dirge of a kiss, but, because their love was such that it went from moment to moment without hesitation, she responded in kind and was carried by his joy. Together they sought no refuge from Paradise. What all the voices had in common was that they did not want anything to be wasted. Everything they'd said, everything they'd suggested, was against waste, and toward something else. Why not call it Paradise? He decided to call it Paradise. He did not think this in words but in kissing.

He knew that others heard voices that wanted everything to be wasted, he knew that the world that called itself "the world" put both kinds of voices in the same category. The world was wrong again.

They kissed in Paradise for the last time, and though they knew that it was the last time it did not matter that it was the last time, because it was Paradise.

A
GUEST

There are screams in Paradise. There is everything in Paradise—*everything* found in the world that calls itself "the world" is also in Paradise. But it's in a different song.

She lay on his chest, face nestled on his neck, she naked, he clothed, but where she had opened his shirt to bite him her breast felt luxurious on his, and a kind of luxury passed between their breasts one to the other. She sang softly, her lips moving on his neck, something lilting and wordless, *la la la la la.*

Gradually they became aware of an insectlike sound, but it wasn't an insect. He was savoring that the voices had visited, and was going to tell her of it, but the sound caught his ear and he tried to remember what it sounded like. At the same time she said sleepily, "What's that? That squeak?"

"Christ. It's my beeper."

"What?" She lifted her head to see her alarm clock. "At three in the morning?"

"I'll go see," he said.

"Let it go. Don't."

"Got to."

She grabbed him tighter and pressed her weight on him: "No!"

"Got to, Lee. You know about 'got to.' "

"Bastard."

"I love you."

"I know. I know, I know. I feel loved. I feel so loved."

"So do I."

"So go to your fuckin' squeaker then," she said, and rolled off him.

First he couldn't find it (their love play had squeezed it between two cushions on the sofa), then it looked so strange to him, for the state he was in, that he couldn't quite grasp it. Then he simply couldn't believe it: the number he was to call was Elizabeth's and Eddie's.

"Is it OK?" Lee said from the bedroom.

"Where's your phone?"

"By the bed."

"I have to call my ex-wife."

"Look at my body while you do. Woooooo! The girl's a bitch, is she a bitch or *what?*"

"Proud of yourself?"

"Sometimes I get drunk enough to know I have a great body."

He punched up the number on the phone.

Elizabeth picked up on the first ring.

She said, "Where in the hell are you at *this* hour?"

"Actually—and really—it's none of your business."

Lee stretched her body, exaggerated the stretch, squirmed, and lifted her pubis toward him, grinning. She couldn't hear Elizabeth say, "Eddie's sick."

"How sick?"

"It's that fever he used to run. Same pattern, a hundred and two most of the night, but now it's a hundred and three, and now he's puked up the aspirin, he's puked up the Tylenol, which means he'd puke up the Advil too. You remember how he gets."

"I remember." He remembered watching the vein in his son's neck bulge hugely with the force of his heartbeat when this fever hit him, and how no test had come up with a diagnosis.

"So you don't have any suppository aspirin?" he said.

Lee's eyes bulged: "Sup-OS-it-or-y AS-pir-in?"

Elizabeth heard her. "My god, Jim. No, I feel like an idiot, I don't have any, he hasn't had one of these in such a long time. I mean, if I *had* them I wouldn't be calling you and your friend, would I?"

"You've had friends, too, Elizabeth."

"I know, I'm being unfair, I *like* being unfair," and she gave a small choked laugh.

"The Kaiser in Hollywood has an all-night drugstore, I'll get them there. I should be at your place in about an hour, a little less."

"No," Lee said.

"If his temperature goes up at *all* give him an alcohol rub, and if you think he's too old for that take him to a hospital. I don't want his temperature to hit a hundred and four in his state of mind; he could get delirious and scare the hell out of himself."

"Thanks, Jim."

They hung up.

"My kid runs fevers. Same as I did when I was a kid. They're pretty—intense. He hasn't had one in a long time. If they get too high—"

He had spoken without looking at her. When he looked now he saw someone he had never seen. Her face had gone colorless—not white, but colorless. Even her eyes seemed colorless, yet they had a terrible force, looking at him un-blinking. It was not hate. It wasn't anything he had ever seen. But it was dangerous—he felt that in his skin. Then sitting there on her knees naked, she said a word that was almost a very soft growl: "No."

"What?"

"No," she said back in her throat, her mouth hardly moved. "No."

"Lee—"

"You," she said, "don't," she said, "leave," she said, "me," she said, "alone," she said, "now."

His body had gone still as if a dangerous animal had stepped suddenly into his path—an animal he didn't know how to talk to.

"No," she said again. "Just—no."

It wasn't that he feared her. She would do him no harm, it wasn't in her to do him physical harm. No, what had been triggered in Lee was dangerous to *her*. If he left her alone now, this thing, this furious colorlessness that now possessed her—it would devour her, devour *them*, destroy all their moments together. It would infect and take possession of her memory; whenever she would think of him she would think of this and be overwhelmed and in *that* way his existence in her would be killed. All this was intuition in him, but his response was instantaneous. He knew what he must do, but he couldn't yet bring himself to say it.

And she was becoming more herself again, saying, "Not tonight, man, no, Doc, no, *James*, please, God, *Jim*—don't spew me out of your *mouth*."

Then she said, in her normal voice, which, because her face had not changed and she had not changed position, seemed strange in the animal naked girl, "I know I'm leaving you, but you gotta let me, you gotta gotta gotta, *you* can't leave me, not *you*. Deal?"

"Deal. Get dressed."

"What?"

"I got a sick kid, Lee. I can't leave him either."

Abbey marveled at how swiftly her face changed and was now the face of the laughing girl at the zoo. She had changed so fast there were no transitions, like quick cuts in a movie. It was hard for him to keep up.

"You'd better hurry," he said, "you're naked, remember?"

"This is great. *Now* we got somethin' to visit."

He watched her dress. She had heard his urgency and was quick about it. The basic costume she'd worn at the zoo—so different from the carefree housedress, so different from the voluptuous nakedness: the lines of her body hidden by the flow of a full skirt, black with green flower patterns, like the upholstery of his childhood, and the full blouse, white with green flower embroidered, and a gypsy scarf, and the incongruous military footwear of her generation.

"Did you not wear underwear at the zoo, too?"

"That's what my heart feels like—a dress with nothing on underneath."

In this world this should not happen. In Paradise it must.

The huge, bleak Kaiser hospital, with the bright "24 Hour Pharmacy" sign, and only a car or two on Hollywood Boulevard, and no one walking—Abbey parked illegally, Lee stayed in the car, he ran up the many steps, and his running echoed down the street. The traffic lights changed from green to yellow to red, and for the moment this was Paradise—because these two people had left the world that calls itself "the world," though they seemed to be moving within it: they cared neither about avoiding pain nor inflicting it (which is almost solely what "the world's" judgments are based on); they cared only about how one moment's beauty demands audacity in order to lead to the next moment's beauty; and they cared about nothing, when together, but fulfilling the demands of that audacity. It is beautiful not to desert a lover to her demons; and it is beautiful to fulfill your loyalty to your son; and if the world that calls itself "the world" demands you choose between them, there is also Paradise, which knows that all paths cause pain, so to choose the safe over the audacious will not give you less pain, only less beauty. As Abbey came out of the pharmacy and stood on the steps of the hospital looking down at the Buick, the only car on the street, and knew Lee to be in it, and imagined Elizabeth's face when she would see Lee, and wondered at Eddie's face, he was neither nervous nor afraid—the three people he loved most would be in one place, and, while he would not have used words like "beauty" and "audacity," and while he did not really know and would never fully articulate the new standards and assumptions that he was beginning to live by, having only the vague words "eternity" and "paradise" and associating them with tigers and giraffes and Lee . . . what he felt, what was clear to him, was deep relief that he had not left Lee behind—that he had not, when he saw her in that state, even considered it. He knew now that he would never be the same man he was two weeks ago. And if he didn't have to be that way, neither did his son.

Lee, for her part, sat in the car not thinking of where they were going, but softly singing, "*It rained all night the day I left, the weather it was dry . . . Sun was so hot I froze myself . . . don't you cry . . .*"

Driving was difficult. It had been many years since he'd had too much to drink. He gave it all his attention, but the trip seemed to be happening in slow motion, and he was afraid for his son.

Lee fell asleep soon after they left the hospital, and was still asleep when he parked in front of the house in Pasadena.

"Lee?"

She opened her eyes slowly but when she focused she was startled.

"Whoa! What are we doing? Where have you taken me?" Then she was furious: "*Why* did you wake me *up?* Shit, my head. Christ, I *drank* too much."

"You drink too much."

"Whatever."

Elizabeth's porch light went on.

"Where in the fuck *are* we?"

The front door opened and Elizabeth stood in it.

"Stay in the car until you remember," Abbey said.

He opened his door and started to get out but she grabbed his arm with all her strength: "*Oh,* no, *hey*—no."

Elizabeth walked toward the car quickly across the lawn in her paint-stained jeans and a white shirt too large for her that hung down like a smock. Her hair was pulled back tightly, accenting the strong lines of her face. Her feet were bare, and she walked carefully on the lawn.

"Who the fuck is that?" Lee said.

James Abbey, in his fifty years, had felt many unpleasant things, but not often had he felt like a complete fool.

The passenger side of the car was at the curb. Lee was whom Elizabeth saw first as she bent to the window. Their first good look at each other was with faces not a foot apart.

Elizabeth's voice was flat with fury: "Well this is original."

"Get outa my face, cunt."

Elizabeth backed away but kept her eyes level and looked at James: "Give me the aspirin and get out of here."

"I'm going to look at Eddie, Elizabeth."

He got out of the car before Lee could grab him again. "God *damn* you people," she said as James walked across the lawn and Elizabeth went after him shouting "James! You *don't* go into my house tonight, that's all there is to it."

"*Nobody* leaves me in a car," Lee yelled, and she was running out of the car after them.

The car was left with both doors open and the interior lights on.

They got to the porch steps and Elizabeth turned on Lee: "Where do you think you're going?"

"Wherever he goes, lady."

Elizabeth turned to James, who'd stopped at the front door.

"If she comes into my house I'm calling the police."

Abbey said, "Do whatever you have to do."

"You cop-out son of a *bitch*," Lee hissed.

"Agreed," Elizabeth said.

James went inside, clutching his small pharmacy bag. Pain shot through his head. He was short of breath. His heart beat madly. The physician in him noted that he was having all the reactions of a human being in intense fear.

"*James!*" Elizabeth yelled behind him. He was standing in the living room, unable to move. He wanted to run away from her voice but it was as though he'd left his power of motion at the door.

"Where's Eddie?" he said vaguely.

"Where do you think he is, he's in his—"

"What? What?" It was Eddie, standing at the bottom of the stairs in his jockey shorts. He was glistening with sweat and trembling.

"Did you paint these?" Lee said to Elizabeth in her normal voice.

James went to Eddie and held him.

"Back upstairs, kid."

"Who's she?"

"Come on, kid." And James lifted Eddie in his arms as he

had not done in years, and carried him as Eddie said again, "Who's the *girl?*"

Elizabeth was so disoriented that she answered Lee's question before she could stop herself: "Yes."

"You're a *real* mom."

Elizabeth would remember those words later and wonder about them, but now she started quickly for the stairs, then stopped and turned: "If *one* thing in this house is missing or damaged when I come down, I'll see you in jail, young lady."

"Yeah, right."

James lay the boy on his bed upstairs. Eddie suddenly laughed, and pulled at James' shirt, opening the collar.

"You've got hickeys, Daddy."

"I've got some shove-'em-ups for you." That was their old word for them. He gave them to the boy. "Now get under the covers and shove 'em up."

"*Mom* didn't give you those, did she?" The boy was smiling.

"Your mother isn't the hickey type."

"That little girl?"

Elizabeth came in, her face white. She grasped the bedstead but her hands were trembling.

"Dad's here, Mom."

"Have you shoved 'em up, kid?" his father asked.

"Yeah, Dad. He's got hickeys, Mom."

Abbey was feeling his son's forehead.

"Christ, Elizabeth. Why did you wait for us?"

" 'Us,' " Elizabeth repeated.

"Where's the thermometer?"

"It was a hundred and four point one just before you came. It was sudden. I was going to take him in when you pulled up. I saw the car from here and said, 'Thank God.' What fun. Hickeys."

"Where'd everybody go?" Lee was standing in the door.

"James," Elizabeth said.

"It's that girl," the boy said sleepily.

"There should be more blankets on him, he'll have chills."

"They're on the other side of the bed, he's kicked them off."

"Get them."

"You get them."

"Want me to get them?" Lee said in an almost normal voice.

"*James*," Elizabeth said. Then she turned to Lee: "What are you doing here, get *out* of here, this is a family matter."

"So? I got a family." She looked at Eddie. "Hi."

"Hi."

James had put the blankets on Eddie and was wiping his sweaty head with a wet cloth that Elizabeth had left on the bedstead.

"I'm going to hate you for this for a long time, James. I'm going to hate you, really," Elizabeth said.

"Why, Mom?"

"Oh," Elizabeth moaned, "shit. James."

"Lee," James said, "this is Elizabeth and Eddie."

Lee tried to smile. She said, "I really fucked up, I'm sorry. I remember now. I just didn't know where I was. I got crazy. Oh, boy. This is bad, isn't it? Oh, man. Sorry, Doc. Just . . ."

She turned from them, went to the door, stopped, looked at Elizabeth: "Sorry about—what I said—out there—I'm . . ." She turned and was going down the stairs when she called back, "I'm not like that!"

"Clearly," Elizabeth said, "she *is* like that."

"When she's like that."

"She gave him hickeys, Mom."

James said, "She'll be alright now, Elizabeth. Please believe me. I'm sure of it."

"Not in front of Eddie, please."

"Right. Hang tight a second, kid."

"You and Mom gonna fight? You gonna fight, Mom?"

"It's way past fighting, honey, we're not going to fight."

Elizabeth and James went down the hall to her bedroom.

"There's nothing to say, James. We're not friends anymore. And I thought we could be. And I *wanted* to be. So much."

"I don't blame you. That's all I can say about that. I don't blame you."

"Big deal."

"I'm not going to try to explain anything—"

"*That's* a relief—"

"—but I am going to ask you for something."

"You're going to what?"

He had not been in her bedroom before. It was so different from the one they'd shared. Bright instead of dark. Playful colors, Pueblo Indian designs, this touch and that touch that spoke of a woman who wanted to be what she decided to be, no more and no less, and whose effort was to make the world accommodate that.

He said, "I want to sit with Eddie for a while alone. I want you to just let Lee be. The shock is over, she won't be any trouble."

"You're amazing."

"Eddie shouldn't be alone now, please—"

"And James, you're drunk!"

"Not as drunk as I was. Elizabeth—"

"I hadn't even considered it, is why I didn't notice it."

"Please, Elizabeth. I'll leave right now if you demand it, but—"

"Because I'll call the cops if you don't. You *do* know that?"

"Yes."

"Excellent. Then leave right now. I'm demanding it."

"Let me sit with Eddie a few minutes. Please."

"No. That's it."

James was suddenly very tired.

"It's probably better. I'll tell him another time. Probably better."

"Tell him what? You're not going to *marry* this child?"

"We gotta get back to Eddie."

"I'll get back to Eddie and you will leave *right now.*"

She allowed him to stop in Eddie's room on the way out. Eddie was groggy. The aspirin were already working. His fever was going down. He was sweating. He seemed oddly happy.

"Good night, son."

"Good night," the boy said sleepily. "Watch those hickeys, Dad." The boy smiled and slept.

As they went downstairs Elizabeth said, "*He* seems to be enjoying this."

"It's the fever. I doubt he'll even remember it."

Lee wasn't in the living room.

"Where the *hell* is she now?" Elizabeth said, and rushed to the kitchen and her studio.

James went to the front door. It was open. He saw his car, doors open, lights on. The huge round Inside Cat was sitting on the front seat, huddled, mewing, terrified at being out of the house. Lee must have petted it, picked it up, come outside, and then, unable to bring herself to come back in, and seeing the cat's fear, left it safe in the car.

James went to the car, picked up the frightened cat. In eyebrow pencil on the front seat beside the cat she'd written:

Forgive me, Doc— Remember me— I love you.

He ran with the cat back to the house, let it drop roughly to the floor, and ran out again, slamming the door (unintentionally) behind him, slammed the car doors, started the car, and sped down the street looking for her. It was a residential neighborhood, half a mile to a street of any size, where she might call a cab or a friend, but she could have gone up and down several streets by now if she was hurrying—she could have zigzagged, doubled back, anything. He took a left, then a right, and went around one block, then another, then another, north then south, east then west. Finally, taking a turn, he saw Lee's unmistakable silhouette and walk crossing the street about four blocks ahead. Not since he was a boy had he burned rubber on a car. When she heard the squeal she looked, knew who it was, and stopped.

He pulled up beside her.

"Get in, Lee."

"No can do, Doc."

He killed the engine. Killed the lights. It would be dawn in not too long.

She said, "I ruined everything."

"You didn't."

"I know I did. But you didn't leave me, didja? Even just now you didn't. You're all right, Doc."

"Please get in. Let me drive you home, at least."

"No can do."

"Tomorrow—"

"No can do."

"Lee."

"The music goes 'round and 'round," she said.

"I feel so helpless," he said.

"I know that feeling."

"Can I at least give you some money for Texas, something that'll—"

"*Oh* I wish I were mature enough. I'm not, man. I'm *really* not. It would ruin everything. *No* fuckin' can do."

"I didn't mean—"

"Oh *I* know. *You're* cool with that. Wouldn't matter. It's me. It's always me."

"Let me at least drive you to a phone, a bus—"

"No."

He couldn't start the car. She couldn't walk away.

"Hi, Lee."

" 'Hi,' he says. Hi, Doc."

"I love you. Will you remember that?"

"I think I will." And again. "I think I will. Hey?"

"What?"

"You just gotta drive off now. Trust me, Doc."

He couldn't do less than trust her. He didn't know how to do more. He drove off.

A
CARD

He made himself eat. He made the calls and such necessary for his return to work. He even looked forward to the knife again. He missed Lee acutely, the power of the emotion stunned him, but in a way it also grounded and even protected him—missing Lee was almost a shield against the shock of returning to what most people called "life."

Neither his receptionist, nor the other doctors, nor the nurses, nor his patients, made any mention of the hickeys that faded slowly on his neck over the next week or so. James Abbey found this extraordinary. It *must* have been a topic between them, spoken of and joked about, at least briefly, but no one said a word to him. He didn't consider himself *that* imposing a man, so he had to take this as the measure of their distance from him. Or was it just their good manners? He would never really know. He felt more a foreigner than ever in the world of his work, but paradoxically more at ease. It had to do with Paradise. The work was no longer his life or his limit, it was something he merely visited, the satisfying fulfillment of a pact he had made long ago (with whom? with the priest he had never become?): a pact to be of service in this world. But the world he serviced was not the whole world, or the only world, and he now knew this not as a concept but as an experience—and this very knowledge worked to loose the bonds that made him feel so distant from everything. As simply a visitor to the world that called itself "the world," and a worker in it, rather than being trapped in it, he could relax and find more enjoyment in his skills. His grimness gradually lifted. He was still "thinking all the time," as Lee would have said, and still kept himself largely to himself, as he always had, but he seemed able to breathe more easily and more deeply, and he sensed that this quality of breathing was the ground note of happiness.

In the evenings he sat in the dark as he had before his "vacation" (he did not know what else to call it); but now he did not even think of fear. He had his tea in the kitchen, or sat in the yard, aware now of skunk and possum, raccoon and owl, cat and cricket and spider and tree and moon, and each one of them meant that he was not alone, and *he* meant that *they* were not alone, nor the mourning dove in the morning, nor the sparrows and the crows and the hummingbirds. The hours spent like this were the strongest of his day, so strong that he knew no need or reason to "do" anything with them, and he came to feel that to be able to have such hours was the one real achievement of his life.

Often during these hours he would think of Lee, wonder about her, question himself (should he go find her? wouldn't that violate what she clearly said she needed?); or the phone would ring and he would expect her voice. The loss of her pained him always, but it was not a dull pain, it was a pain that connected him to the most crucial of his experiences; thus the pain itself carried a sweetness that consoled and went beyond pain into a gentle feeling that did not hurt and had no name.

So the elements of his life remained largely the same, but they were in a different song.

On an afternoon before the hickeys had quite faded, not many days after the last time he saw Lee, a coincidence of cancellations gave him the rest of the day off. He drove to Pasadena. It was neither a plan nor an impulse; it was merely something that had to be done and was long overdue. He hadn't attended the most recent session with Dr. Benjamin, in part because he was busy again, but more because he didn't want to be put into a position of having to defend the actions of the other night. By Elizabeth's lights, the other night was indefensible, and she was right; by his lights, it didn't need to be defended, and he was right. What was it the physicist Niels Bohr had said? "The opposite of a correct statement is a false statement, but the opposite of a profound truth may be another profound truth." Something like that. She had a right to her world and he had finally found his, and there was no point arguing—which is what the "discussion" would surely be. They had never been married, not really, but that night they had become truly divorced.

He hadn't tried to see Eddie on the last visiting day either; hadn't even called. He knew what their next meeting had to be, and he wasn't ready for it on that visiting day, and he didn't want to make excuses. But now, after these two conspicuous absences, he was driving to Pasadena unannounced.

It was a bright day. The colorless brightness that is the very air of L.A. The streets where he'd last seen Lee looked grotesque in this light—only in the dark would they ever seem themselves again, to his eyes. But now the light somehow stripped them to the bone, and he hated to think of Eddie in this place where so little *really* happened, so little but the repetition of small intentions.

And there was the house. And there was where he'd parked. Another car was in the space, a BMW. Elizabeth's car wasn't in the driveway—a fact which made him proud of his intuition to come at this particular hour. Curiously, he had never doubted Eddie would be home, and he felt a thrill when he tried the front door and found it unlocked—the sure sign that Eddie was home, he rarely locked the door behind him in daylight.

As he walked through the living room toward the stairs he missed Lee terribly. It was a different house to him now that Lee had been in it. How strange that now he could come *here* for the memory of her.

He should have called out, he didn't mean to scare the boy. Eddie's voice trembled when he called from upstairs, "Who's there?"

"It's me, Eddie," Abbey called.

"Dad?"

"Yeah."

Now Eddie was on the top of the stairs, looking down at his father who stood on the first step.

"Mom's gonna kill you if she finds you here."

"I've been killed before."

"That's what you think."

The boy seemed glad to see him, in his way.

"Can I come up?" Abbey asked.

"Why not?"

As Abbey climbed the stairs Eddie looked carefully at him with a slight but definite smile.

"They're still there, Dad—those hickeys."

Abbey, to his surprise, blushed.

"That girl gave you those hickeys?"

"Yes."

"Did you give her hickeys?"

"I—think so."

"Is she in the car outside? 'Cause Mom—"

"No. She's gone. Lee's gone."

"Her name's Lee?"

"Yeah."

"Will I get to see her again?"

"That's not up to me."

"Who's it up to?"

"I wish I knew."

They stood awkwardly in Eddie's room.

"How're you feeling?" his father asked. "Fever's gone?"

"Yeah."

"And things—are OK, more or less?"

"More or less?"

"Yeah, more or less."

"I don't know what to say," Eddie stated, and sat down on his bed.

His father sat down on the floor where he'd slept not long ago, and looked up at his son. Behind his son, on the walls, were the animal photographs he'd noticed the last time.

"Who put those up? Those photographs? They your idea, your mother's?"

"Dad, like— *I don't know what to say.*"

"I love you, son. And I'm not out of my mind. That's—a lot of what I wanted to say."

"Great. You love me and you're not out of your mind." Then, in a smaller voice, and looking off to the side: "Love you too."

"You don't remember whose idea it was, those pictures?"

"Like, what *is* it with the *pictures*, man?"

"Those hippos—you know they kill more people in Africa than any other wild animal?"

"Oh boy, no, I *didn't* know that." Then, in spite of himself: "Seriously?"

"Seriously. Apparently they're angry all the time—when they open their mouths wide and look like they're yawning? That's how they roar. People don't take it seriously. And people don't know that on land hippos can run really fast— thirty-five miles an hour, in short spurts, plenty fast enough to catch you or me. They get angry and just—run people over. You know how hippos die?"

"Is this, like, kind of 'knock knock who's there'? How do hippos die?"

"They live about twenty-five years, that's how long it takes for those big teeth of theirs to wear down. When the teeth are too worn, they can't bite and chew anymore. They starve to death."

"Dad? You're kind of weirding me out, OK?" The boy's eyes were very uncertain. "I mean, who cares about hippos?"

"I do. That's part of what I'm trying to tell you. I guess I'm not doing it very well."

"You oughta go before Mom gets back."

"Don't worry about it."

"Don't tell me what to worry about, OK?"

They sat there not knowing what to say. Abbey had been afraid, since the night Elizabeth had told him about Eddie's voices, that this conversation might do more harm than good, and he didn't know what to say now except to follow his impulses, and his impulses appeared not to be helping. But he had nothing else to go by.

"Can I say one more thing about the pictures?"

"I guess. Fuck. Dad—say what you *want*, I guess."
Abbey sighed loudly.

"Does that sigh, like, mean, like, I shouldn't say 'fuck' in front of you?"

"Eddie—"

"*What?*"

"OK. In zoos, tigers are pretty quiet, but in wild nature—"

"How do you know all this shit?"

"Been watching a lot of television."

"Like, The Learning Channel and shit?"

"The Discovery Channel, PBS. Taping shows."

"You? Taping?" Then: "Dad, you oughta go, you know?"

"Five more minutes."

"And you're not crazy, right?" Eddie said sarcastically.

"I'm really not. I'm just not playing by the rules."

The boy heard that. His face went from petulance and fear to seriousness and inquiry, in just a heartbeat.

"Yeah?" the boy said.

"Tigers are pretty quiet in zoos. They make about six sounds, I think it is. So for a long time people thought those were the only sounds they made, because—"

"Who's gonna crew with tigers in jungles and listen?"

"Right," Abbey smiled. "But a couple of guys in India managed to do it. And they talked about 'the complex and elaborate language of the tiger'—forty-fifty sounds at least, and they're not random, those guys watched, and the sounds are like words that elicit definite responses. They say you have to call that a language, there's nothing else to call it."

The boy actually turned around and looked at the photo of the tiger on his wall.

"OK, they have a language. Is this gonna be on the quiz? I mean—yeah, it's kind of cool, OK."

"Eddie, I've heard voices too."

"What's that got to do with tigers?" Eddie shot out, before he'd taken in what had just been said—or as a way to delay taking it in. "Dad— I—"

"I've heard voices too. The same kind you hear."

"And *you're* not crazy, right?" the boy said with desperate humor. "The same kind?"

"Yeah. My name. Just the same. Right between sleep and waking. The same."

"So I get it from you? This isn't my fault?"

The weight of his question pulled at his father's heart.

"Nobody's fault, kid. It's just something that happens."

"And—" but Eddie's voice trailed off.

And Abbey told him that his voices had been from his earliest years, so he hadn't been frightened because he thought it happened to everyone.

"Then how come this happened to me now, and not when I was little?"

"I don't know. Nobody knows. They happen when they wanna happen, I guess."

He explained that his voices had left him in his twenties, and he didn't know why. As he was speaking he remembered a thought he'd had at Dr. Benjamin's: that the only safety is to be given sufficient skills for the dangers one will meet. The world that called itself "the world" was now equating safety with *no danger*, but a condition of "no danger" is not possible; safety can be found only in the capacity to meet danger with enough skills to have some chance. What skill could he give his boy?

"I just mean," he was saying, "about the tigers, I mean—there are many languages, there are many voices, and a lot of them we don't know about—" and now his voice trailed off.

"Why—why did your voices leave?"

"I've been thinking maybe they just got sick of me."

"*What?*"

"I think they don't want—"

"Hey, man, they're just in your head. They're just in *my* head."

"I don't know, kid. It was all so clear in *my* head on the way over here."

It was clear now he couldn't tell Eddie about the tiger at the zoo. The boy wasn't ready, and would think his father mad.

"So what did you start to say?" The boy wouldn't let it go.

"They don't want us to waste our lives. That's what I think. For what it's worth."

"Oh, man, 'they,' like—where do 'they' come from, like—
Fuck." Then: "Dad, they just say my name, you *know?* It's
getting a little boring."

He had made a mess of it. He wasn't going to be able to
pass on his vision. At least not this way. But he'd done, finally, what the good doctor had suggested and what he'd
known from the first he would have to do. Whatever his son
thought of him, the boy could see he had survived. And that
the voices weren't, as he had put it, his fault. But Abbey
couldn't pass on a skill he didn't have.

That's what he felt and thought, but he misjudged. His
willingness to risk the awkwardness of speech, the profound uneasiness of such a talk, was itself a skill, and crit-
ical for the meeting of many dangers. They didn't call
disease "dis-ease" for nothing. Nevertheless this talk was
not, could not have been, what he had hoped.

He said, "They're getting a little boring, huh?"

"It's good to know it's not, like, sort of, my fault—you
know?"

"You can blame it on your old man."

"I didn't mean it like that."

"I was only kidding."

"No, you weren't."

"Half kidding?"

Abbey got up from where he was sitting on the floor.

"It was me, Dad."

"What was you?"

"The photographs. On the wall. That wasn't Mom, that
was me."

A strange elation went softly through his father's body.

"Why—didn't you tell me before?"

"It's embarrassing. I mean—it's such a little-kid thing to
do, cut out animal pictures."

"Why'd you do it?"

"Just felt like it."

"Thanks for telling me."

Many years later Eddie would remember all this vaguely,
and only in terms of his own struggles (very different from
his father's). What he'd remember most vividly would be
what he called "that night of the hickeys," seen always in

memory through the giddiness of his fever. As a middle-aged man he would say that he went back in memory to that night for what he'd call "the humanity" of his father. His father had seemed hardly human to him before; hence he was enormously grateful for that night but never understood what was really going on, he'd say. So, in Paradise, it is hard to know who a given moment is truly for.

Nearly a year passed. James Abbey received a postcard from Lee at his office. ("Doctors are easy to find," she'd said.) It was an aerial view of Austin where the river cuts through the city. Once he realized what it was he could barely bring himself to read it, his heart beat so. In a tiny yet strong, thick-lettered handwriting, it read:

"Hi. It's me. You OK? I'm not much of a letter writer, but somebody just gave me this great rap about how they got this great zoo in San Antonio. That's not too far from here. Maybe I'll see you there one day. Say hello to the tiger for me—and the giraffe—and the 'reindeer,' oops, I mean gerenuk. I miss you, Doc. Love, Lee."

A feeling of almost unbearable loveliness filled him. He had been so afraid that their last hour had murdered, in her, what they'd shared. She was writing to tell him that wasn't so. Everything was all right now. There was no return address.

Several months after her card, he was driving on Sunset and he thought he saw her. By the time he'd doubled back, the glimpse of dress and scarf had gone. But he couldn't leave the moment. The next afternoon he went to the zoo for the first time since their last walk. He walked that walk again, in reverie, not expecting her to be there, not really, but as an act of loyalty to the two people they had been— two people who'd left him such gifts.

The loveliness descended on him as he walked ("You're a *sweet* man, did you know you're a *sweet* man?"), a gentleness such as his father used to speak of: the half-distracted air of those who had been touched "by the *little* people, Jimmy, the faerie people, you know." The giraffes were as he remembered them. The chimpanzees were as he remembered them. And he remembered his panic that ninety-nine percent of their DNA was the same as ours, that one percent is enough to change everything—but he couldn't remember why he'd been afraid, for if merely one percent could mean such massive change, then everything was always waiting to change. Fundamentally change. Even the end of the world itself waited to change into a beginning. And so I was wrong that day, that the few could not stand against the mighty, for the mighty always want what is not possible, which is that things not change that they may stay mighty. What am I thinking of? Getting carried away again, Lee. Here at the gerenuks again, where you first saw me. The gerenuks are dancing, Lee. So delicate, so graceful, with their thin thin legs and long supple necks and large bright eyes, they are dancing, three of them, standing upright on their hind legs—they really are, standing on their hind legs and their forehooves reaching up like arms and their necks extended to reach the leaves on the low-hanging branches, branches that hang down over the wall of their captivity— and they take small steps on their small hind hooves, little steps to keep their balance, and they look like they're dancing to something Viennese. We never saw that. There. Now they are as we saw them again.

I've come to the tiger now. Here is the tiger. Asleep. All mammals dream. The tiger is dreaming in the sun. Let us stand guard over the tiger as it dreams. You and I could watch a tiger sleep for hours. Soon even the sleep of the tiger will be gone from the world.

At home he checked his messages. Some work calls. One from Eddie. Could they change the day they were going to the movies? He called back and said they could. Eddie's voice sounded good. James Abbey made his meal. A salad and a sandwich. It was beginning to get dark. He made his tea. He turned off all the lights in the house, and went to sit outside and watch the lights on the hills.

ABOUT THE AUTHOR

Michael Ventura is the author of *We've Had a Hundred Years of Psychotherapy and the World's Getting Worse* (with James Hillman) and *Letters at 3 A.M.—Reports on Endarkenment*. *The Zoo Where You're Fed to God* is the first book of a trilogy titled *The Tiger, the Rock, and the Rose*. Ventura has also embarked on a series of novels about Las Vegas. He divides his time between Austin and Los Angeles.

Printed in the United States
By Bookmasters